THE FIRES OF PARIS

ZACHARY HUGHES

A JOVE BOOK

THE FIRES OF PARIS

Requests for permission to make copies of any part
of the work should be mailed to: Permissions,
Jove Publications, Inc., 200 Madison Avenue,
New York, NY 10016

First Jove edition published January 1982

First printing

Printed in the United States of America

Jove books are published by Jove Publications, Inc.,
200 Madison Avenue, New York, NY 10016

Why should we care if Paris is destroyed? The Allies at this very moment are destroying cities all over Germany with their bombs.

—Adolph Hitler
August 1944

1

AS THE RATHER battered Rover rolled to a stop at the edge of the abandoned sod landing strip in Norfolk, the man in the passenger seat lit a cigarette and looked up. The sky was just beginning to show the cast of dusk; the breeze was crisp with the tang of the North Sea and the premonition of winter, though it was only August. There was, in the delayed dusk, the old and often forgotten reminder that he was a long way from home, that this field was on a latitude with central Canada, that he had not smelled the arid drylands of west Texas in more than four years.

He checked the time again, and again was momentarily startled to see a cheap Swiss watch on his wrist instead of his good gold Bulova. His dark and somewhat soiled slacks were of wartime French manufacture, and his worn shoes were Luftwaffe issue.

"You have everything?" the man at the wheel asked.

"*Jawohl.*" By now it was natural to answer in German, even when the question was in English.

"We have a few minutes. Care to go over it?"

He shrugged. No trace of his Texas accent emerged in his flawless German. His German-born grandfather had insisted he learn it well: "The German language is an exercise in reason. You develop the muscles of your body by exercise. Learning German will develop your mind." And learn he did—often reluctantly at first, but then, as he grew older, with an interest that had never left him, even as he shot down those other Germans, the Nazis, from the skies over England. Now, after a week of crash briefing during which he had not spoken a word of English, he was at home in the language of his ancestors. He even managed to speak his high-school French with a German accent.

No longer did he have to remind himself to forget that he was Teddy Werner, third-generation American. He checked his identification papers for the twentieth time. He was beginning to believe them: He was Theo Werner, medically discharged from the Luftwaffe after being shot down over the Channel coast; Theo Werner, Swiss national, a volunteer for the glory of the Third Reich, slightly embittered at the luck that had put him out of the war.

A distant drone came in with the breeze. "Ah, there he is," the driver said.

The aircraft that swept in from the sunset was an incongruous-looking beast, slow of approach, high-winged, its big radial engine protruding. It floated down from the west, waffling a bit in the cross wind, landed with a short roll—that's why it had been selected—and revved up to taxi toward the waiting Rover. It was a Westland Lysander, a relic, a plane from early in the war; its old-fashioned fixed landing gear was housed in streamlined wheel-pants and braced by thick struts. He could see the face of the pilot as the plane wheeled, sent propwash into the open windows of the Rover.

"Well then," the man beside him said.

"*Wiedersehen*," Theo Werner said. He stepped out, holding the canvas bag containing a few extra clothes and a German-made shaving kit.

"Good luck," the man said, coming to stand beside him, extending his hand.

"*Danke*," Theo said.

He was still strapping in when the Lysander roared, lurched, and leaped into the air. He looked back once to see the man standing beside the Rover, hands in pockets. He put on the headset.

"Are you there?" the pilot asked in a young, splendidly Oxonian voice.

"*Jawohl*," Teddy-Theo said.

"Sorry, old man, I don't speak German," the pilot said. "Do you understand English at all?"

"A bit," Theo said. Even that had a German accent.

"It's a good evening for it," the pilot said. "The weather is good all the way into Normandy. I just hope the fighter lads are keeping Jerry in his hole."

"*Ja*."

"If I tend to ramble on a bit, don't mind me," the pilot said.

"*Ja*, OK."

"This isn't what I wanted, you know," the pilot said. "I applied for Fighter Command, after all. Too young to be in on the big show, worse luck, when Jerry made it easy and came over here. The old boys had all the luck, getting their kills within ten minutes of home, and—''

With a sigh, Teddy took the headset off and put it on his lap. He could hear the tinny voice of the pilot yammering on, but it soon became just another part of the airplane's roar.

Lucky. Yes, perhaps some were. Lucky to be alive after that terrible summer of 1940, when the Luftwaffe poured its overwhelming superiority against a pitifully few Spitfires and Hurricanes, when you sometimes flew five deathly draining sorties a day from a sod strip like the one back there, to take on the 109s and the twin-engined bombers—and saw your friends die one by one.

Lucky? He had once thought he was lucky—lucky to have had the vision to volunteer before the United States got into the war, lucky to be one of the Americans who were among old Winnie's ''few.'' But he'd seen friends flame and die, and he'd seen the Mad Pole parachute into the cold Channel to die in the frigid waters. And later, briefly grounded by a wound, he'd heard the English civilians, in their ignorance, cheer when a Spit flamed and fell like a falling leaf from the high sky. And those same people—the pretty girls in bathing suits, the noncombatant old men, the chubby housewives and smelly tradesmen—had killed the woman he loved. Rushing for shelter in an air raid, they had panicked and pushed and fallen, filling the subway stairwell, crushing down upon her loveliness, to squeeze and smash the life from Jeanna. The very people he'd been fighting for had killed the only woman he could ever love.

But he'd gone on flying, bitterly, doggedly, through

the end of the Blitz in the winter of 1940–41, and through the long, depressing years of German triumphs. And when the United States entered the war, he could have transferred to the American Army Air Corps; he'd been tempted to do so; but somehow that would have been denying *her*. Jeanna. She was dead, but he could still see her in his mind, could remember her as she'd been when they walked the bomb-littered streets hand in hand. So he'd stayed with the RAF.

Then, not long before D-Day, he limped back from the Continent with his Spit coughing its last and with two German machine-gun bullets lodged in his back. One was so near the spine that he was, indeed, lucky to be alive.

They gave him another medal for that. This one he kept; he was too tired to throw a second one back at their feet. Too dogged, too bitter.

But they told him he would never fly again, and that hurt. "To hell with that," he said. "The war isn't over." It wasn't over, but it had changed. Now London and the industrial cities cowered and shuddered under the buzz-bombs and the silent and deadly V-2 rockets. The Spits and Hurricanes and American-built Mustangs were no longer defending English skies; they were taking the war deep into Germany, guiding the devastating Allied bombers, while on the ground, Patton's Third Army was just breaking out of the Normandy beachhead at Avranches, beginning to give lessons in blitzkrieg, lancing across the hedge-rows and flatlands of France, threatening to encircle entire German Army groups.

And Teddy Werner wanted part of the action. He had only one thing left in his life—killing Nazis. But his body wasn't ready for him to go back after the machine-gun bullets had done their work; he'd lost strength, and his coordination wasn't what it should be. No more flying.

Then, when he was finally almost ready to throw in the towel, to say to hell with all of them and go back to Texas, the man in the Rover came to ask him to go into occupied Paris.

"Naw," he said, surprised at the stupidity of the proposal. "Sorry, but I don't even like the French. Didn't like studying the language in high school, and don't much like the people."

"Oh?"

There was a long silence. He was talking to a man who knew his psychology. If one man is confident enough, he can force the person he's with to talk merely by being silent.

Teddy talked. There was a time when the West Wall was manned by old men and boys, when all the French had to do was roll over in bed and they'd be across the Rhine. The best of the German troops were in the east. But the Frogs were too civilized, too rational to fight such a brutal war. They sat behind their blessed Maginot Line and reasoned that Hitler "would just go away."

The man let a moment of silence pass, then said, "At Dunkirk, two French divisions were pretty well wiped out, but they held off the Panzers long enough for us to evacuate half a million men." What the man said was true.

"And the bastards fought the Americans landing in North Africa." That was true, too.

"I can agree that some Frenchmen are a sorry lot," the man conceded. "But aren't they like all of us, a mixture of good and bad?"

"I don't care to risk my ass for France." Teddy said it with finality.

The other man smiled deprecatingly, nodded as if he accepted the refusal, and musingly filled his pipe. "Group Leader Werner," he said, "do you know the single largest problem our Allied forces are going to be facing in France?"

"I would imagine that it would be a few Germans."

"Oh, yes, that too. But your General Patton seems to know how to handle Germans." He held a match to his pipe, drew deeply, and was rewarded with a cloud of smoke. "Our forces, now that they've broken out at Avranches, seem to be free to go where they wish. The problem is that Patton is beginning to move so swiftly, so powerfully, that we won't be able to keep him supplied. I'm told he is on the telephone several times a day screaming for more petrol, for more food, for more supplies. Mainly petrol, though. If we can keep his tanks on the move, the Third Army will be at the Rhine within weeks."

"And you want me to go to Paris and find gasoline for Patton?" Teddy laughed mirthlessly.

The other man chuckled with more appreciation. "Find it?" He produced another cloud of smoke for emphasis. "No. Save it."

"Save it?"

"Let me explain. The situation is, shall we say, volatile in Paris. There are those who want to start an uprising against the occupying Germans now, when the Allies are practically at the gates of the city. Political motives, infighting among various Resistance groups. But a rising now would be premature— it would probably bring stiff reprisals from Jerry, and we'd have to step in and take a hand."

"Why not go in and help them?"

"Bad timing, my boy." His pipe had choked out, and he held another match to it. "Even if the place could be taken without a battle—unlikely in any case—the city, once liberated, would soak up supplies like a basket of several million sponges. Food, clothing, transport, you name it—including General Patton's petrol. An army at war, an army on the march, can't afford to keep an expensive mistress like La Belle Paris." He tried yet another match. "Let Jerry enjoy her charms for a few more weeks, and foot the bill."

"Logical. If everyone will just lie down and behave, now . . ."

"Precisely. If."

"Is it likely?"

"No. But we've got a chance. You say you don't like Frenchmen; there's one in particular that I could do without. But de Gaulle is on our side, and he has some control of part—just part—of the Resistance Movement."

Teddy waited, then, as pointedly noncommittal as he could be, said, "That's nice."

"Very nice. He's agreed to help us keep a lid on there, as long as he can. That will save a lot of lives—not only French, but British and American, too. We need to get that message through."

"That should be easy enough, if he's got such good control."

The man drew on his pipe, nodding slowly. "Should be; probably will."

Teddy waited a moment, avoiding the bait. He could see the hook attached to it. Finally he said, "And?"

The smoke wreathed the smile. "And you, my

lad, go in and tell them. Pick up a bit of information, send it along to us. We're not quite sure about what they're telling us. It will help that, with your German, you can do a bit of eavesdropping on Jerry, too. De Gaulle's men will be easy to contact. The fun will be with the others.''

2

DOWN BELOW HE saw the French coast. God, it was familiar! He'd flown a hundred sorties over that coast. Just down there, past Cherbourg, he'd scored his only triple of the war—two 109s and a Focke-Wolfe 190 in the same action.

By now the Lysander was flying low, and they could see the darkness of the French countryside, with patches of highter darkness for the ripe wheatfields that had survived the battles. An artillery battle was underway near St.-Malo, the flash of the guns momentarily lighting the darkness. He knew that elements of Patton's Third Army were lancing back from the areas of Rennes and Nantes in an effort to encircle a German army.

The young pilot was good. He had not deviated, had taken the most direct course. His voice still buzzed tinnily now and then on the headset; Theo-Teddy put on the set and heard the pilot say, as the plane started down north of Le Mans, "There we are."

He saw tiny pinpoints of light on the ground, outlining a landing area.

"Hope they haven't picked one with rocks," the pilot said. Gingerly he lowered the Lysander in the darkness, feeling his way down. When they were almost on the ground, Theo saw the pastureland rushing underneath, felt the shock of wheel contact. He had the canopy open before the plane had stopped rolling. Using the struts, he stepped out, and dropped to the ground.

The man in the U.S. Army combat gear did not speak at first. He motioned Theo to follow. Now, so close behind the American front lines, it was more important than ever that he think of himself as Theo Werner. He followed to a half-wrecked barn.

Inside, they gave him a tin cup of black coffee, and the American captain briefed him, spreading the map on a rude table. Theo knew the area well, for it had been the subject of intense study these last days. He nodded, sipped his coffee.

His transportation to Paris was a rusting but sturdy French bicycle. Its basket held a few scraggly raw vegetables and a scrawny pair of sleepy rabbits in a cage. He left the barn and followed a silent and grim-faced group of GIs into a nearby woods, pushing the bicycle. The night seemed to be thick, darker then usual. Now he wished that he had insisted on going in by parachute, even if the man he'd left back there in Norfolk had felt that it was too dangerous, and that he might reopen his scarcely healed wounds upon landing. He didn't like the night and the woods and the darkness. Especially, he didn't like having to cross over the lines into German territory.

"OK, buddy," the young lieutenant leading the patrol whispered into Theo's ear, "this is it. You go straight up that little slope. At the top is a road. Take it to the right. It goes to Chartres, then on to Paris.''

"*Danke*," Theo said.

And now he was alone. He pushed the bicycle up the grassy slope, around trees. From behind he could hear the muffled roar of the big guns. And ahead there was only the darkness. When he found the road he continued to push the bicycle, not wanting to risk riding into a shell hole or making too much noise. He walked for two hours. There were no Germans.

He slept in a haystack. At dawn he resumed his journey. He was Theo Werner, a Swiss national who had volunteered to serve in the Luftwaffe and he had his medical discharge in his pocket. He had the wounds in his back to justify the discharge. He was Theo Werner, just recently released from a field hospital, making his way to Paris with a few vegetables and a pair of rabbits, because food was scarce in Paris. There he would look for a job. All those things he would tell to any German who stopped him. He would not tell them that his employment was already assured.

It was a long ride, but, in spite of the circumstances, a pleasant one. The August sun was warm. The countryside was delightful. Unless one looked up to see the contrails left by the day-raiding Fortresses, it would have been hard to guess that there was a war on. The peacefulness of the countryside, the lack of Germans, was eerie; all the action, he knew, was further north and west, and he was in what seemed a peaceful void.

He grew more confident of his disguise. Partly to test it, to see how he would fare as a German, he stopped at a village inn for a midday meal. He ordered in German, and was served efficiently but truculently. He need not have worried about people seeing through his disguise; to the French people at the inn, he was a faceless German, to be served as quickly as possible and overcharged as much as possible.

In the late afternoon he reached Chartres; there he saw a few men in German uniforms. It was strange, but it didn't bother him. They went about their business, not paying any attention to the tall blond man in baggy French pants who pedaled his bicycle toward Paris, with a bit of food to sell on the black market.

The capital was out of reach for today, though. Ten miles beyond Chartres, Theo found another haystack, fed the rabbits some fresh grass, and spent the night.

In the morning, he joined the traffic merging toward the city—a sparse collection of wagons and bicycles and horses and, rarely, cars drawn inward to the city he could still not see. Now and then someone would nod, or speak. He nodded in return, but would not answer otherwise. He, Theo Werner, did not deign to speak French. He was Swiss-German, a member of the master race, so he had no need of French, had even refused to learn the language required in all the schools of trilingual Switzerland. Let the French learn German, for, in spite of the presence of the Allied armies on the continent, in spite of the worrisome situation with the Russians on the Eastern Front, the Führer would salvage the situation—and the city just ahead of him would remain a part of the Third Reich for a thousand years.

As Teddy monitored Theo's thoughts, he could almost laugh about it. He'd been indoctrinated so thoroughly that, as he began to see more and more people, he could feel quite arrogant.

He had never been to Paris. Like most, he'd heard the glories of Paris sung since he was a boy. Paris, City of Light, Paris the beautiful. So here it was—and it was one hell of a sad-looking place. He halted and removed a battered city map from his canvas bag. A German half-track roared past, its machine gun manned by soldiers with unsmiling faces under their coal-scuttle helmets. He almost wished they'd stop and question him. He felt secure that he could face the most suspicious Gestapo agent and pass muster.

The route was simple—through the Porte St.-Cloud, along the Avenue Versailles, following the curve of the Seine to the heart of the city. He folded his map, put it away, and once more joined the traffic of the city. A feeling of unreality suddenly gripped him. What the hell was a Texas boy doing in Paris? Man, there were one hell of a lot of Germans in Paris. There, up ahead, he could see the garish red flag with the black swastika of Nazi Germany flying from the top of the Eiffel Tower—and that sight, more than even the sight of various German uniforms, brought it home to him that he was in an occupied city, a military man out of uniform, a spy. And if he were caught he'd be killed without hesitation.

But there was something in the air, a feeling, a knowledge. Perhaps he didn't dislike all of France as much as he'd suspected. As he pedaled along the riverside quays, he was already falling under the spell of that most seductive of cities. As an exercise of mind—*yes, Grandpa, you were right*—he was reviewing what he'd learned.

All of France would fit inside the state of Texas—
all of her, not to mention a couple of French islands
thrown into the bargain. But this wasn't France, this
was Paris. There was the river that boasted thirty-
two bridges, and somewhere around were dozens of
museums, and a man could take a leak right on the
street in one of the five hundred or so street urinals
named *vespasiennes* after the Roman emperor.

He detoured out onto a bridge and looked up the
muddy river. Even the bridges were works of art,
with statues on the piers and on the center columns.
Up here he could see Notre Dame, on the island
where the city had been established by a wild Gallic
tribe known to the Romans as Parisii. The Romans
moved in and called the town Lutetia.

One rattling and chugging automobile passed him
as he rested there in the middle of the bridge—a car
equipped with a burner, made from a washtub, which
allowed it to use wood for fuel. The other traffic was
made up of bicycles, horse carts, and carriages, and
the curious velo-taxis—small, improvised vehicles
towed by men and women on bicycles. And there
were, of course, pedestrians, Germans in uniform,
some taking snapshots like good tourists, acting on
the whole as if Patton's Third Army was still back
in England, and not less than a hundred and fifty
miles away.

He rode back to the right bank and consulted his
map again. The wide boulevards here seemed so
empty, compared to London's teeming streets. And
now he began to notice the dullness of the faces of
the French people who passed him. They were a
people conquered. It was hard to believe, looking at
those sullen faces, that there was even the threat of
an uprising.

Concrete pillboxes had been built into the pavements. And they were manned; the conquerors were there, and meant business. Signposts at intersections gracelessly pointed the way to such un-French points as German military installations. Motor traffic consisted mainly of German military vehicles, with the occasional exception of a puffing wood-burning *gazogène*.

But Theo-Teddy also saw a young couple holding hands as they rode side by side on their bicycles, a group of fresh-faced young women—and he realized he *was* in Paris. The women were beautiful, trim, lean—probably, he thought, as the result of walking, riding bicycles, and the continual shortage of food. He was in Paris on a lovely summer Sunday, at the Place de la Concorde, with more gawking touristlike German soldiers and the *obélisque*. Feeling touristy himself, he rode around the square, looked up the Champs Élysées, where, he had been told, each day at noon the Germans paraded from the Arc de Triomphe to remind Paris who was in control.

It was afternoon by the time he entered the wide Rue de Rivoli and, having consulted his map once again, turned left into the narrower Rue Castiglione. A Luftwaffe staff car honked imperiously and he pulled to the curb to let it pass, saw the smart uniforms of the men in the automobile, caught a glint of light from an arrogant monocle. The staff car moved swiftly ahead and, as he pedaled into the Place Vendôme, came to a halt in front of the building that was his own destination.

"You must be kidding," he'd said, when the quiet man with the pipe had told him that he'd be living and working in a place that had been largely taken over by the Luftwaffe. The Luftwaffe! His own personal enemy. When you fight an air war you're fighting a very personal war, because you're up there, sometimes three miles high, and there are times when it's one to one, when it's just you and some impersonal German in a very personal battle to the death. Because air aces make news, they're publicized—so it comes to the point where you know that a certain German ace has shot down thirty British aircraft. And you realize that the Germans know from checking the British press that an American named Teddy Werner has shot down fourteen German aircraft.

If Teddy had ever been shot down over German-held territory and picked up by the Luftwaffe, he'd have been treated with a certain sort of respect—until they turned him over to the Nazis who ran prisoner-of-war camps. But he knew that if the Luftwaffe, or anyone else, caught him sneaking around Paris in civilian clothing, not even the respect one aerial warrior has for another would save him from a Gestapo torture room and the firing squad.

He gulped a bit, watched the natty Luftwaffe officers dismount from the automobile and enter the splendid building, and then he pedaled forward.

He'd seen pictures of the building. The main facade on Place Vendôme was, indeed, elegant. But a man looking for a job doesn't go in the front door. He goes to the back, the employees' entrance, the service entrance.

Theo-Teddy was, however, still a bit reluctant. He had reached the point of no return when he left the American patrol in the darkness of night in a strange French woodland, but now he was about to reach a crisis point. He was on the verge of putting his fate, his life, into the hands of people he didn't even know, people who had stood quietly by when Germans marched into Paris, people who had lived under German rule for four years. People who had proved their cowardice, if nothing else.

Among the papers he carried was a letter of recommendation signed by a Luftwaffe *oberst,* a colonel who had conveniently been killed only weeks earlier. The finely forged letter said that Unteroffizier Theo Werner had been an outstanding crewman on a German bomber and was worthy of any consideration that could be given in reward for his service and for his wounds. Theo—and from that moment he must not think of himself as Teddy—took the paper out, his hand shaking only a little, and looked at it. Then he followed the instructions he'd been given back in London and made his way to the service entrance of the building he'd never seen to deliver himself into the hands of people he didn't know.

"Your contact will be a member of the Resistance," he'd been told, "who, not incidentally, is a Gaullist. She will be expecting you."

At the proper entrance, he went inside, carrying the rabbits and the vegetables, and finally attracted the attention of a harried-looking man in the white uniform of a cook. "I am to see the head housekeeper," he said in German. The cook looked at him in contempt, counting out a few francs for the food he'd brought. "The head housekeeper," Theo repeated. The cook pointed a finger. He moved toward a door. Behind him he heard the hissed word, "Boche." In an area of scuttling uniformed maids he repeated his request and, after some confusion, was ushered into a small office. The woman there looked up, her lips pursed.

"I was told that you could help me," Theo Wer-

ner said, extending the letter of recommendation
from the Luftwaffe colonel.

The woman behind the small desk took the letter,
scanned it. "God helps those who help themselves,"
she said in a highly accented German, her face
unsmiling.

So that part of the game was over. She had responded with the proper phrase. She lifted her finger
to her lips in a motion of silence, a motion of
warning.

"Yes," she said. "We can always use good help.
I will speak for you."

"Thank you," Theo said.

"At least," she said, "since you're German, they
won't ship you off to Germany for the labor battalions just when you start earning your keep here."

"Yes, that is true," he said.

So he'd done it. He was now committed. The
woman in the smart but slightly faded dress now
held his life in her hands.

She was writing. Finishing one note, she handed it
to him: a name and directions within the building.
"He will take care of you and furnish you with a
uniform," she said.

"Thank you."

She was writing again. This time the note was
more immediate. It gave him a time and instruction
on how to get to a particular room.

"I remember Oberst Müller well," she said. "He
stayed with us often. It is a sorrow to us that he is
dead."

"Yes," Theo said. Was she merely making conversation, or had she known the colonel whose sig-
nature had been forged on his letter? And if she had
known Müller, how well had she known him? She

was a striking woman, clear of skin, a face of true French beauty, a full, pretty, feminine mouth, large dark eyes, hair that framed the face well. And she was lithe and slim and proud of posture as she rose and indicated that the interview was over.

She extended a hand. "Welcome to the Ritz, Herr Werner," she said.

"Thank you. I am sure I will enjoy my work here," he said, with no hint of flirtation. He was German. He was all seriousness. And, truly, he had no interest in her as a woman. The woman he'd loved was dead.

He left the office, looked at the note she'd given him, and tried to figure out the way to the office where he would, assuredly, be hired to work in one of the most famous hotels in the world. The Paris Ritz. The symbol of luxury. Puttin' on the Ritz. A "ritzy" place . . . a place taken over by the Luftwaffe. A place where he would stay until one of several things happened—until the Germans destroyed Paris as they'd destroyed Rotterdam and Warsaw; until the Resistance groups within the city rose up and fought the German garrison house to house; until the Allies captured the city.

He was there and he was not in control of his fate. He was known as a British spy by at least one person, the rather attractive woman who had warned him to silence in her office. And how many others would know? In spite of all the publicity the French Resistance got, they hadn't done one hell of a lot. They had waited for over a year after the fall of France, to kill their first German soldier and from what he knew they seemed just as intent on fighting each other for the prize of the bones of France after the Allies liberated the country as in fighting Germans.

Hell no, he had no respect for Frenchmen. Maybe a few of the Free French with de Gaulle and Leclerc, but not those who had calmly and supinely lain down and opened their legs to be raped by Hitler's panzers. He didn't like Frenchmen at all.

3

BLAISE DESCHAISES, a slender, dark, un-smiling young man of a scant eighteen years, had seen the blond stranger enter the service area of the hotel and ask for the head housekeeper. Blaise worked in the kitchen as a chef's helper; it was he who spat the word "boche" as Theo Werner walked away. As much as any citizen of France, Blaise had reason to hate the Germans. And more than most Frenchmen, he hated those men, those politicians and generals who, in 1940 and before, had allowed France to be so weakened, so demoralized, that it was but the work of weeks for Guderian's panzers to subjugate the country.

Blaise was a fourteen-year-old cadet when the Germans astounded the French generals and moved heavy armor through the Ardennes. Even then he had been a bit more advanced in his thinking than the generals and the politicians. He could well remember the day, in the late spring of 1940, when he had pointed to a map of France, there in the old and honored Cavalry School at Saumur.

"A child can see it," Blaise Deschaises then said. "The Germans will strike here."

It was after hours and two young cadets were poring over a large-scale map of the Republic by candlelight.

"If you can see it, yes, a child surely can," said his friend Philippe, for Blaise was the youngest cadet at Saumur.

"It will come here," Blaise insisted, punching a finger to an area to the north of peaceful Saumur.

"You are still thinking of another war."

"No, no! Guderian will strike across Luxembourg, here. And the high command will be unprepared. The area is defended by old men and boys."

"And trees," Philippe said, with a smile. "The Ardennes is scarcely the terrain for tank warfare."

"But that is exactly why," Blaise said. "Because they know we will not be expecting an armored thrust through the Ardennes."

"Perhaps you should telegraph Marshal Pétain and warn him," Philippe said.

"He would not listen." Blaise knew that his friend's comment had been touched with sarcasm, but he was quite serious. "He would not listen to those who advised an offensive along the Germans' Western Wall when the best of the German troops were occupied in Poland. If he had listened, we could be beyond the Rhine at this point."

Neither of them heard the quiet approach of a uniformed member of the cadre. "Such wisdom in one so young is commendable," the instructor said. "We admire your exercising it. But since it is after lights-out, you must pay the price, cadets."

"*Merde*," Philippe whispered. Once again he had listened to Blaise, and once again there would be fatigue detail. Someday he would learn not to let Blaise Deschaises lead him into trouble.

Now, four years later, as Blaise cleaned rabbits for the gullets of the hated boches who had occupied the Ritz and used it as a Luftwaffe Headquarters, he could remember it all, for it was engraved on his heart in the blood of his friends.

As he had predicted, Guderian struck through the Ardennes. The French armies were far away, expecting the lunge to come in country more favorable for tanks. The generals enjoyed their feasts far from the front, meanwhile toying with the idea of striking along the sea to meet the Germans in Belgium.

The Nineteenth Panzer Corps smashed over the trees of the Ardennes. Guderian, who had been astounded by the lack of offensive action from the French when the Western Wall was as its weakest, poured overwhelming force against the weak forces, pushing, as the Germans had pushed in another war, toward Sedan. Guderian—and Blaise Deschaises— knew that, one to one, the French tanks were superior to Germany's best, but instead of exploiting their superiority, the generals had dined happily behind their Maginot Line and had given Hitler time to return his crack units from Poland.

As the French tried to hold at Sedan, Blaise lectured Philippe, as they once again cleaned the stables as punishment for being up past lights-out. "Only eight percent of the German invasion force is there," he said. "Just eight percent—a mere ten armored divisions—and the front has collapsed in six days."

"We will stop them," Philippe said.

"Where?" Blaise asked with a shrug. "Now the sea is open to them. They will reach the Channel coast in ten days."

For once, Blaise was wrong. As Rommel and Hoth's Corps blasted toward the sea from the north, Guderian reached the sea beyond Abbeville at seven in the evening of the May 20, only one week after Sedan.

The Cavalry School at Saumur, built in 1768, stood on rising ground dominated by the château of the Dukes of Anjou. Across the Loire, it was a hundred and sixty miles, as the Stuka flies, to Paris. In his first term at the school, Blaise became known to his instructors as a somewhat overconfident young man with some very adult opinions. For example, he had read *the* book when he was twelve. As the now-fatherless son of a decorated veteran of the Great War, he had earned his appointment to Saumur at an unusually tender age, and in his first days there he had questioned why de Gaulle's book wasn't used in classes. The book had sold only about a thousand copies in France, but it was more widely read in German military circles; men like Guderian and Rommel had studied it. In Guderian's thrust through the Ardennes, Blaise recognized some of the theories which a young officer named Charles de Gaulle had developed in the 1930s, before the theory of the blitzkreig had gained favor in Germany. In his youthful confidence, he took pains to point this out.

In Tactics class he held the pointer in his delicate hands, his youthful face seemingly swelled by his high, tight collar. He was taking his turn in analyzing the current military situation.

"They are too far extended," he said, pointing to the forces of the Nineteenth Panzer Corps. "There is not enough support for the tanks. We can cut them off here, or here, or here, and isolate the Nineteen Corps. Guderian will then have his back to the sea and we can eliminate the Nineteenth Corps as a viable force.''

The instructor was an old man, a veteran of the most terrible battle of the Great War, Verdun. ''And what do you do about the main thrust through the Low Countries?'' he asked.

''Sir,'' Blaise said, *''this* is the main thrust. Now they will consolidate and swing back to crush the southern armies here, then move to surround the northern armies.''

''Perhaps the High Command has plans for that contingency,'' the instructor said. ''Have you considered that possibility?''

''Yes, they have plans,'' Blaise said. ''Many plans. The problem is, sir, that before they move to implement the plans, the Germans have moved on. We seem to continue to think in terms of the stationary battles of the Great War. It is this mentality which is defeating us.''

The old man's face reddened. He was one of the famous Black Cadre, entrusted with keeping traditions alive. He, too, had read *the* book, and in spite of it he believed that tanks were useful mainly as support weapons for the men who won wars, the infantry.

Blaise failed to see the warning signals and plunged blithely on. ''Hasn't it been proven that we are wrong? Isn't it clear that the entire nation, with few exceptions, has developed a defensive mentality? Pétain tells us that a continuous front cannot be broken, that defense is less wasteful of the blood of French soldiers—and now we have, in still another war, French dead at Sedan. The Maginot Line has not been broken, no. It has simply been ignored, flanked. And our generals still plan in terms of the great battles, such as Verdun.''

"Ah," said the instructor, his voice low, "so you understand the battle of Verdun?"

"With all due respect, sir," Blaise said, knowing that he was treading dangerous ground, "in all respect to you, and to all the brave men who fought there, Verdun is a stain on the national character."

There was a mass intake of breath from the cadets in the classroom.

"Be silent," the instructor told them. "Let the all-knowing one continue."

"If we could suddenly bring back to life all those who died at Verdun," Blaise said, "and place them there, on the battlefield, there would not be room for them to stand. And yet we called it a victory. The Great War was called a French victory, was it not? But was it? It was an Allied victory, true, but it was a French defeat, and that defeat marks us to this day. We have not yet recovered from the horror of seeing one French citizen in twenty-five die, of the horror of a million and a half dead. Because of those great losses, we have become perhaps too civilized, too weary of war; and we are determined never again to see the carnage of a Verdun. So we build our magnificent wall. The Germans laugh, and bypass it. The French armies are now cut in half, but still the generals do not understand what is happening. If they had only read the book—''

Philippe felt quite brave, emboldened by Blaise's words. "Sir," he said, "he has a point. De Gaulle outlined the very tactics used by Guderian and Rommel back in 1936."

"I have read the book," the instructor said. "He had some good ideas. However, I think it is not the function of a cadet to question the decisions of the General Staff. Therefore—''

Blaise sighed. The stables again. He therefore did not state, in the classroom, what he said to Philippe over a steaming shovelful of horse droppings. ''General Gamelin is the best general the boche have.''

''But he is a French general!'' Phillippe protested.

''Yes—and he moved his troops into Belgium, thus opening the door for the Panzer thrust on the Meuse.''

''If you keep saying things like that you're going to be in big trouble, Blaise!''

''We are all in big trouble.'' Blaise heaved another shovelful onto his cart and pushed it toward the gardens.

They never left him, the memories. At eighteen, he was at work in the kitchen of the Ritz, but the memories were always with him, and in his mind he could see the German paratroopers falling from the skies over Holland like mushrooms, leaping from a mighty fleet of Ju-52s. On that day in 1940, a boche lieutenant colonel had jumped from the leading Ju-52 in command of the Third Battalion of the Sixteenth Regiment of Airborne Infantry. It was that man who had ordered the bombing of Rotterdam, after the city had shown a willingness to surrender, but had not acted swiftly enough to meet his two-hour deadline. Now that man was in Paris. Blaise and some of his friends knew the reputation of the new commander of Paris, now General Dietrich von Choltitz—the destroyer, the man who had, in covering German retreats, razed cities. At Sebastopol he'd used the largest mortar ever built, which could fire a two-and-a-half-ton shell more than three miles and penetrate eight feet of reinforced concrete. Von Choltitz had leveled Sebastopol with it, and now he was in Paris. There could be only one reason for von Choltitz to be in Paris. Blaise knew that it was an ancient military maxim that he who controls Paris controls France; if the Germans were forced out of Paris, they would leave behind smoking ruins. He who controls ruins controls nothing.

The prospect saddened him. But he had seen his friends die, and he had seen the generals waste time over huge and sumptous feasts in Paris while the panzers rolled toward the sea. There were times when he thought he could not bear seeing his city in flames, but the city was less important than the honor of France.

Never again should the politicians and the generals allow France to be overrun. No. It was time to do something. Allied armies were near. Never again should Paris and France fall into the hands of the ambitious, the traditionalists, the cowards who fought so briefly, saying, "We will attack," with a mouth full of *mousse au chocolate*.

Yes, he could remember. "We will attack," said the French generals, but the British saw that it was now hopeless and they fell back to Dunkirk to salvage what they could.

And in the midst of that defeat there had been one moment of glory. The man who had written the book led his Fourth Armored Division into an attack near Abbeville. He had, after all, invented blitzkreig. He advanced. The superior French tanks gave the Germans a rare beating—but when he had advanced for fifteen miles he was given orders to retreat. France fell because the old generals were still living the glory of 1918. The southern armies were surrounded.

Quiet old Saumur could hear the Germans before

it saw them. Blaise Deschaises, praying in the ancient church of Notre Dame des Ardilliers, could hear the Stukas as they flew over, the same Stukas that had been so decisive at Sedan. Later, standing on the rise of ground, he could see the distant smoke and hear the German tank guns.

"Sir," he said, standing at his maximum height, dressed in his best, "we require the keys to the arsenal."

"No, no," the old veteran of Verdun said.

"The boche will be here within hours," Blaise said. "I do not intend to surrender. There are others who feel the same."

"But that is an entire Panzer division out there!"

Blaise shrugged. "We will require the keys."

The young cadets who fought at Saumur had the advantages of high ground, and they had a splendid collection of modern arms, for they were being trained to be the future warriors of the armored forces. They spent the few remaining hours preparing their positions, and when the Germans came, expecting another undefended French town, the sound of battle rivaled the spring thunderstorms of that hot and sultry June. Boys who did not yet shave dared death, and in that cauldron of steel and smoke the character of Blaise Deschaises was toned, tempered. He saw his friends fall one by one, by the third day, the ranks of the cadets terribly depleted, he commanded a squad composed of himself, Philippe, and three other cadets.

Philippe, who had been wounded in the leg, limped up to him. "We have held them for three days," Philippe said, grinning proudly.

"Yes, my friend." Blaise nodded.

"We will hold."

But Blaise knew. He shook his head. His eyes

were burning, bloodshot, and his ears rang continuously from the shellbursts. "My dear friend," he said. "It is time. Take the others and go. Find a cave along the river. Find civilian clothing and hide until the Germans have passed, then make your way home."

"Will you come?"

Blaise shook his head. "No, my friend. I have no plans to leave Saumur."

A company of German infantry was moving up the hill under the cover of the guns of the tanks. The others did not leave. Philippe and another cadet manned a machine gun. Mortar shells exploded closer and closer, seeking the range of the gun. The school was in ruins, but shells continued to stir the rubble, to detonate among the dead and desecrate their already mutilated bodies. Most of the cadre were dead.

It was the old veteran who survived longest. Now he was on the verge of being overrun. He looked around him and saw only a pitiful few. And he carried a treasure in his pack. He crawled toward the machine-gun position, remembering that other war, so long ago, feeling himself to be, once again, in no-man's land, with German shells bursting around him. He was hit a few yards away from Blaise's position. At the same time, another shell burst the barrel of the machine gun, killing Philippe and the cadet with him.

Blaise was screaming and firing as fast as he could. When the shell burst, he felt a numbing blow to his shoulder. He looked around. Alone. All the others were dead. Nerves taut, he prepared to make a last charge into the heart of the German advance. Just then he heard his name and turned. The old instructor was beckoning. He crawled over to him, feeling the characteristic whiz of bullets passing just over his head.

"You must go, Deschaises." The instructor was bleeding from the mouth. He had not long to live. Blaise tried to ease his position and shook his head in negation.

"In my pack," the old man whispered. "My pack."

There was little time, but an old man was dying. Blaise humored him and opened the pack. The golden object seemed to blaze in the mixed light of the cloudy, sultry day. It was the unofficial symbol of Saumur. It had been brought to the school by an officer of Napoleon's army, freshly back from the ill-fated expedition to Egypt. It was a horse, the tool of cavalry, the symbol of the school, a golden horse fashioned by ancient craftsmen in an alien civilization which had, like poor bloody France, known conquerors. The Egyptian Horse was priceless with its gold and emeralds and rubies—more priceless because of its symbolism. The horse *was* the Cavalry School, all that was left of it.

The old man was emphatic, though barely audible. "Take it! Hide it well, protect it. The Germans must never have it."

Blaise would always wonder if he had used the horse as an excuse to leave. It weighed heavily in his hand as he watched the old man die. The shouts of the approaching German infantry grew louder. Quickly he tucked the horse into his tunic and began to crawl. The countryside surrounding the school was familiar to him, so escape was relatively easy. His shoulder did not begin to hurt until he gained the rough country along the river, but then the pain from the mortar wound slammed into him, making him gasp aloud.

He knew a cave nearby—one of the caves that line the cliffs of the Loire, where, in ancient but vivid color, strange sticklike men chase antique beasts to speak of the distant past of the original Frenchmen. His was not one of the more famous caves, but only a small one, little known. But in two areas there were tiny paintings which, as he moaned aloud in pain, seemed to dance and come alive.

When he had rested a bit, he crawled deep into the darkness of the cave, and there he buried the horse. He covered it well, marking the spot in his mind. If he lived, he could pass his knowledge to others. If he died, at least the Germans would not have it.

He cleaned his wound with his handkerchief, and could feel that it was not mortal. The piece of shrapnel had torn through the flesh of his shoulder without striking bone. He bandaged the wound, curled up on the floor, and slept.

When he emerged, it was hunger that had awakened him. He swam across the Loire by night. He walked a few kilometers before dawn to dry his clothes and lay down in a copse of trees to pray that his wound did not become infected. He took civilian clothing from a clothesline in a farmyard and began to walk by day.

He walked into panic and confusion. The Germans were coming from his rear, and entire villages were being emptied. The roads were crowded with fleeing civilians, and here and there a disorganized unit of the French Army. The air seemed filled with the constant echo of German jackboots, clunking, marching, advancing. He considered joining one of

the Army units, but he scorned their panicky disorgani-
zation. He had killed his Germans, and he had a new
mission—to pass along the knowledge of the location of the Saumur horse. Someday the Germans
would be thrown back and the horse would take its
place, once again, at Saumur Cavalry School.

Stukas came to bomb and strafe the Army and
civilians with equal enthusiasm. A horse pulling a
farm cart screamed in agony and fell to thrash its
legs into the legs of screaming, running people. At a
small river ahead, a unit of French engineers were
placing explosives on the span of the bridge. Bodies
bloated in the water. A flood of fleeing villagers
fought, pushed, screamed to get off the bridge as a
Stuka, the fearful siren yowling, dived to strafe the
bridge. Blaise would not take the exposed bridge.
Though his shoulder was stiff and quite sore, he was
not feverish; he had already swum one river and
could swim another. As he watched, the soldiers
placed the last charges on the bridge.

The officer barked an order, but it took a moment
for it to penetrate Blaise's dazed brain. The bridge
still swarmed with people, farm animals on leads, a
horse pulling a two-wheeled cart. Some of the people on the bridge heard the order and went mad with
fear. A young girl was pushed over the rail; she fell
and fell an interminable instant, hitting the water
with a huge splash. A woman holding a baby was
crushed against the rail, and the baby's head broke
open, to ooze a strange pinkish substance mixed
with blood.

Blaise leaped for the nearest soldier and sent him
sprawling. With the soldier's rifle ready to fire, he
crouched and told the officer, "If you fire the charges,

you will die before the sound of the blast is out of your ears.''

Like good Frenchmen, they negotiated in heated tones, but Blaise prevailed. The soldiers blocked the road and waited until the bridge was free of people and then there was the blast and the span toppled. Blaise gave the rifle back and apologized. The officer said that he understood. Blaise picked his way down the riverbank and swam across the river.

It was a long walk. At first he did not hear the war news. He was not there to hear the sound of jack-boots on Paris pavements, did not see the Parisians swarm from the city to the country roads, where they were bombed and strafed by German aircraft. Only later did he learn that, in an old railroad carriage where once the victorious Allies had dictated peace terms to the Kaiser's generals, Adolf Hitler had now closed the books on the Treaty of Versailles with a humiliating set of conditions for the surrender of France. He did not know, at the time, that his idol de Gaulle was among the French troops that were taken off the beaches of Dunkirk by a ragtag navy of small boats.

When he reached Paris he was halted by an arro-gant German. ''I was caught in the bombings,'' he said. He found it easy to weep. If the German who questioned him took that to be the fright of a teenage boy, well, the misconception served a purpose. He was not detained.

So he heard German laughter in Paris streets. He heard the sound of jackboots. He saw Germans climb-ing the Eiffel Tower and he saw the swastika flying there, and everywhere. His last food had been taken from the body of a dead soldier two days previously. He was delayed in crossing an avenue by the passage of a very sharp unit of German infantry on parade. Their boots rang against the Paris street in unison. Their stern, expressionless faces continued to float before his eyes, as if they were figments of a delirium.

Later he learned that two million French soldiers had surrendered. And for a long time he would wish that he were back on the hill at Saumur, to kill one last German and then to lie there with his friends, perhaps with a neat little stone on his grave with the words, MORT POUR LA FRANCE. For they, the generals and the politicians had sold France, had betrayed her, had abandoned her, had allowed the boches to come traduce the symbol of France, Blaise's home city, his Paris.

On that hopeless day in 1940 he had but one place to go. He was only a boy. His country was dying around him; Marshal Pétain said it must give up the fight. It was entering a period of darkness from which, to his young eyes, there seemed no escape. He was hurt and he was hungry and he was weeping. He made his way to the service entrance of the grand hotel which fronted on the Place Vendôme, the place where his widowed mother worked.

A chef looked up to see a young scarecrow, clothing in tatters, face soiled, shoulder stained with blood.

"Monsieur," Blaise had said, long ago, "I am Blaise Deschaises, would you please—"

He fainted, there in the kitchens of the Ritz, but he did not give up the fight. He immediately began to seek a way, and he found it. Not instantly, but as the time went on, he found it. He had revered one man, the little-known general who had advanced when all of France was retreating; at first he sought out those who felt as he did, that de Gaulle was the one hope for France. But as the months passed and became a year, the Germans still paraded down the Champs Élysées each day at noon, Paris still bowed and scraped to its German lords. Slowly it became evident that Charles de Gaulle was no hero—was, after all, merely another politician whose one goal was to rule France after the British and the Americans and the Russians had defeated Germany.

In Paris, the vaunted French Resistance played games. Not a single German soldier was killed. Paris was much talk and no action. In Holland the Underground did things. They blew up trains and helped Allied airmen escape. In Paris they talked, endlessly. They printed little ragtag newspapers calling the Germans boches, while in public they said, "Yes, sir."

"We must *do* something," he said to a new friend, one day when he was fifteen. "We must."

He was introduced to a man. He was unlike any man Blaise had ever known, a man who had a new vision. And suddenly Blaise's world changed. Here, at last, was a group with plans. Here were men and women who were active, who were *doing* something. It filled him with tremendous pride when he met, face to face, an American airman who had been hidden by this particular Resistance group for months.

"So, you want to kill Germans," the man said to him.

"That I have already done," Blaise said.

The man laughed.

Insulted, Blaise turned his back arrogantly and started to leave.

"Yes," the man said gently. "I know of Saumur."

He stopped, but did not turn back to face the man.

"I did not laugh because you want to kill Germans," the man said, "but because your spirit pleases me. Come with me, my young cock, and you will kill Germans. Not now. Now, if we kill a German they kill a dozen of us. The few we could kill now would not make the difference."

"So we talk until the Americans come again?" Blaise addressed the door.

"Perhaps we should talk, first," the man said. "For example, what is your primary goal?"

Blaise whirled to face the man. "To free France of the boches," he spat.

"And then?"

He was silent. Already he had begun to wonder what would happen when the Germans were gone. Would the generals and the politicians become too civilized again? Would they forget the lessons of this war, as they'd forgotten the lessons of the one before?

"You see, my young friend," the man said, "we think not only of today. We think not only of the day when we, with guns and grenades, will wipe the honor of France clean once more. We think of the day after that, and we intend to have a strong say in just who will control the destiny of France. I promise you a change, my friend. I promise you that France will never again fall under the control of those who have shamed her. Never again will she be weak. We will see to that."

He liked it. He listened. And when he learned who the "we" to whom the man referred actually were, he was past shock. The man whose talk was convincing, the man who was *doing* something, was known as Colonel Rol. He was the primary leader of one of the two Resistance groups in Paris. He was an avowed Communist.

No one, other than Colonel Rol and two others,

knew that Blaise Deschaises, son of a decorated hero of the Great War, had embraced the Communist belief. It was in fact somewhat ironic that he should be working at the Ritz, for he knew well that the Ritz, in the service areas, in the basements, in the hidden nooks and corners, was a strong cell of the Gaullist Resistance. He sometimes suspected that his own mother knew of the Gaullists, that she even sympathized with them. She would not talk about it. She insisted that he keep aloof from the movement, warning him that the help of one teen-age boy would not remove the heel of the German dictator from Paris. It suited his purpose to let her think that he was content to be in training as a chef. He did not tell her the details of the battle at Saumur. He let her think that he had been so young that he did not participate. She had been so thankful, that day in 1940 when he staggered into the kitchens of the Ritz, to see him alive that she had not questioned him too deeply.

It was not to his mother that he confided the whereabouts of a certain *objet d' art*, but to Colonel Rol. The location of the horse was recorded safely in several secret places now, and he had Colonel Rol's word that after the war, should Blaise not survive, the horse would be returned to Saumur.

Now it was August of 1944, and the Allied forces were pushing inexorably closer to Paris. Now, after four years of talk and planning and hiding a few Allied airmen, it was time. Now, here and there in the city, Germans were dying. He himself had had the satisfaction, only two nights past, of seeing a German sentry topple and die with one well-placed shot from his own weapon, a stolen Luger.

Yes, the time was near. He felt both joy and dread, for Paris would suffer. Von Choltitz's reputation was clear; he would suppress any insurrection ruthlessly. But Blaise would follow the orders of Colonel Rol, defying the Allied wishes, and rise up to kill Germans wherever he could find them. Paris would fight. If Paris suffered, well, perhaps, as Colonel Rol stated, it was worth it. He would fight with the Communist Resistance, and he would fight afterward to see to it that Paris did not fall under the control of a man who had once been brave but who had fled and then put politics above country. When the Allied armies arrived in Paris, he and his friends would be in control. And he who holds Paris holds France.

If he had needed any more convincing that Colonel Rol was right, the Vercors affair would have done it. He had heard the sincere voices on the radio, after D-Day, calling upon the Resistance to rise up, to fight the Germans. And he had wanted to fight then. In the mountains, near Grenoble, the Resistance had risen. There the French Tricolor flew proudly, and for days the brave men withstood everything the Germans could throw against them. And all the while, believing the promises of help, they had called for help. What was largely a French army had come ashore in the south, between Cape Cavalaire and Agay. There were aircraft there, and the brave men of Vercors had called upon them for aid. German planes strafed and bombed, but there were no Allied planes over the Vercors. The heroic men who had risen, convinced that they would receive help, were told that they were beyond the range of the aircraft. Had not Fernand Grenier, Minister for Air in the Provisional Government, himself called de

Gaulle an opportunist? Had not Grenier pointed out that for days the heroes of Vercors had begged for bombing strikes on the Germans' airfield—and been refused?

"Consider this," Colonel Rol had said. "The generals said that Vercors was beyond aircraft range. And yet there were planes available at Calvi, two hundred twenty-five miles away, planes with ranges of eight or nine hundred miles."

So, once again, the generals and the politicians had deserted Frenchmen who were fighting for their lives and their country. It would, if Blaise had any say in it, never happen again.

4

ORDINARILY, THE DISTINGUISHED but often harried director of the Ritz would not have been involved in the hiring of a mere steward. M. Claude Auzello had other things on his mind—not, he would have clarified, more important things, for the level of service at his hotel was as important as any. However, the hotel was experiencing trying times. The traditional formula of two employees to each guest was suffering from the wartime manpower shortage. Only a few days past, one of the hotel's stewards had unwisely violated the curfew and had been taken to the quarters of the German Military Police. He spent the rest of the night shining shoes. That might have been the end of it, but he was one of the unlucky ones. Violating curfew, while not always severely punished, was an offense not necessarily free of serious consequences. The Germans, with their delicate irony, liked to select from among curfew offenders those who were to be shot in reprisal for the death of German soldiers in the increasing Resistance activity.

M. Auzello had no way of knowing if his steward had been shot, or if he'd merely been shipped off to Germany to join the labor battalions. He knew only that he'd lost still another man from a staff already seriously depleted. Of course there were plenty of women available for work, but for some jobs, women were simply not suited. He did his best with what he had though, and in fact was quite pleased with the work of his "girls" in particular, with the work of his head housekeeper, Mady Deschaises.

As it happened, the man who normally hired and fired the lowlier help had been struck, while riding his bicycle, by a speeding German motorcycle side-car and was in the hospital. Claude Auzello was a man who was capable of handling details with precision and dispatch, so he handled still one more when he was told that a Swiss-German with a medical discharge from the Luftwaffe was seeking employment.

"Please send the man to me," Auzello said.

While he waited, he leafed through a sheaf of papers that were of great importance. The papers represented an idea for which he had little hope, but he was increasingly aware of the growing Resistance activity, of the nearness of the Allied armies, and of a definite threat to Paris and, in particular, to his hotel. He had spent the morning talking about the plan with the senior Luftwaffe officer in the Ritz, General Schläfer. Schläfer, interested, was sending his valet to collect the proposal from Auzello, so the dirctor made one last check to be sure that all of the papers were in order. He was just finishing when the general's valet appeared at his open door.

The man had been in the Ritz for over a year, yet Claude Auzello could still not even begin to guess what went on behind that thin, almost ratlike face, what thoughts motivated the dark, piercing eyes. The man was an enigma, and for more reasons than one. First, Auzello could not understand why a high-ranking Luftwaffe general, who could have had his pick of enlisted servants, would travel with, and in effect live with, a congenital cripple.

It seemed incongrous to Auzello that the Germans, who boasted of being the master race—and, it was said, quite casually destroyed malformed children at birth—should be represented in his office by a small, wiry man with a withered arm and one leg shorter than the other. And yet he was there, staring down at Auzello with his characteristic arrogant gaze, a small man in the uniform of a Luftwaffe corporal.

"Ah, Monsieur Wolf," Auzello said. He was never sure whether Wolf was the valet's given name or surname, but it was the only one the man ever used. "I have the papers ready."

Wolf allowed a small smile to alter his expressionless face. "It is a good plan, Director."

"Thank you."

Wolf shrugged. "It will not, of course, work."

"Well," Auzello said, spreading his hands, "we can but try. The hotel is worth the saving, don't you think?"

Wolf did not answer immediately. Instead, he moved forward, picked up the papers on Auzello's desk, and riffled through them. "If you repeat this I will say you are a liar," he said, with that twisted little smile. "But shares in a Paris hotel will not be worth much when von Choltitz is finished."

"We can but try." Auzello reinforced his patience, when it flagged, by repeating himself.

"It is too bad." That smirking little smile played on Wolf's face. "Paris is a beautiful city."

"You seem rather pessimistic."

"Can you really believe that the Führer will allow Paris to stand to fall into Allied hands?"

"Surely even he must have some shread of decency left."

Wolf shrugged again, dismissing such human failings as decency and hope. "As you say, we can but try. I myself will speak with the Herr General."

Auzello raised an eyebrow ever so slightly. Did the man think that a mere servant, a servant in a corporal's uniform, could influence a man so powerful as Schläfer? He was at a loss for words. For over a year now this man, this strange little man with his heavy-soled left shoe, had acted as spokesman for the high-ranking Luftwaffe officers who had occupied most of the Ritz. It seemed that the officers considered it beneath them to speak to staff and management about mere matters of personal comfort. That had been left to Wolf. Although the director had talked with the crippled corporal many times, he still was a bit uncomfortable in his presence. There was more than a German arrogance about Wolf. There was also a constant hint of threat. His mildest words seemed to carry hidden meaning. Usually distinctly nasty.

"I will appreciate any help you can give me," Auzello said with diplomatic grace. "As you know, I am prepared to go to great lengths to spare this hotel the destruction which very well may come to our city."

He was silent then, waiting, wanting the man to

leave, but Wolf shifted his weight and turned his head at the sound of footsteps. An older man in the livery of a steward appeared in the doorway.

"Sorry, Monsieur Director, I did not know you were occupied," the old steward said.

"We are just finished," Wolf said, casually usurping the director's authority.

Auzello missed only a beat before saying, "Come in."

"It is the new man," the steward said.

"Ask him to come in." Auzello glanced at Wolf, who showed no inclination to leave. Instead he moved to stand against one wall, his steady, burning eyes on the old steward.

"Yes, sir," the old steward said. "His name, sir, is Herr Theo Werner."

Wolf's faced changed slightly, and he looked at Theo with narrowed eyes as the tall blond man entered and snapped to Germanic attention in front of Auzello's desk.

"*Herr* Werner?" Wolf asked, having to look upward to see Theo's eyes.

Theo did not move his head, stood at strict attention.

"Relax, man," Auzello said. "You are not in a military office here."

"I'm sorry, sir," Theo said, in German, "I have little French."

Auzello repeated his words, his German quite satisfactory. Theo relaxed to the extent of standing at rigid parade rest. He did not look at Wolf, although he had noticed the Luftwaffe uniform.

"Your papers?" Auzello asked.

Theo handed them over. Wolf leaned, took a match from the director's desk, and lit a cigarette. Auzello read for a moment. "You have an enviable war record, Herr Werner,'' he said. ''Have you experience in hotel service?''

''Very little, sir,'' Theo said. ''My uncle has a small inn near St. Gallen. But I have a desire to learn, sir. It is a career that has captured my interest. I must confess that I have never even been inside a hotel of the quality of the Ritz.'' And, saying it, he remembered another grand hotel, the proud old Savoy, where he'd spent so many lovely hours with the woman who became his wife, the woman who was now dead. ''I was advised, by my commanding officer, that service at the Ritz would be invaluable training.''

''Your commanding officer?'' Wolf asked.

Theo allowed his head to swivel stiffly, giving Wolf a cold glare. The dark little eyes did not shift away.

''Herr Werner had long and honorable service with the bombers of Luftflotte Two,'' Auzello said. ''He has been medically discharged. I trust that your wounds, Herr Werner, are not too bothersome to hamper you in your work.''

''The doctors have advised me to refrain from heavy lifting for some time,'' Theo said. ''That does not preclude my lifting a serving tray, sir.''

''So you were with Luftflotte Two?'' Wolf asked. ''Your years of service?''

''Since early 1940,'' Theo said.

''You must have visited our friends across the Channel a few times,'' Wolf said.

''I know England quite well,'' Theo said, unsmilingly. ''At least the way it looks from a gunner's turret.''

''Your commanding officer who sent you here?'' Wolf demanded.

"Herr Oberst Klaus Müller," Theo said, putting respect into his voice.

"Who is dead," Wolf said flatly.

"*Ja*," Theo said.

"There is a strange quality to your German," Wolf said. "I've been trying to place your accent."

"I am German," Theo said. "I am, however, a Swiss national. I am here by choice."

"Very commendable," Wolf said. He turned and left abruptly. Theo returned his gaze to a point inches above the director's head, wondering why a Luftwaffe corporal had been in the office, feeling free to ask questions of a prospective employee. He decided that he'd have to watch that one.

"To be frank," Auzello said, "in ordinary times I would not hire you, Herr Werner. We like to have French employees here. However, as you must know, we have guests who . . . are not French. I think that it will work out quite well, if you have no objection to doing your service in the part of the hotel occupied by our Luftwaffe guests."

"Thank you, sir," Theo said.

"It would help if you learned French."

He almost smiled. He didn't think he'd be there long enough to work much on it. "I shall try, sir. No one who wishes a career in an international hotel can be without French." With the director, of course, he must appear a bit less arrogant.

"You will report to M. Alexandre, the chief steward—the man who brought you here. He will try to find a uniform to fit you. You're a large one, and you might have to make do with less than perfect fit for a while. I think you know that you are being employed by one of the great hotels of the world." He smiled when Theo nodded his awed agreement.

"Even under such adverse circumstances as we now suffer, the Ritz has maintained a certain quality of service and elegance of living. What do you know of our establishment?"

"That it has a most excellent reputation," Theo said.

"Give me your impressions," the director said.

"Sir, I have seen little. I was impressed by the appearance of the facade. It is quite elegant."

"That is only the facade, essentially uniform with the rest on the Place Vendôme," Auzello said. "It is the people who work here which make this a great hotel. We have a tradition second to none. Our founder, César Ritz—a countryman of yours, by the way—is still judged the greatest of all the great hotel men. He put his stamp on the Savoy, in London. He brought there the king of the chefs, Georges Auguste Escoffier. From the Savoy he and Escoffier moved to the London Carlton to establish even higher reputations, reputations so great that when César Ritz decided to establish a hotel in Paris, he had no trouble getting the backing."

Once Claude Auzello began speaking about the one love of his life, the Ritz, he was able to forget the war, the long years of shortages and occupation and humiliation, the danger that threatened all of the city and his beloved hotel. Talking about the hotel was his own private opium, his escape. For to merely think of what had been done by one man, back there in 1898, was enough to mist his eyes. And he was quite expressive.

He spoke of the man, César Ritz, who believed in the pursuit of the good life, the man who, while managing the great Carlton, heeded the complaints of the elite—who spent business months at the Savoy or the Carlton in London and the social seasons at such luxurious hotels as Lucerne's National, Baden-Baden's Brenner's Park, or the grand old Adlon in Berlin—that although they would like to spend time in Paris, the city simply did not boast a hotel that offered the proper amenities, that held to adequate standards.

Auzello loved the story, and it mattered not whether it was totally true, that the site of the Paris Ritz had been determined by accident. Lost in his subject, he took valuable time to tell the new steward how César Ritz, walking along the Place Vendôme, saw a delivery boy taking a bathtub and hot water to an elegant private mansion. Upon questioning the delivery boy, Ritz learned that the bath was for the Prince of Wales—later to be Edward VII. With no hesitation he decided that if the mansion was good enough for the Prince of Wales, it was the proper site for his hotel.

The affair seemed to be favored by the fates from the beginning. The mansion, once home of the Ducs de Lauzun, was, in fact, on the market. Upon inspection, it proved ideal for the rather small but elegantly comfortable watering place Ritz had in mind. He needed nothing more than money—and that was simple, too. He knew a man named Marnier La Postolle, a little man who had just invented a particularly meritorious orange-flavored liqueur. Both men, Postolle and Ritz, gained when Ritz asked for backing, for in the course of the talks Postolle mentioned that he needed a name for his new liqueur. The tall and elegant Ritz, with a trace of humor, looked down upon the short man and said, "M. Postolle, I suggest that you call your creation Grand Marnier."

The combination of Ritz and the great chef, Escoffier, the impeccable taste of both, the drive of the man who *knew* the good life and knew the needs of those who could afford it, was a guarantee of success. Ritz's faultless service and Escoffier's superlative cuisine brought the elite to Paris to be cosseted at the hotel that made its name a part of several languages.

Compared to some of the other great luxury hotels, the Ritz was small. There were only two hundred and ten rooms. There were no overweening displays of space and opulence, merely an atmosphere that made the word "luxury" seem inadequate. Even in the darkest days of the war, it remained the sort of place that could give hints on how things should have been done at Versailles. Its turn-of-the-century richness of Baroque decor included hundreds of floor-to-ceiling wall mirrors reflecting quietly strolling ladies and gentlemen in perfect dress. There were two staff members to each guest. As at the Savoy, where Ritz himself had established the traditions, a guest had only to state his preferences once, and they were tended with meticulous care forever after.

The Ritz had seen its royalty and its important personages. The Ritz Bar had witnessed events that had profound effects on the government of France and upon the world.

And now, with the Allied armies so near, with the Germans, in their impending defeat, revealing themselves as the barbarbians they'd always been, Claude Auzello knew that he would be a very lucky man if he did not live to see the Ritz in ruin—burned, razed, bombed, destroyed. The thought was an ache in his breast, an almost unbearable fear of seeing that treasure of woodwork and tapestries and paintings looking like Warsaw or Rotterdam or Stalingrad.

But time was important, and the pleasure of talking about the past glories had to take second place to the necessities of today. He had used enough of his time talking with a mere steward—and a boche, at that.

"It is said," he concluded, "that our kitchen is managed from the grave by the great Escoffier. Remember that. You will be serving the best food that it is possible to serve. Fortunately, our German guests are often quite helpful in obtaining for us some of the nicer things. Just remember, Herr Werner, that you are a part of the Ritz, that when you give service, even to German officers, you are upholding a tradition."

He was a bit doubtful about that last statement, that "even German officers," but the new steward didn't blink an eye.

"If you are sincere in your desire to learn a career, you are in the proper place," Auzello said.

He stood. Theo, taking that as a dismissal, clicked his heels and stood at attention.

"And please, Herr Werner," Auzello said, forgetting caution, "stop that infernal soldiering!"

Theo found M. Alexandre, who have him a uniform—a somewhat frayed one, but clean and pressed neatly.

"The jacket seems a bit tight in the shoulders," the chief steward observed. "We'll have a seamstress take care of that tomorrow. Meantime, Lucien can begin introducing you to your duties."

Lucien proved to be a younger German-speaking steward, who guided Theo through the service areas, the upstairs halls, and the storerooms and laundry in the basement. He demonstrated and described the duties, manners, rules, prohibitions, and schedule that defined the life of a steward at the Ritz. It all reminded Theo-Teddy of his recent week-long indoctrination in England; he absorbed the information, filed, and classified it, determined to make his cover as perfect as he could.

He ate with other stewards and kitchen workers at a large table in a staff dining room near the kitchen. Lucien was still occupying his attention, with more descriptions of of what a steward must and must not do; but once Theo looked up to see a dark young man glaring at him from the other end of the table. When Theo caught his gaze, he frowned and looked away.

"Who is that?" he asked Lucien.

"Who? Oh, Blaise. Don't worry. He's very young. He doesn't like to hear German. Fortunately, he works only in the kitchen."

After supper, M. Alexandre took Theo aside. "Do you have a place to stay?" the old steward asked.

"I haven't had a chance to find a place," Theo said. He knew that there were limited facilities for housing Ritz employees in various odd corners of the hotel, and he was banking on the help of his contact to see to it that he would be assigned a bed in the building.

"Well, we must think about that, then," the old steward said.

"There is someone with whom I can discuss it," Theo said. The note with the head housekeeper's room number was in his pocket.

"Do that," the old steward said. "Meanwhile, I will speak with others."

"Meanwhile," Theo said, "I stand ready to work."

The man laughed. "Not even a German begins service at the Ritz without proper training. First we must find you a place to sleep for the night. Then, tomorrow, we will begin your real instructions."

5

THE ROOM THEO sought was near the Cambon end of the hotel, away from the elegant facade on the Place Vendôme where the finer areas of the building had been taken over by the Luftwaffe. He walked down a dark little passage to an unprepossessing door—perhaps, he suspected, in the old servants' quarters. It was early evening. Outside, the light was growing dim. He stopped in front of the door and knocked. There was a long pause before the door opened and he looked into a face made more feminine by the removal of the light makeup she'd worn when he first saw her in her office.

She looked up and down the dark corridor and jerked her head, telling him to enter. The room was small, the furniture old and rather nice, the one bed made neatly.

Her German was charmingly accented. "Any problems?"

"None," he said.

She had removed her simple working dress, and a

frilly little dressing gown now framed her face with lace. She motioned him to sit. He took a chair that looked as if it might collapse under his long-legged Texas frame.

"I will be in contact with others," she said quickly, standing before his chair. "I must know the intentions of the Allied High Command regarding Paris."

Theo was startled. "The High Command doesn't consult with me," he said with a little smile.

"Then why are you here?" Her voice was low and somewhat angry. "We have sent message after message. The Communists are planning rebellion. You know what that means. De Gaulle has sent word to us to avoid angering the Germans at all costs, to wait until the armies are here. You know that if we fight, the Germans will destroy all of the city."

"I am here merely to gather information and send it out," Theo said.

She made a spitting sound. "We have sent out information. Do they feel that they have to check on us, to see if we are lying?"

He shrugged. "I have my orders," he said. Among them was the advice to be very cautious, and Theo wasn't ready to come clean. "They include collecting information regarding the number of able-bodied men that the Resistance can put on the street at the last moment. The only thing that I can tell you, Madame Deschaises, is that no one wants to see Paris razed. It is my guess that the Allied armies will bypass Paris, to avoid staging a battle of armor and artillery in the streets—to avoid, above all, the destruction of the city."

"But don't they see?" she asked, beginning to

pace back and forth. "That is exactly what we cannot allow. The Communists are determined to be in control of Paris when the Allies arrive, and they are willing to sacrifice lives—and the city itself—to assure that goal."

"Do you know of any plans to start fighting?"

"Not in detail. I—we—know only that those who claim to be 'true' Frenchmen, those who compose a significant portion of the Paris Resistance, are determined to keep de Gaulle from being the ruler of France after the Germans are gone."

"I consider that to be internal politics," Theo said, "and beyond my responsibility. My duty is primarily to get as many facts as possible about the situation and relay them. I trust you have the facilities?"

"There are radios."

"When will I be able to meet with others in your movement?"

"Soon enough," she said. "Have you a place to stay?"

"Not yet. I wanted to speak with you about that. I think I should be here, in the hotel, if it is at all possible."

"Yes. I will see to it." She ceased her pacing and looked down at him. Without makeup her face looked younger. There was, about her dark eyes, something almost vulnerable.

He rose. "Thank you," he said. He turned toward the door and halted when an imperious knock sounded. He looked at her questioningly. She raised a finger to her lips. The knock was repeated, along with a harsh voice calling her name.

She moved to Theo swiftly and whispered. "Take off your shirt, quickly. Get on the bed."

He understood. He ripped off the shirt, lay down on the bed, jerked the coverings from their neat tucks under the pillows to give the bed a rumpled look.

"Madame Deschaises," the harsh voice repeated.

"A moment," she called, her voice breathless. She moved toward the door, ripping open her dressing gown to show faded underthings. A quick gesture mussed her hair. As she opened the door she began to draw the dressing gown closed, but not before Wolf saw a flash of lacy underwear.

"Yes?" she asked.

Wolf made to push past her and she blocked his way.

"I have instructions for the maintainance of General Schläfer's room," Wolf said.

"It is late. I will speak with you tomorrow."

"I am intruding?" Wolf asked, with a knowing leer.

"Yes, you are," she said flatly. She stood with both her hands on the door, holding it so that he could not see into the room.

"Perhaps I shall speak with the director," Wolf said. "He might be interested in knowing that his head housekeeper is more interested in her pleasures than in serving the guests."

"Do as you please," Mady said. "Please state your problem quickly and I will see to it."

"Ah," Wolf said, trying to see past her, his eyes dropping to the area of smooth skin exposed by the not completely closed neck of the dressing gown. "You are interested in your guests?"

"Of course," she said. "What is the problem?"

"It concerns the general's sheets," Wolf said. "They have not been starched properly."

"Tell your general that if he will supply us with starch, we will be happy to use it for him," she said.

"Is there no starch, then, for others?"

"No."

"I will see that you have starch, at least for the general," Wolf said.

He moved suddenly, before she could brace herself. He pushed against the door, using one hand to shove her aside and, as the door flew open, he stepped into the room.

Theo sat up, glaring at him.

"You waste no time, Madame Deschaises," Wolf said, his face expressionless, but with a tightness to his mouth.

Theo swung his legs down from the bed, stood, stretching to his full height. He used the voice of the German *unteroffizier*. "Corporal, you may go."

"Ah, and who gives orders?" Wolf asked.

Theo took two steps forward. "You are intruding, Corporal," he said, his voice tight, cold. "You have two choices. You will leave immediately or be tossed out on your miserable ass."

Wolf's eyes narrowed. For a long moment he looked up, unblinkingly, into Theo's eyes. Then, with a grunt, he turned. He left the door open. Mady closed it and leaned against it. She was shaking. When she turned, her cheeks were wet with silent tears.

There was something about her that touched him, some vague, feminine quality that brought to him the memory of Jeanna, silent tears wetting her face when he had to leave to fly against the endless hordes of German planes. Without thinking, he stepped forward, enfolded her in his arms. She was a long-legged lady, and her head came just under his chin and he found himself patting her on the back, in total silence.

Just that gentle pat and his tenderness unloosed something in her, for no one had held her thus in years, since her husband died, ten years—ages—ago, of his Great War wounds. The sobs came, a torrent that she was helpless to control. Her soft body shook with the force of them, and he held her close, close, his lips and nose brushing the fragrant hair.

He was thinking that she had reason to weep. He knew nothing about her, only that she was a woman, a soft, attractive woman who looked younger than she must be. He could only begin to imagine her reasons. Four years of occupation. Four years of Germans. Four years of having to serve Germans in the hotel—and judging by Wolf's attitude, four years of demands and lust from the conquerors. She was, after all, only a woman, and she was involved in activities which, even though she was a woman, could result in her death.

Her sobbings diminished. She lay weakly against his chest and then, her body stiffening, she tried to push away.

"No," he said. He bent, put his arm under her legs and lifted her. He carried her to the bed and put her down. She did not resist. The ease with which he'd lifted her in his strong arms made her feel weak and helpless. She had not been afforded the luxury of feeling like a woman for a long, long time.

"All right, now?" he asked, standing, moving back a pace.

"Yes, thank you," she said. "I'm sorry."

He grinned. "You don't have to say that you're not the sort of woman to do that often. I suspect that it's been building a long time."

She sighed. "Ah, the power of a sympathetic ear, of a friendly shoulder to cry on."

"You don't have to belittle yourself," he said. "To use an Army phrase, you're doing one hell of a job."

"Thank you, nevertheless," she said, sitting up.

"Just tell me where I can find a place to sleep, and I'll go. Let you get some rest."

She mused for a moment. "He won't like it," she said. She nodded, a look of decision coming to her face. "But he will have to live with it," she said. "Go to the room at the end of the hall." She gave him a number. "You will find a small cot there. If the young man in the other bed gives you trouble, tell him that I said you should sleep there until we can find better accommodations."

He nodded. "Good night, then."

"Yes, good night," she said, coming up from the bed, giving him a flash of lovely leg as she swung off, stood to face him.

Why was he reluctant to leave?

"We will talk again, tomorrow," she said.

"Yes." He turned, put his hand on the doorknob, turned it.

"Herr Werner?" she said, in a small, lost voice.

He turned. "Just Theo," he said.

"Theo—"

"Yes?"

"You don't have to go. Not just yet." She was breathing oddly, the lacy dressing gown rising and falling over her full breasts. He knew. He felt a mixture of emotions. He had a body memory of her, close to him, weeping, her chest heaving. He also had other memories. He had not so much as kissed a girl since that terrible day in the winter when he'd walked aimlessly away from the crush of bodies with his wife's inert form in his arms, not wanting to put her down because she was still warm and it was so cold, so cold. And then he saw in the eyes of this woman whom he'd met only hours previously a look, the look of a woman wounded, a woman hurt, a woman in need, and there was that need in him. He had been alone so long.

"Are you sure?" he asked.

For answer she came forward. This time her arms lifted. She fitted so beautifully. Her body curved to his as if designed for his, and her lips tasted of woman, no lipstick, just woman and the sweet wetness of desire beyond, on the probing tongue, and a sigh that told him everything. They seemed not to know what was happening, and it happened so swiftly, so swiftly, as the dressing gown went, piled in a silken heap to be joined by other garments. And then they were together in a rush, a clinging, tossing, frantic union that was more need than desire.

6

AT FIRST, AS he lay there in Mady Deschaises's bed, her head on his arm, her eyes closed, he could hear the sounds of the hotel. The room was near the service areas, and there were muffled voices, once the sharp crash of a dish breaking, the movement of a room-service cart down the hall, and then it was quiet. He could not sleep. It had been an eventful day and he was tired, but there was a bitterness inside him that prevented his eyes from closing.

She had left a small bedside light burning as they made love frantically, desperately. The act had risen to an immediate frenzy and ended with mutual explosion. And now he could see the delicate veins in her closed eyelids. She breathed evenly. Her head was on his arm; the slight weight of it cut off the blood to his hand so that his fingers tingled, but he did not move. It was as if he were frozen in time. He could squint his eyes and her hair would darken, her complexion lighten, and she would be another woman, a woman who had slept with her head on his arm in a finer room in another luxury hotel across the Channel.

His first night in Paris and already he was forgetting his purpose. The sadness inside him grew, threatened to become larger than he could bear. Not quite four years had passed since he held the body of his wife in his arms, and now another body, a living, soft, feminine body was pressed against his. Now another woman breathed softly in sleep, taking comfort from his warmth. He tried to tell himself that she would understand, that most wonderful of women who had loved him. If she could somehow look down and see, he told himself, she would nod and smile and be pleased that he had found the sweetness and softness of love once again. It didn't work.

He eased his arms from under Mady's head. She sighed and turned to face him, her breath warm and moist on his shoulder. Sleeping, she looked even younger.

There was one advantage. He didn't have to worry about a place to sleep, at least for the rest of the night. She had made no indication that he should leave. She'd made one unexplained reference to placing him with some other hotel employee in a room, but she had not mentioned it again.

He examined her sleeping face. It was a very nice face. And the smoothness of her body, the firmness of breast and length of leg and flatness of stomach brought back to him with vigor the need he'd felt, the sudden and overwhelming and unreasoning need he had sublimated for almost four years. He smiled. It is true, man is not intended to be celibate. But the smile faded and he was, once again, not too happy with Teddy—pardon, Theo—Werner.

He closed his eyes, and when he opened them she was awake. She looked at him with a soft little smile, which faded. Her eyes widened, almost as if in alarm, as if, for a moment, she did not remember.

"Ah, God," she said, "what you must think of me."

"I think you are very much a woman," he said.

"Yes. I am not really this way. The cry of all fallen women: This is not my usual self," she said. "But it doesn't matter. You can't sleep?"

"I've been doing some thinking."

Yes, he had. And into his thoughts had crept the question of the German corporal who had come to Mady's door. How many Germans came? It was a popular conception that women involved in undercover work during war used their bodies as weapons. Hers was a nice weapon, and it would, he felt with some cynicism, be quite effective. For a moment he wanted to break away from her touch, from the warm leg that pressed against him, thought of her as being, well, unclean. But she was looking into his eyes.

"She must have been a wonderful woman," she said.

"She was," he said, accepting the fact that women have a sixth sense, can feel it when a man is thinking of another.

"At home?" she asked.

"England." He didn't want to talk about Jeanna. She did not exist, except in his memory, and there she would exist forever, and be totally his.

"The German bombs?"

"No," he said. And, to get off the subject, "You'd better sleep. Am I to stay here the rest of the night?"

She smiled. "My reputation is ruined. Yes. It will be less trouble."

"I didn't mean to trouble you."

"Nor did I intend to leap into bed with you," she said. "But here we are."

"Yes."

"We can talk, if you're not sleepy," she said.

He shrugged. He reached for a German cigarette, offered her one, lit two. They leaned up on elbows, flicking ashes into a tray she'd placed between them, she casual in her nudity, her body looking warm in the dim light.

"What are we to do, then?" she asked.

"I need to speak with those who control the Resistance organizations in Paris," he said. "As quickly as possible."

"You do have information, then," she said.

"Not information, advice. Orders, if one can give orders to the Resistance."

"I don't blame you for not trusting me immediately," she said.

"One way or the other I am in your hands," he said. "The British and the Americans think it is vital to the hope of saving Paris to prevent any activity from the Paris Resistance. They think that any uprising will be put down forcefully and give the Germans the chance to begin the destruction of the city. That is all I have to say to them. However, I am to say that such advice comes from the highest commands and that General de Gaulle agrees."

"How much do you know about the situation here?" she asked.

"Only what I was told in briefing."

"In effect, there are two Resistance groups, one favorable to de Gaulle, the other intent on keeping de Gaulle and anyone connected with old France from gaining political power after the war,'' she said.

"The Communists?"

"Yes. It is said that they are willing to sacrifice lives and, if necessary, Paris herself, in order to be in control when the invading Allies have driven the Germans out of France. Are your generals and politicians aware of this?"

"I don't know. I would guess so. These Communists—is there any way to get a message to them?"

She laughed without humor. "I think there is no trouble at all in doing that. It often seems that they know when we breathe."

"Spies within your organization?"

"Without a doubt," she said. "What can we do? We both fight for France. That we will have to fight each other seems assured, but meantime we combine forces to rid France of the boches. What we need is a swift move, a dash to Paris by the Allied armies."

"And tank battles on the Champs Élysées?" he asked.

She shuddered. "Is there no answer?"

"The answer was to fight a bit harder in 1940," he said. "Or even in 1939, or 1938, or when the Germans had their best armies in Poland."

"You sound like my son," she said.

"You have a son?"

"A boy of eighteen."

He grinned. "You must have married young."

"Yes. I was quite young. Sixteen."

"And your husband? The war?"

"Another war. He was older than I, and carried old wounds that finally killed him. I have been widowed since 1934."

"You've done well," he said.

She smiled. "How can you know? Ah, but I suppose I have. I had the pension. It was not enough, of course, so I sought work. I knew languages, so I came here, beginning as an assistant housekeeper. My son grew up here, in and around the Ritz."

"Where is he now?"

"Here. I have prayed. I have tried to convince him to stay hidden, as much as possible, right here in the kitchens. There has always been the danger that he would be selected for the work battalions in Germany. Now it seems that it will be over and he will be safe, for which I will always be thankful."

Theo was wondering what sort of boy she'd spawned, a boy content to hide in a hotel kitchen, but he did not voice his thoughts.

"You will meet him, for it is his room number that I gave you," she said.

Gee, he was thinking. How cozy. Bed the mother, then room with her son. *You're a fine lad, Werner.*

He changed the subject. "When will I be able to speak with the Resistance leaders?"

"I will send out messages tomorrow, first thing," she said.

"Is there Gestapo in the hotel?" he asked. "Anyone to watch out for?"

"We know of none. However, it is well known that the Germans watch their high officers, especially since the attempt on Hitler's life. I have often suspected that the man who was here earlier is more than a valet to a Luftwaffe officer."

"Anything solid to back up your suspicions?"

"No, not really. It's just that he seems to be everywhere. He seems to have more time than a general's valet should have. He appears in odd places.

He speaks for the German officers in connection with hotel affairs.''

"He seemed to be very cocky for a mere corporal,'' Theo agreed. "I'll keep an eye on Corporal Wolf.'' He covered a yawn with a fist. "Guess I'm sleepy after all.''

"Sleep then,'' she said. She stubbed out her cigarette and leaned to kiss him, her mouth soft. "Forgive me for being weak,'' she said.

"Weak?''

"It won't happen again.''

"I'm not sure I like that,'' he said.

"You're just being nice,'' she said. "It was a moment of weakness. It seemed as if Wolf's appearance at the door was the last straw. Perhaps I merely sensed that you were strong and sympathetic. Perhaps I have been strong too long and needed, for only a moment, to be a woman again. It will not happen again.''

"There, you've said it again.'' What the hell was going on? Was he being a small boy at heart, wanting what was being denied to him? He reached for her and held her close. "If you're so determined it won't happen again, perhaps we'd better take this opportunity.''

She sighed. His mouth covered hers and she melted to him, all warm and soft and woman. This time it was not swift, not frantic. This time she rose to it slowly, and when it was over she clung, saying, "Unfair, unfair, you are unfair, because you will make me want you again and again.''

7

ABOUT A HUNDRED miles to the west of Paris a lanky American war correspondent was having his Monday-evening meal with a group of tank crewmen. He was the butt of good-natured jokes because his German was better than his French.

"You should be covering the German retreats," said a smiling young tank commander.

"But then I would not have the pleasure of this splendid French cuisine" Ed Raine said, looking rather doubtfully into his tin tray to see the heated American C-rations. "I came all the way back from Washington just to get another taste of this food."

"Soon we will treat you to dinner at Maxim's," the tank commander said.

"Which brings up a subject," Raine said. "There's something going on around here, and I'd like to know what it is."

"It is a war," said a French captain, to a quick burst of laughter.

But there was something very definitely going on.

The French Second Armored Division hadn't progressed very far since the breakout, but it was having relatively easy going. The Americans were beginning their circling movement, waiting for the Brits to move down and trap the German armies in the Falaise pocket. And there was Paris up ahead, apparently lightly protected.

Ed Raine had seen a lot of war since he'd left England in 1940 to cover what was, at the time, considered to be a sideshow to the real war, the action in faraway Africa. At the time, he hadn't considered himself to be lucky. A combination of circumstances had convinced him that he should leave England. First, since he worked for one of the lesser-known news organizations, he has always, seemingly, relegated to writing what were essentially color stories, while the well-known newsmen of the major news services got all the headlines. Second, always unlucky in love, he had felt the need to get away from a disintegrating relationship. He'd been a second-rate newsman working for a second-rate news service when he went to Africa. For a while, the small but often strategically important battles gained him little space in the stateside papers. Then the glamour battles in North Africa, in a country designed for massive and impressive tank movements, brought the names Rommel and Montgomery to the lips of the world, and Ed Raine was no longer second-rate. He stuck with that story to the end, until an Italian celebrating his surrender sent him to England, with the bullet hole in his butt, for a hospital stay and another dose of his on-again, off-again love affair. After North Africa he could have named his price and his job, but he was basically loyal. He chose to stay with ANA, the American News Association, going to Sicily and up Italy to Rome.

He managed to hop from Rome to England in time to make D-Day with the French divisions of the invasion force. He knew that the British and the Americans would garner most of the headlines, but he had a nose for a good story, and he'd met a man who had sworn to liberate Paris. That, he felt, would be the biggest story after D-Day and before the fall of Berlin. There was an additional advantage to being with the French, for the big names were following Patton and Montgomery. A writer of some little repute, a big hairy fellow called Papa, was in and out of the French areas of combat, but Hemingway seemed to be more intent on being the man among men, in playing soldier, than in writing. Essentially, the story of the French advances were told on the battered portable typewriter belonging to Ed Raine.

All of that was good planning, but within a few days he was disabled back to England with another flesh wound. Again, Bea ran hot-cold, so in disgust he'd accepted Elmer Davis's offer of a job in Washington with the Office of War Information. He had tacked on one proviso—that he be allowed to come back, once the troops broke out of the Normandy beachhead, to join the march to Paris. He wanted to be in on that liberation.

So he had brushed up on his French. He'd just returned to the French Second Armored, now moving freely away from the Normandy beachheads. He knew how the French soldiers felt. Many of them thought they'd been sold out in 1940, and all of them had one burning desire, to avenge French loss of honor and to have a direct part in the liberation of France, and most especially, Paris.

Therein lay the problem.

Ed had seen a lot of battles. He'd followed a lot of armies during four years of war, and he had developed a nose for the feelings of a unit. This one was no different in that relationship from the units he'd watched through the rough days of the North African campaigns, when German superiority won victory after victory, no different from those, later, who began to turn the tide. There was a feeling about a real unit; and in this camp in the French countryside there was an undercurrent that Ed could not quite define.

He finished his food and washed his messkit. Around him the division was beginning to turn in for the night. Off in the distance he could hear the sounds of a fire-fight. Here, in an apple tree, a nightbird sang as if the huge tanks that crouched darkly under their camouflage netting were no more deadly than the cows that had once grazed on the grass between the trees. He made his way toward headquarters. He knew he had little chance of talking with the commanding general. Jacques Leclerc was a private man, a man with a mission. Few of his followers even knew that Leclerc was not his real name, that he was Philippe de Hautecloque, that he had taken the name Leclerc when he rode a red bicycle away from the German advance in 1940, leaving behind a wife and six children to live in occupied France. He had changed his name to protect his family, and he had made a vow, a vow that he was near completing. He was only a hundred miles from Paris.

And, Ed Raine knew, he had orders to bypass the city.

Leclerc was not in his headquarters. A French colonel told Ed politely that there was nothing new, that the division would move, as always, with the dawn, that some resistance was expected up ahead, that no major distance was expected. No news there. Ed said good night and went in search of one of the two American liaison officers with the Second Armored. He found Captain Bob Hoye soaking his feet in a helmet. Hoye was always glad to see the newsman. As one of only three Yanks with the division, he sometimes felt a bit isolated.

Hoye told the sad story of two blisters on his heels and offered Ed a drink of liberated red wine, which was gratefully received. In the dark—the blackout was complete—only the glowing tips of the two men's cigarettes were visible in the darkness. It was a moonless night, the sky inky black, the stars seeming to be far away.

"I heard the man, himself, is coming to France," Ed said. He knew that Hoye was a friendly fellow, eager to help, but was kept in the dark as much as possible by the careful and suspicious French officers.

"It'll hit the fan then," Hoye said.

"I'm surprised that Ike is allowing it," Raine said.

"What's his other choice?" Hoye asked, taking a sip from the bottle. "France seems to be short of leaders just now."

"But de Gaulle hates everything American and everything British," Ed said, priming the pump, just talking in an effort to get Hoye to open up. "He hates Churchill for not sending in the RAF in the Battle of France, and he hates the Americans for winning a war France couldn't win."

Hoye shrugged, the motion unseen in the darkness. There was a comfortable silence. "You're not going to mention it, are you Bob?" Ed asked, after a while.

"What?"

"The fact that Leclerc is building up supplies."

"Is he?" Hoye asked.

"You know damned well he is," Ed said. "You know damned well he isn't reporting any vehicle losses, so that he can go on drawing rations for tanks and trucks that the Germans blasted days ago."

"You've been reading too many cloak-and-dagger tales," Hoye murmured.

"I went with a group of men the other night to a supply dump. If you think the American Army has moonlight requisition artists, you should see the Frenchies in action," Ed said. "They almost cleaned the place out. The way I hear it, Patton's running out of gas. He's screaming for more, but I saw with my own eyes yesterday the Second's fuel trucks take on a double ration—four tons instead of two. I think Leclerc has Paris on his mind."

"I suppose he has. He'll follow orders, though," the liaison man said.

"Yeah, but whose? Ike's or de Gaulle's?"

Hoye lifted one foot and dried it on an invisibly dark towel. "I can almost agree with de Gaulle and Leclerc. I love that city up there. I spent my honeymoon there in thirty-eight. Beautiful town. And there are times when I wake up in the middle of a nightmare, seeing all those fantastic monuments and all those beautiful buildings coming down under German guns. How would you feel if this war were being fought back home and you had a division of armor—sixteen thousand men and two thousand vehicles—within striking distance of New York and the enemy was in a position to blow up the Empire State Building and Grant's Tomb and the Met?''

"I see what you mean," Ed said. "So, in your opinion, what's going to happen?"

"Off the record?"

"Off the record."

"We're going to bypass Paris on one side and Patton's going to bypass it on the other. We'll cut it off, leave the German garrison intact, not risk causing street battles there—and hope to hell that when the Germans are cut off they'll be at least a little bit civilized and surrender without razing the city."

"You know Hitler has declared Paris a fortress city, and that he's sent von Choltitz there to command," Ed said.

"Yeah, I'll admit, it doesn't look good," Hoye said. "But all we can do is hope."

"Hoye? Can I ask you a question?"

"Sure. Shoot."

"When was the last time you saw a war won on hope?"

8

THE KITCHEN STAFF was accustomed to seeing the general's valet in the kitchens. He was resented, because it seemed that the Germans were questioning the skill and art of the Ritz's chefs, but some of the wise ones merely shrugged. Wolf, they felt, was merely being the typical overbearing German, seeking new places to demonstrate that he was of the masters. He selected the general's fruits and salads himself. He said it was because the general was a very picky eater. But he seldom came as late in the day as this.

Most of the time, Blaise managed to hide his hatred for all Germans. He, being only an assistant chef, had little contact with Wolf, so he was surprised to see the little corporal limp over to where he was working, using a large cleaver to sever neckbones for tomorrow's soup.

"I visited your mother last night," Wolf said, grinning at Blaise.

Blaise looked up, resisted the urge to severe Wolf's neckbones, and continued with his work.

"She is a very charming woman."

"Thank you," Blaise said, hitting the chopping block with the cleaver with more force than necessary.

Wolf grinned again, more hungrily. "At least one other German has found her to be so."

Blaise felt his face flush. He halted his motion, the cleaver held high in front of him. His look must have given Wolf pause, because the corporal took a backward step.

"Perhaps you've met him," Wolf said. "He is now an employee of the Ritz."

Blaise fought to control his temper. He remained silent.

"You don't seem upset that the untouchable Madame Deschaises has suddenly developed a love for the boches," Wolf said.

The German's life was saved by Henri Morlaix, the chef under whom Blaise was training. Henri, having heard Wolf's opening remarks, had moved to stand slightly behind Blaise, and when the younger man leaped, bringing down the deadly cleaver toward Wolf's head, Henri put his considerable weight and the strength of his massive arms into seizing Blaise's arm. The cleaver whistled down short of the startled German and banged deep into the block of wood.

Wolf recovered his composure quickly. He smiled as Blaise struggled in the grasp of the burly chef.

"He shows spirit," Wolf said. "I wonder if he would keep it in the labor battalions." With that he left.

"You fool," Henri Morlaix was saying, as Blaise gradually stopped trying to go after the German. "He can do as he says. He can send you to your death in the labor camps."

"The boche told lies about my mother," Blaise said. "No one, not even a German, can do that and live."

"Yes, that would be very intelligent," Henri said. "Kill the boche and die yourself, just when you will be needed on the barricades." Henri was a member of Colonel Rol's Resistance group. He and Blaise constituted the Ritz cell of the group, at least to their knowledge. It was possible that there were others, for the organization worked in small groups, with no man knowing more than two or three others in case of detection and torture by the Germans.

"It is the family honor," Blaise said.

"And I speak of the honor of France, of the future of France."

"I'm sorry, Henri, I can't let it pass. I can't let that cripple, that boche, insult my mother."

Silently, and with a strong arm, Henri pulled the deeply buried cleaver from the block and handed it, handle first, to Blaise.

"Why?" Blaise asked, surprised. "Do you agree?"

"No," Henri said sadly, his big, watery eyes looking at Blaise tenderly. "I have watched over you, Blaise. I am your comrade. Will you use the cleaver on me when I tell you that the words of the boche are true?"

Blaise's knuckles tightened on the cleaver handle, but he made no move to lift it.

"I will say only this. It is not for me and you to judge, boy. Perhaps she had her reasons."

"Who?" Blaise asked.

"Will you kill him, too?"

"Who, damn you?"

"The new steward. The one called Theo Werner.

I can only guess that she knew him previously. He is a Luftwaffe veteran, a Swiss.''

"A boche," Blaise spat.

"I tell you this because, my boy, the time is near. Soon the call will go out. *Aux barricades*. We will need your fiery temper then. We will need your fighting skills. You have killed your Germans. You fought well at Saumur, when you were only a lad. I tell you this because your sternest test is yet to come. Your mother has arranged to have this Theo Werner share your room.''

He heard it, but he didn't believe it. For years his mother had been all he had, with his father dead, with his world falling apart. She had always been the rock upon which he based his continued existence. It pained him, when he became a member of the Resistance, to withhold the information from her. He longed to talk with her, to tell her his reasons, to explain to her that it was only the Communists who really cared what happened to the ordinary Frenchman, the people who had suffered most from the coward-ice of the generals and the politicians in the 1930s. But he loved her so much that he could not, for he knew that knowledge of his own danger would be painful to her. He had been assigned, at her interven-tion with the German officers in the Luftwaffe sec-tion of the hotel, a status of necessary occupation. That and that alone had kept him from conscription into either the German Army or the labor camps. And she was so gentle, so delicate. She had been father and mother to him, and his one desire was to see the war through, see France liberated, and then to go to work to support her, as she'd supported him for so long.

Now this. A boche. Dirty and terrible pictures came to his mind.

"Remember," Henri said again, seeing the expression on his face, "she must have had her reasons."

But to think of her in the arms of a German! To think of her with the dirty and filthy little passions of the women who had given their bodies to the conquerors. Ah, to think of her as she would be, when it was over and the Germans were thrown out, for there would be those who would point the accusing finger. She, like the others who had collaborated, would be punished.

"Are you all right?" Henri asked.

"Yes."

"Will you remember that the time is near? Will you hold your anger until then, to vent it on German soldiers?"

"Yes."

"Look at me. Promise me."

He looked into the chubby, friendly old face. He swallowed, and felt his stomach rise in acid anger. "I give you my word," he said.

The immediate object of Blaise's hatred was undergoing a crash course in being the type of steward demanded by the high standards of the Ritz. His mentor, M. Alexandre, who had taken him to the director's office, was pleased by his quickness and his retentive abilities.

"Good, good," the old steward found himself saying repeatedly, as Theo Werner practiced serving from a room-service tray. "Soon you will be ready."

The work went on. There was much to learn. Each movement was orchestrated by tradition. It was necessary for him to practice naming the various

foods in French, for not even the Germans could
alter the tradition established by the godlike Escoffier.
When in France, one ordered in French—not German, not English, not any other language. And not
even a German-speaking waiter could escape that
tradition.

Theo concentrated, but his mind was elsewhere.
He was thinking of his night with Mady, of the
suddenness of it, the power of it, for she had been
with him all through the morning, all through the
day. He had found himself wanting to see her, to
simply look at her and wonder if she had been as
sweet as he remembered. And there were other considerations. Somewhere in the basement, hidden from
the nearby Germans, there was a radio receiver, and
in spite of his being German he had overheard two
employees speaking of hearing the BBC's evening
war news. The Allies were on the move. The Second
French Armored Division was advancing against light
opposition. He knew that time was short. He had to
know soon. He had to talk with the Resistance leaders and impress upon them the necessity of keeping
the peace in the hope that the Germans, once Paris
was surrounded and cut off, would surrender without
doing terrible damage to the city.

If he could have heard Henri assuring young Blaise
that the time to man the barricades was near, he
would have been more concerned.

9

"HOW WOULD YOU like to go to Paris?"
Otto Schellen asked, standing just behind the desk of
the blonde girl, whose slim fingers tapped the typewriter keys with delicate speed.

She stopped typing and turned, using one hand to
brush back her long blonde hair. Schellen had been
watching her for a long time, for the several weeks
since she had been assigned to his Amt-VI group in
Berlin.

"I have my work, Herr Schellen," she said, but
her smile belied the negative.

Yes he thought, I have read her right. He had
suspected she was ambitious, desiring to be more
than a mere office worker. He smiled. "I'm the one
who assigns you your work," he said, "even if you
get the orders through my office supervisor."

"Yes, sir." She had the look of a ripe peach, all
pink and juicy. Her hair was worn in a deliberate
looseness, giving a first impression of untidy mass—
until one looked closer and recognized the art that

had gone into that casual hair style. Her lips were reddened only lightly and her natural coloration made facial makeup unnecessary. He guessed her to be in her early twenties.

As head of Amt VI, the foreign intelligence agency of the Main Security Office, Otto Schellen was a powerful man. He ran a good organization, even though he had been losing agents quite often in the past couple of years as the Allies won victory after victory. He still had his people in England, although he'd lost the best agent he had there in his abortive attempt to kill Churchill. And he still had agents in a half dozen other countries, feeding him information that was convincing him more and more each day that the end of the war was near, that Germany was, for all practical purposes, a defeated nation.

The war years had been kind to Schellen. There was an attractive maturity to his face, and his close-cut hair was showing a tint of premature gray, making his Aryan blondness more striking. He had the eyes of a man who knew himself, and knew self-confidence as a result. The small laugh lines around his mouth spoke of one phase of his character, and the grimness of his lips when he was angry of another.

"I will need an assistant in Paris," he said. "Of course, if you're not interested—"

"I am most interested in my career," Silke Frager said.

"Good." But, he was thinking what career? The Allies were pushing toward Paris. If he was lucky they'd move in and take the city before he could get there, making his errand unnecessary. He was not thinking of careers, not even his own. He was thinking of forcing some luckless Luftwaffe officer from his plush room at the Paris Ritz and occupying that room with pleasant company while he conducted some business with the commander of Luftflotte 3, the Luftwaffe unit near the city.

"Such an assignment would, indeed, carry with it a promotion," he said. "As a matter of fact I've been watching you, Fraülein Frager. You show great promise. I take it that you are willing?"

"Of course, sir," Silke said. "May I ask when?"

"We'll leave this evening, and be in Paris from Wednesday through Friday—maybe even over the weekend. How long will it take you to pack?" he asked.

"An hour, no more."

"Good. Give me your address and I'll have you picked up at seven." She did, writing it longhand on a piece of paper, the letters flowing and feminine. "There is one thing I should mention," he said, with a lopsided little grin. "The nature of this trip demands certain subterfuge. If you are to go, you go as my mistress."

Her peach-colored face flushed only momentarily and she took only a second to answer. "If that is necessary, sir, it is necessary."

He winked, and went to prepare for the journey. What the hell, he was thinking, if he was to be involved by orders in an undertaking so distasteful as the destruction of a beautiful city, he might as well enjoy it. He didn't really need an assistant for the trip. What he needed was the slim and lovely body of the girl he'd been watching for some time.

Of course, her unhesitating agreement to sleep with him made him want to vent a cynical chuckle. For when he had put in his requisition for more office help and had interviewed her, she had told him quite openly—since it was listed in her brochure—

86

that she had previously worked at Gestapo head-quarters.

"And why do you want to leave?" he had asked.

She had looked at him with wide eyes, that peach-blossom face serious. "For a women there is no advancement there."

"I thought," he'd said, suspecting that this beautiful package was merely being sent to him so that the Gestapo could have another set of eyes in his office, "that perhaps the continual screaming bothered you." In a way, it was a test. She did not blink an eye.

"Pardon?" she'd asked, as if she did not know what he meant.

Well, Gestapo agent or not, she was one hell of a package. And he'd seen them come in various packages. He'd had no steady woman for quite some time, not since the most fantastic woman he'd ever known had decided to go abroad again, to work more actively for the victory of her adopted fatherland. Just to remember her sent little trembles of desire through him, and this Silke would have to work hard to be half the woman Margo Ostenso had been. At least, if the Allies stayed out of Paris for a few days, the atmosphere would be favorable.

He knew from experience that nothing excited a woman more, made her more willing, than being in a luxury hotel. From his experience, too, he knew that the serene and luxurious Ritz was the most comfortable of all. He would take her for a drink to the Ritz Bar, still open to the public, and then feed her and bed her. After that there'd be plenty of time to speak to the Luftwaffe about certain plans that not only the Führer but others wanted carried out.

* * *

In mid-August of 1944, travel was quite an adventure. Night and day the bombers filled German skies. By day the fighters roamed, and, in the absence of German fighters, used their ammunition strafing trains, trucks, any target of opportunity. Schellen had called upon his Navy friends for aid, and so it was that he and the silken Silke boarded a comfortably outfitted admiral's plane near Berlin at dusk. The trip, as it turned out, was uneventful. There were others in the cabin, so he could do little to begin the process of getting acquainted with Silke. He spent the time doing routine paperwork, and found her to be, at least, an efficient secretary. But now and then, as they sat side by side, a movement would cause her leg to brush his, and his thoughts would be diverted from his work.

A Luftwaffe staff car was waiting at Orly. The enlisted driver stowed their baggage. In the back seat, Schellen edged close to Silke. She wore a dress which, in material at least, was prewar, a dress to match her name, with a smooth, silky feeling. He could detect the warmth of her body and his thigh pressed against hers and his hand sought hers to enlace fingers and squeeze.

"Will we have a chance to see the city by day?" she asked, as the car began to move.

"I have a feeling that this job will take several days," Schellen said archly. "Depending, of course, on a Yank named George Patton. Yes, my dear, I will consider it my duty to show you Paris."

Even in darkness, the facade of the Place Vendôme impressed Silke. She clung to Schellen's arm and gawked upward at the huge columns. A polite doorman admitted them, and a steward directed them to the room that had been prepared for them. Silke looked around at the magnificent decor, removed her light jacket to show that her dress was low cut, showing a lot of shoulder and breast. She oh-ed and ah-ed at the turn-of-the-century furniture, the huge and comfortable bed.

"I have to call to make," Schellen said. "Perhaps you would like to refresh yourself?"

She smiled and disappeared into the sumptuous bath. He soon had the valet of General Schläfer on the telephone.

"I am sorry, sir," Wolf said, "but General Schläfer has retired. I will tell him you called and you can expect—"

When necessary, Schellen's voice could be icy. "I can expect you to waken the General immediately," he said. "I have not flown from Berlin to cool my heels while the Luftwaffe sleeps."

There was a silence. "One moment, please," Wolf said. And then the General, his voice blurred by sleep—and perhaps by wine—was on the line. When told that Schellen wanted to see him immediately he grumbled, but said, "Give me a few minutes, Herr Schellen."

"You're leaving?" Silke asked. She had changed into a lovely black nightgown, a garment that increased Schellen's pulse rate immediately. He held her for a moment, letting his hands savor the softness now covered by one layer of silk. And inside, that cynical little voice was asking where a mere secretary got the money to buy such a garment, obviously non-German and of a luxury available only on the black market or, perhaps, in Switzerland or Spain.

"Ummm," he said, letting his lips play over the

fragrant skin of her soft neck. "Duty, my love. Wait for me."

General Schläfer, looking slightly put out, was dressed in an ornate dressing jacket and pajamas. Wolf admitted Schellen, his hard eyes not dropping when Schellen glared at him. He introduced himself, shook Schläfer's limp hand, and turned to look at the man in a corporal's uniform. "Your presence will not be necessary," he said, in his iciest tone. "But before you go I shall ask General Schläfer to see to it that you are, in the future, taught some manners."

"Thank you, sir," Wolf said, with a sardonic little grin.

Well, Schellen thought, so they are here, too. For the man had to be more than a Luftwaffe corporal to have the courage to be insolent to the head of Amt VI. He turned his back and did not look to see if Wolf left.

"I hope this is important," the general said.

"The Führer thinks so," Schellen said. "May we sit? I wouldn't object to some good French brandy, if you have any."

For a moment it seemed that the general would summon his valet, and Schellen waited interestedly, to see if the man had that much backbone. When he closed his mouth and went to a bar to pour two glasses himself, Schellen had his measure. He was a survivor. That, Schellen thought, was not all bad. It was time for the survivors to emerge, to begin to look forward to the time when Hitler and the Nazi fanatics no longer controlled Germany. No, not all bad, but the general's easy caving-in to Schellen's strong personality told Schellen that this was not the man for the job the Nazi leaders had in mind.

He took the brandy, not rising, one leg crossed.

The general sat opposite him, on an Empire couch, his legs close together, his back straight.

"I am here on high orders," Schellen said. "I want you to summon the commander of Lutflotte Three as quickly as possible."

"Tonight?" Schalfer asked, in surprise.

Schellen spoke gently. "If you send the order tonight, he can be here tomorrow, is that not true?"

"True," Schläfer said, starting to rise.

"Later, please," Schellen said. "I want you to know the reason for my, ah, request." The general subsided.

"As you perhaps know, the Führer considers Paris to be vital," Schellen said. "You have seen, perhaps, his orders on this subject?"

"I spoke with General von Choltitz just today," Schläfer said.

"Good. You know, then, that the Führer has demanded that if Paris is taken, the Allies will take nothing but rubble and fire." He did not give the general a chance to answer. "Therefore, Luftflotte Three will stand ready, at a moment's notice, to bomb Paris."

"My God," Schläfer said, then went white.

"If He were listening there would have been no bombing," Schellen said quietly. "I do not originate the orders, Herr General, I merely relay them. I confess to you that were it my choice I would leave this city intact. It is French, but it belongs to the world. I fear that the Führer knows of this mentality, that he suspects that even his city-destroyer, von Choltitz, will weaken at the last moment. Therefore, I am here to implement a back-up plan. If the Army fails, the Luftwaffe will accomplish the Führer's wishes in regard to Paris. Is that understood?"

"It is understood," the general said. "I will send for the commander of Luftflotte Three immediately, as you wish."

"Thank you," Schellen said. "Now that that is done, what of the war news? I have been out of touch since early afternoon."

"It is bad," Schläfer said. "The American Army all but has the Normandy forces encircled."

"And the British?"

"The fighting is fierce," Schläfer said, "but so far our forces are holding."

"Yes, the Führer would be extremely upset if the submarine pens were taken," Schellen said. "He still stakes his hopes on the new secret weapons. Your new fighter, for example."

Schläfer went stiff, covered his confusion by raising his glass. Schellen laughed. "My dear General," he said, "Your secret is safe. I am, after all, head of a very important department. It is my business to know that soon the Luftwaffe will deploy an aircraft with a radical new power plant, an aircraft that flies without a propeller and has a speed far superior to anything that the Allies have. I only hope that the factories produce enough, in time to make a difference."

"I was surprised that an, ah, civilian knew," the general said. "But yes, we are all quite hopeful. And I, too, pray that the factories remain in operation. When we have the jet in the air—"

He went silent as the door burst open and a Luftwaffe colonel burst in, came to a dead stop, slicked his heels, and stood at attention.

"Yes, yes, "Schläfer said. "Have you forgotten how to knock?"

"Forgive me, General," the Colonel said. "We have captured a Resistance spy."

"How melodramatic," Schläfer said. "Must you bother me with such matters?"

"Forgive me, Herr General," the Colonel sputtered. "We felt that you should know, since she was caught prowling your office."

"The devil you say," Schläfer said, rising, his face going red. "Perhaps I should know. Bring her to me."

Schellen was interested. He asked permission to stay, and it was granted. And then two men were half dragging a frightened girl in the uniform of a Ritz maid into the room. She was, Schellen thought, quite an unlikely spy. She was only a child—not over sixteen, he estimated—and quite plain, with large, thick-lensed glasses, stringy, greasy-looking hair, and a face made more unattractive by her undisguised fear.

"What were you doing in my office?" the General thundered.

"I wasn't doing anything, sir," the girl whimpered. "I was only cleaning."

"You know that there are orders against maids being alone in my office," the General said. "What were you after?" He moved forward, thrust his thick neck down and put his face near hers. "Tell, me, damn you, what were you after?"

"Perhaps we should call the Gestapo," the officious colonel said.

General Schläfer glared at him, his mouth open.

"It is their province," the colonel said.

"I want no Gestapo butchers—" Schläfer paused, looked quickly at Schellen.

Schellen laughed. "I feel the same way, General. However, the child must be questioned.

"Yes, yes, damn it," Schläfer said, looking undecided.

"Perhaps I can help," Schellen said. "It happens that I have a female assistant with me." Yes, it would be interesting, a test to see if his suspicions about Silke were well founded. "She has experience interrogating criminals. And a girl such as this would speak more readily to another woman."

"Yes," the General said, obviously relieved. "You're very kind, Schellen. I'd appreciate it if you'd look after this thing. If the girl is innocent—"

"We will find out," Schellen said. "I will need a room, someplace to conduct the questioning."

"Take him to the gym," the General said.

"I'll use your telephone," Schellen said, moving to do so without waiting for permission. Silke answered on the first ring. "Sorry, my dear, duty calls. I'll require your presence—" He told her the location of the gym that had been set up for the Luftwaffe officers. "Work clothes, please. This could get messy."

He followed the two Luftwaffe men and the weeping, sobbing girl. In the gym, amid the rank smell of old sweat, he said, "I can watch her. You may go." The two Luftwaffe men looked uncertain, then wilted under his gaze. Alone with the cringing girl he motioned for her to sit down at a little table. She halted her sobbing for a moment and looked at him with an expression of hope on her plain face.

"Before my assistant arrives," he said, "we can have a little talk."

"Please, please," she said, threatening to cry again.

"I think I went to the wrong room. The head house-keeper told me—"

"Don't lie," he said gently. "It will do you no good. You knew what you were doing. Have you stolen information before?"

"Oh, sir, I'm just a maid. I know nothing of war, of politics."

"And which group do you represent?" Schellen asked. "Let me see. You're one of Colonel Rol's, I'd say."

He thought he saw a flicker in the girl's eyes. He smiled. "It will only go harder on you if you lie to me."

"I know nothing," she wailed.

Silke had dressed in record time, he thought, as he looked up to see her come in a plain skirt and a white blouse.

"What's this?" she asked, looking first at the girl, then at Schellen.

"The girl is a member of the Resistance," he said calmly, ignoring the girl's quick protest. "She was caught in the general's office. I thought that perhaps another woman would encourage her to be truthful. I hate to think of a mere child in the basement of the Gestapo headquarters." He shook his head. "All that screaming."

"Oh, God," the girl sobbed.

"Silke," Schellen said. "What we need to know is her contact in the Resistance, who ordered her to the general's room, if she has conducted similar chores before. Do you think you can speak with her?"

In answer, Silke moved with surprising swiftness, her palm ringing once, twice, on the girl's cheeks, the girl's head jerking. "Talk, you little French bitch," Silke said.

The blows seemed to sober the girl. She stopped sobbing, looked defiantly into Silke's eyes. "I merely went to the wrong room to clean."

"Who sent you there?"

"I was told to clean by the head housekeeper," the girl said. "I am not too smart. Perhaps—yes, I am sure I got the wrong room number mixed up in my head."

"Take off your dress," Silke said. Had Schellen not been looking directly at her he would not have recognized her voice. The girl looked startled, then began to obey. Silke moved and helped, ripping the uniform. The girl wore old-fashioned underclothing. "Off," Silke said.

"Oh, God," the girl wept. "Not in front of the gentleman."

So Schellen knew all that he had to know. Disrobing a suspect, reducing a woman to nakedness and shame before beginning serious questioning, was standard Gestapo procedure. He knew that the graceful blonde was, as he had suspected, a plant in his office. He shrugged, the motion not seen by Silke, who was intent on the girl.

"Shall I leave you for a few minutes?" he asked.

Silke didn't look at him. "It won't take long with this one," she said.

The girl watched him go, the last hope fading from her eyes. As he reached the door she tried to bolt, and he watched with bemusement as Silke moved decisively, throwing the hapless girl back into the small, straight chair and hitting her with her fist at the same time. The situation, Schellen thought, was well under control.

He stood outside the door. The scream began as startled yell and became the kind of scream he'd heard from time to time, the protest of a human who is being subjected to humiliating and unbearable pain. He lit a cigarette. So it had come to this. Woman torturing woman. In the silence he thought to leave, to go to his room. Suddenly the thought of spending a few days in Paris with the blonde secretary from his office seemed less interesting, but, ah, well, he was into it. Now he had no choice.

The scream came again and was cut off suddenly.

Now he heard a sobbing voice, coming through the closed door with not enough force to be understood. Than another scream and a long silence. He opened the door. The girl was lying atop the table. Silke, one hand dampened, fist still clenched, stood over her.

"The bitch fainted," she said.

"Did she speak?"

"She denied everything," Silke said. "But she will awaken."

He saw, then, what had been done to the girl, knew why Silke's clenched fist was moist, glistening. For there was a trickle of blood on the inside of the girl's open thighs. A woman knows how to hurt another woman and not leave a mark, at least not on the outside. For a moment he was sickened. Then he spoke. "Revive her. Help her get dressed and let her return to her work, if she can."

She looked at him, startled, her eyes wide and her lips drawn back. Then she seemed to relax. "Perhaps you're right. Perhaps she is innocent."

Ah, her orders were to report any suspicious leanings on his part. They were all getting paranoid, these Nazis. And he'd shown a weakness.

"Not at all," he said. "The girl has been frightened. She is young. She will go immediately to her superior in the Resistance. We will have someone watching?''

"Ah," Silke said. "Yes. Yes. Very good." And then she remembered that she was feminine, that she was supposed to be merely a secretary. "I wouldn't have thought of that."

The girl began to revive and Schellen turned his head as Silke forced her to get dressed. When she stood, she clutched her lower abdomen, her torso bent forward, a grimace of pain on her face.

"Consider yourself lucky that we have no time to pursue this," Silke said. "Get out of here."

The girl left, walking as if she were very, very fragile. "I'll meet you in the room," Schellen said. "I want to see where she goes."

He followed. The girl, obviously in pain, did not look back. In the part of the hotel near the service areas, she arrived at a door. A rather attractive woman opened the door, saw the girl's condition, put her arm around her to help her to the bed, leaving the door open while she quickly picked up the telephone.

Schellen stood in the shadows and watched. He could not hear the voices of the women from where he stood, but there was nothing to indicate that there was anything more than concern from the attractive woman who had opened the door marked HEAD HOUSEKEEPER. When he saw the hotel doctor arrive, he left.

Silke was, once again, in the black nightgown. He wondered if she'd bathed.

"And who was her contact?" Silke asked.

"I don't think it was a contact," he said. "I think she was merely going for help. She went to the room of the head houskeeper, who called a doctor."

"She mentioned that the head housekeeper had sent her to clean a room," Silke said.

"Is that not natural? She is a maid. She takes orders from the head housekeeper."

"Yes, I suppose you're right," Silke said.

"I think we have had enough unpleasantness," Schellen said.

"Yes," she murmured, going suddenly coy. He shrugged mentally. Somehow she did not have the attractiveness that she had possessed before the incident in the gym. But what the hell.

On the bed, the black nightgown silky under his hands, she whispered into his ear. "I'm not experienced. You'll have to tell me what to do."

He felt that inward tug of cynicism. He knew—for he had a sense about those things, a sixth sense that made him good at his job—that she was lying about this as she'd lied about not knowing about methods of interrogation.

And yet, when he had removed the nightgown, when he had allowed his hands to explore a slim and proud young body with its delightful curves and swellings, he could forget and, after one of the most skillful lovings he'd ever received, he could forgive her lie there, too. For there are some things to which experience brings certain delights.

10

OTTO SCHELLEN HAD just indulged in one of the more pleasant morning rituals between man and woman—the quick and mutually satisfying action that lasted only moments—when his telephone rang.

"I have not seen the Luftwaffe move so swiftly since Poland," he told Silke, as he hung up.

She made a face. "Oh, Otto," she said, "you mustn't allow business to interfere with pleasure. After all," she said, trying to pull him back into the bed, "this is Paris."

"Ah, Schellen," General Schläfer said, as Wolf opened the door of Schläfer's suite. "You're just in time. I took the liberty of ordering breakfast for you."

The tall blond waiter at the service cart aroused Schellen's curiosity immediately, for he could not be French, not with those eyes and that Teutonic blond hair.

"Can that delicious smell actually be fresh eggs and sausage?" Schellen asked.

"Indeed. We are in luck. My valet has a way of finding such things, even with the situation as it is," Schläfer said. "Before you draw up a chair, however, meet the new commanding officer of Luftflotte Three. You share a common given name: Herr Otto Schellen, Generaloberst Otto Dessloch."

Dessloch was a vigorous-looking man, Prussian in preciseness as he rose and gave Schellen a firm handshake.

"And what of Generalfeldmarschall Sperrle?" Schellen asked.

Dessloch grinned wolfishly, but said nothing. Sperrle had long been known as one of the most ineffective Luftflotte commanders. Yes, Schellen thought, things are changing. All over what was left of the Greater German Reich, the hungry ones, the lean and desperate ones, were coming out of the obscurity to which they had been relegated and were taking one last shot at glory. And they were too pleased with their advancement to question the timing, to realize that they were mounting the war stallion just before the last, long, unreachable jump.

"I have not had the opportunity to tell General Dessloch the purpose of your visit," Schläfer said, "leaving that pleasure, as is fitting, to you."

"Thank you," Schellen said.

Wolf was in the room, standing unobtrusively beside the door leading to the General's bedchamber. The blond waiter stood, as if invisible, waiting to perform his functions when needed.

"I think I have an inkling," Dessloch said. "In fact, I have made a special trip into Paris to make some suggestions of my own."

Schellen's smile spoke of an inner amusement. The swiftness of Dessloch's appearance was not efficiency, then, but accident.

"I have an appointment with General von Choltitz this afternoon, to present my compliments," Dessloch said. "I am going to tell him that my Luftflotte stands ready to help in the event of trouble in Paris. Or in the impossible event that the Allies should enter the city."

"Commendable," Schellen muttered, taking his seat. The blond waiter moved skillfully, aiding him in selecting fat, hot, aromatic sausage and a helping of eggs Benedict. There were fresh fruits, tomatoes, slender loaves of good French bread.

"I have been in the wrong service, General," Schellen said, savoring the eggs, lavishing fresh butter on a piece of the crisp bread. "Perhaps, if things were not in such a state, I would ask for transfer to the Luftwaffe and request assignment in Paris."

There was a general laugh. "It isn't all fine living," Schläfer said. "There is responsibility as well."

"Of course," Schellen said, making his voice sincere. Out of the corner of his eye he was watching the blond waiter. The man stood at Germanic attention, but he wore the uniform of a Ritz steward.

"I have a hundred and fifty Heinkels at Le Bourget," General Dessloch began, and Schellen put down his fork.

"Excuse me, sir," he said. "Perhaps it is the nature of my business that makes me cautious." He cast a meaningful look toward the blond waiter.

"Oh, it's all right," Schläfer laughed. "Every man and woman in Paris knows that there are bombers at Le Bourget. Moreover, if you're concerned about the waiter, I had Wolf check him out. In fact,

I've requested that he be assigned to duty to this suite.''

He turned his head and motioned to the waiter, who snapped his heels, stepped forward, and came to attention.

"Tell Herr Schellen who you are, son," Schläfer said.

"Sir," Theo said, "Unteroffizier Theo Werner, formerly of Third Squadron, Luftflotte Two, sir." He snapped his heels again, then walked back to his post.

"The boy flew over a hundred missions over England," Schläfer said. "I don't think we have to censor our conversation in front of him."

Schellen looked openly into Theo's face, smiling.

And that Texas-born RAF throttle-jockey was feeling cold tendrils of nervousness creep into his gut. He was, as they used to say back home, in tall cotton. Two Luftwaffe generals and a German spymaster talking about the fate of Paris. He leaped to pour more coffee for General Dessloch, returned to his place.

"I have orders to get Luftflotte Three back into the skies over the Western Front," Dessloch said. "However, I am aware of the critical situation here. As I said, I stand ready to help. I know that the Führer has ordered the Wehrmacht to hold Paris at all costs—and, in the event of being pushed back, to leave Paris in smoking ruin. I think we can all understand the necessity of this, however sentimental we might feel about the city." Dessloch looked not the least sentimental as he gazed first at Schläfer, then at Schellen. "The factories here could be turned around to produce war material to be used against the Reich within days, if they were taken intact. And there are other considerations, as well. I am from Hamburg. I have seen the bomb damage there. I could not sleep at night if, knowing what the American and British bombers are doing to our cities, we left Paris untouched."

"You touch on my mission here," Schellen said. "You might wonder why the head of foreign intelligence is in Paris. I am simply a messenger. I do, however, have certain powers given to me by the High Command. I am here to assure that, should the Wehrmacht fail to level Paris if it is lost, the Luftwaffe will do the job. You sound, General Dessloch, as if you're the man for the job."

"I stand ready," Dessloch said. "I could put my bombers into the air at night, when they would be safe from the Allied fighters. From the nearby airfields, the bombers could make many sorties during the night. We could shuttle-bomb the city, load after load. Delightful! There would be no antiaircraft fire from the ground to hinder the operation. We could erase"—he hissed the final *s* sound longer than necessary, and smoothed the imaginary buildings off the tabletop—"the city methodically, block by block."

Schellen felt a cold shudder work its way up his spine. However, he nodded.

"If you could have your man bring a map," Dessloch said, wiping his mouth on a delicate linen napkin.

Wolf leaped into action, spreading the map over the dishes on the table. Dessloch used his finger to point to a working-class section of Paris. "The factories in the northeast would have first priority, of course. From the slopes of Montmartre eastward to Pantin and then from Buttes-Chaumont north to the area of Porte de la Villette. As you can see, Le

Bourget is only five miles away. There are enough bombs stored there to give this group roughly ten bombing runs each. That should do the job.''

"Perhaps," Schellen said, "there would be time to warn the civilians in the area.''

Dessloch snorted. "A commendable sentiment, Herr Schellen. "But my wife and children had no warning before the fire raids in Hamburg.''

"I see," Schellen said. He shrugged. "Well, gentlemen, we all have our orders. I am reassured, General Dessloch.''

"Meanwhile, as we saturate the industrial areas," Dessloch said, "my other bombers can be working along the Seine. When we are finished, they will know how it feels to see a beloved city in flames.''

"Of course, the bombing cannot be started until our own troops are in the clear," Schläfer said, motioning for Wolf to take the map away.

"*If* they are forced to abandon the city at all.'' Schellen was testing, for he himself had no doubt that Paris would fall.

"If, indeed," Schläfer said, but without conviction.

"Ah, another thought," Dessloch said. "It would increase the accuracy of the bombing if Choltitz has men mark the target areas with flares. Wonderful! And I would suggest that he destroy the water mains, so that the fires will burn unchecked.''

"Brilliant," Schellen said, not expressing the sadness he felt.

Theo Werner, standing at parade rest, waiting to clear the table, felt that he would be sick. He'd seen what German bombs had done in London. So far he hadn't seen much of Paris, but he knew it was a city of great and delicate beauty. To hear the three Germans speaking so calmly of razing it to the ground brought home to him, once more, why he'd been fighting them for over four years. Now he felt a burning need for action, and he could not move—could not find Mady and insist that she put him into contact with the resistance leaders—until he had cleared the table of the remnants of the hearty breakfast the Germans had eaten with gusto, even as they talked of killing thousands of people. When Schläfer stood and beckoned to him, he leaped forward and began his task.

Otto Schellen watched him. The waiter moved like a soldier, it was true. He lit a cigarette and watched, and just as Theo was about to hoist his tray he spoke.

"And why are you *formerly* of the Luftflotte Two?"

"Sir," Theo said, coming to attention, "I still have a British machine-gun bullet embedded near my spine."

"And yet you are healthy enough to hoist a load of dirty dishes and leftovers," Schellen said.

"I begged them to let me stay on active duty," Theo said. "It has something to do with altitude, and strain, sir."

"I see. Well, carry on, man."

He loaded his rolling cart and left the room. Time, he knew, was desperately short. He took the cart to the kitchen and reported to M. Alexandre. Another assignment delayed still further a chance to seek out Mady. He passed by Blaise Deschaises's post and nodded, but received scant recognition in return. He had spent the previous two nights in the young man's room, sleeping on a surplus French Army cot. His attempts to engage the boy in conversation had been rewarded by only grunts and monosyllables.

It was interesting to look at the sullen face and see

there the shape of nose, the delicacy of eyes, that were the distinguishing features of Mady's face. It gave him a strange feeling to see the resemblance, to think that this boy, who obviously hated him as a German, had sprung from Mady, was loved by Mady.

Once again, he pushed his cart to the Luftwaffe section and he spent an hour there, serving breakfast to another group of Luftwaffe officers, who apparently had no urge to get to work. Their conversation was mainly about women and wine, and it gave no hint of any awareness that the good life in Paris was in its last days.

On the way back to the kitchen he made a detour, even at the risk of being reprimanded by M. Alexandre, or of running unexpectedly into the German, Wolf, who seemed to be everywhere. Corporal Wolf, Theo felt, did not like him at best, and at worst might harbor suspicions about him.

He stopped his service cart just outside Mady's office and peered in through the open door. She was talking with a housemaid. She caught his eye and nodded, quickly dismissed the girl. She gave him an angry look as he entered and closed the door behind him.

"You shouldn't be here," she hissed.

"It is vital that I meet with your people," he said. "No later than tonight. You said you were sending messages on Monday. Now it's Wednesday—what's the delay?"

"I am trying to arrange it. Now go, quickly."

"Yes. Tonight. I'll be waiting for word from you."

"Get out, get out," she said, pushing him. He

grinned, looking down into her face. She was quite beautiful in anger. She saw the look in his eyes and let a wry smile twist her full lips. He leaned, pecked those lips quickly, and then left her.

11

THE MIDDAY RUSH at the Ritz was over. Theo had found time to eat his lunch—a rather nice one, since extra food had been prepared for the Germans. Now, he sat in a secluded corner, leaned back and closed his eyes. The work was not heavy, but it was wearing—especially the standing at attention. And the underlying tension of his being there as a spy was getting to him. Especially since he wasn't *doing* anything. He was not at all satisfied with himself. His main accomplishment in Paris, up to that Wednesday afternoon, was the seduction of a widowed Frenchwoman who had a teenage son who hated him.

He felt a deep need to move, to do, to complete his assignment. But the men he was supposed to contact weren't being very cooperative. Not much action there. He knew he'd probably be stuck in Paris until the city was either destroyed or liberated. Either way, he had to make plans to survive. If the Germans started demolishing the city he would do his best to get out. That prospect did not attract him, for, after all, his French was primitive, and he had no way to identify himself as an American. As a German, he would be in trouble outside of German-occupied territory. All in all, it would be best if he could remain hidden, perhaps simply stay on, working at the Ritz, until the Allies encircled Paris and the besieged Germans were finally starved into surrender, if that's how things were going to work out.

He had just begun to realize the true danger of his position. He was safe as long as the Germans were there—unless he was exposed as a spy. And, as far as he knew, only one person, Mady, knew his true identity, so in the event of an uprising he would have to depend on her to protect him, to reveal his true character to others, to hide him if necessary. It would be pushing irony a bit too far to survive being a spy in occupied Paris only to be killed by angry Frenchmen upon the liberation of the city.

He heard someone near him and opened his eyes. He jerked upright in the chair, for he had looked up into the eyes of a man he'd seen only in pictures. He was staring, wide-eyed, into the distinctive Gallic face of a famous man, Charles de Gaulle.

"Jesus Christ," he said, before he could stop himself.

The man who stood before him, tall to the point of gauntness, strong mouth and weak chin accented by a mustache, ears large and protruding, grinned down at him and did not speak.

He saw, then, that the man wore the uniform of a Ritz porter. He spoke to Theo in French, and with an accent so provincial that Theo caught only a word or two. The gist was, he thought, that the man was asking if he had a cigarette, so he reached into his pocket and took out a pack of German cigarettes and extended one.

"My name is Michel," the lanky man said.

"You could have fooled me," Theo said, in German, and the man grinned again.

"Yes," he said, also in German, "I have fooled many. In uniform, as I was once at a masquerade party, I drew salutes."

"I'd stay away from the other Germans, if I were you," Theo said. "They might make a mistake."

"On the contrary," Michel said, "I have many German friends. I see no reason to hate."

"An enlightened attitude," Theo said, rather doubtfully. He'd received nothing but hate from most of the other French employees.

"You are quite an advanced people, you Germans," Michel said. He shrugged. "I know that most feel differently. I happen to like Germans. All this fighting—I don't see why we can't live in peace."

There was, upon close examination, a strange look in the eyes of the tall man who could have doubled for Charles de Gaulle. And, as the conversation went on, Theo began to assess the man's intelligence as being somewhat below normal. He was to learn, later, that his assessment was generous, for Michel Skop, somewhat of a mascot at the Ritz, had been injured severely in the early days of the war, taking shrapnel in his head, suffering some brain damage. The damage had left him with an unusual talent—an uncanny ability as a mimic. He could memorize the most complicated message, deliver it accurately, in a fair imitation of the sender's intonations—and then, apparently not having understood anything, forget it all. He had enough intelligence to do his job, to keep his mouth shut when near patrons of the hotel.

"Actually," he confided, the first day when he sought out Theo, "I don't really like Germans, but I like to make people feel good."

"Thank you, Michel," Theo said. "I don't have many cigarettes, but you're welcome to share them as long as they last."

"Ah, you are a fine man, even if you are German," the porter said, taking another cigarette.

It was an odd coincidence, for Theo was to see the lanky porter once again that day, not over an hour later, when Theo had returned to the kitchen areas. He was thinking of seeking out Mady again when Michel Skop came running up from the basement levels, his face white, his voice doing strange things. He made frantic motions. Theo was of the first to see him and he ran to the man.

"Terrible," Michel was saying, making motions toward the stairs. He turned and ran down the stairs, Theo following, and behind them others from the kitchen staff.

She was hanging from a network of pipes in a laundry room, a young girl in the uniform of a hotel maid. Her face was bloated, pushing against the thick glasses. The others came up behind and halted with an intake of breath. Skop was pointing, making a sobbing sound in his throat.

"Do you have a pocket knife?" Theo asked, and the tall porter reached into pocket. Theo pulled up the stool she had stepped from, and climbed atop. "Some of you be ready to help me lower her." Michel moved forward, along with Blaise Deschaises. Theo cut the rope with which the girl had hanged herself and let the limp body slide down his until the

others could get their hands on it. Her dress had
been pulled up by the slide down his body and he
saw legs covered in thick work stockings, old-
fashioned underwear. The two men placed her on the
floor and stood back.

"We must send for the doctor," someone was
saying, repeating it over and over.

"She is dead," Theo said.

"The director," someone suggested.

Mady appeared on the scene. She took one look,
covered her mouth with her hand for a moment, and
took charge.

"All right," she said. "You have seen. Now
return to your work. I will handle this."

Blaise and Theo stayed, the boy giving Theo a
hard glare of hatred. "Do you know how this happened?" Mady asked.

Blaise was silent, looking from one face to the
other. "The porter, Michel Skop, discovered her,"
Theo said.

"Blaise, will you please go to the office and tell
the director what has happened? While you're there,
have someone call for a hearse."

When they were alone, she looked at Teddy, shaking her head.

"Any idea why she would commit suicide?" he
asked.

"She was questioned, just last night, by the Gestapo," Mady said. "A woman. She was hurt, and
shamed, and she was afraid."

"Why would they question a maid?"

"She was caught in General Schläfer's room, going
through his papers."

"My God!" A thought came to him. "One of
yours?"

"No. I hired her, but she was not, as you say, 'one of ours.' She was not the most brilliant of girls. She said, when she came to me for help, that she'd gone to the room by mistake. She said she was merely straightening the papers on the General's desk. I think I believe her."

"She came to you?" Theo asked, beginning to be concerned.

"Yes."

"Will they suspect you?"

"I don't think so."

"You're sure she was not in your group?"

"Of course." She opened her mouth to speak further, but she heard the sound of heavy, irregular footsteps on the stairs, and stopped.

In a moment Wolf limped into the laundry room. "I understand there is trouble here," he said.

"Yes," Mady said. "This poor girl—"

Wolf had approached. The girl's bloated face was not recognizable, but the glasses were. "Well, well," he said. "The Resistance girl who was in the General's rooms." He looked up at Mady, then brought his eyes to rest on Teddy's face. "I imagine that her fellow criminals killed her to prevent further questioning."

"I don't think so," Teddy said. "It appears that she merely knotted a piece of clothesline around her neck, tied it to the pipe, and stepped off this stool."

"Oh, yes, it could have happened that way," Wolf said. "But it could have been set up, couldn't it? You must admit that it seems suspicious for the girl to be questioned and released and to die so quickly afterward." He smiled at Mady. "I understand, Madame Deschaises, that she came to you?"

"She was hurt," Mady said. "I was her supervisor. She came to me for help."

"Ah, of course," Wolf said, making it plain that he had his own opinions. He smiled. "These are trying times, Madame Deschaises. No time for one to become involved in matters that might become, suddenly, quite serious."

"Corporal," Theo said, "the girl was frightened. Perhaps she feared they would hurt her again. Who can say? I assure you that neither I nor Madame Deschaises knows anything about it."

"So, the steward speaks for Madame Deschaises?" Wolf asked. Without waiting for an answer he turned and left the laundry room. Teddy knew that he would have only a few moments alone with Mady, and there was a lot to say. His first concern was the seriousness of the barely veiled threats Wolf had made.

"Mady," he said, "there's going to be trouble. The man is suspicious. I'd suggest that if you have anything incriminating in the hotel, you get rid of it immediately. I know, for example, that there's at least one radio receiver somewhere in the basement."

"There are at least two, probably more," she said.

"For God's sake, don't go near them," he said. "Can you be connected with them in any way?"

"No," she said.

"These Germans are like an injured snake," he said. "Soon they're going to start lashing out in all directions. Somehow we've got to survive these last few days."

In spite of the grim circumstances, she was touched.

She gave him a fleeting smile and, taking a clean sheet from a stack of finished laundry, spread it carefully and tenderly over the body of the dead maid. "She didn't survive," she said. "God, how I hate them!"

12

REPORTING TO HIS station a few minutes
later, Teddy was given an order to be delivered—a
late lunch. He took it to the assigned room, knocked,
and, hearing a feminine voice call out, pushed open
the door. A blonde woman with a flowing silken
dress sat, a book in her hand, looking up at him. He
set down the tray, laid things out neatly.

"Will this be satisfactory, madame?" he asked.

She merely nodded. He moved to stand against a
wall as Silke took her place at the table and examined the offering. She was in a sour mood—Schellen
had been gone all morning and into the afternoon.
She wanted to see Paris, and all she was seeing was
the inside of hotel room. However nice it was, that
was not her idea of how to spend a day.

She had been out of the room only once, to walk
down to the lobby. There she'd been the object of
admiring glances from uniformed officers, but she
was accustomed to that. While there, however, she
noted the arrival of a policeman, who hurried through
toward the back of the hotel.

She sampled the asparagus. It was delcious, but not even the good food could overcome her resentment at being left alone.

"I understand there was some sort of incident in the hotel," she said.

"It was nothing to cause concern, madame," Teddy said. He was looking at her back, at a shock of rather nice hair worn in a casual, loose style which gave, almost, the appearance of untidiness but, upon closer examination, showed a cunning artfulness.

"Had I not been interested, I would not have asked," Silke said curtly.

"Forgive me," Teddy said. "A maid committed suicide, madame. That is all."

"That is all?" She laughed. "For the maid, the event was not so casual, no?"

"Yes, it was quite a serious incident for the maid," Teddy said, tongue in cheek, but in a respectful voice.

"Damn it, when I speak to you, stand around here so that I can see you," Silke said.

"I beg your pardon, madame," Teddy said, moving to stand at parade rest at a slight angle from her face. She looked up at him, her cat-gray eyes squinting slightly.

"You are no garlic eater," she said. "Your accent is Swiss-German."

"Very astute, madame," Teddy said. "Yes, I am Swiss."

"German, in the eyes of the French," she said. "How do you come to be working here, in Paris?"

"It is my desire to make a career of hotel work after the war," Teddy said.

"So, you think there will be hotels standing?" She smiled. "Well, without hope, where are we? Tell me about yourself as I eat. I hate being alone."

"There isn't much to tell," Teddy said. "My father took Swiss citizenship before I was born. However, I have always been German at heart. When the war started I came home."

"Home?"

"To Germany. I was given the honor of service with the Luftwaffe."

"Ah. A war hero?"

"Not really, madame," Teddy said. He did not look at her directly, but he saw enough to know that she was a beautiful woman. The dress she wore showed a creamy cleavage and the beginnings of nice breasts. And there was a look in her eyes. He had the feeling that she was measuring him. For a moment he wondered, with an inner laugh, what the rules of the Ritz were regarding fraternization between staff and guests. But it was an idle thought.

"This maid who committed suicide," Silke said. "Tell me about her."

"I know little," he said. "I've been here only a short while. I don't even know her name. She was young."

Silke looked thoughtful. "Rather plain? Heavy glasses? With a large rump, skinny shoulders, no breasts?"

"Perhaps, madame," he said, his interest aroused.

"And with a sort of growth, a wart, just to the side of her nose?"

"I believe so, madame," he said, trying to remember.

"An amazing coincidence." Silke was silent for a moment, and her lips parted to take a bite of paté. She shook her head, as if to dismiss the matter.

"Do you know Paris well?" she asked.

"No, madame. I've only just arrived."

"I don't either," she said. "And I'm cross because I was supposed to be out seeing the city before it is too late."

"Too late?"

"Have you forgotten the war?" She smiled. "No, I suppose you haven't. Perhaps we should go and see Paris together." She smiled and gave him a challenging look.

"A lovely thought, madame."

"Well?"

"If your suggestion is serious, madame, I am overwhelmed. However, I have my job."

"I could arrange it," she said.

The most noncommittal answer he could think of was a click of his heels and a murmured, "Madame."

She mused for a moment. When she spoke again her voice was different. She had, he felt, decided that she could, with her beauty, command him. "Do you know the head housekeeper here?" she asked.

He tensed. "I know her by sight. My work doesn't put me into contact with her."

"Tell me—what is your name?" He told her. "Werner. Tell me, Werner, do you think we will win the war?"

"I have trust in the Führer, madame," Teddy said. "He has promised us secret weapons to throw the Allies back into the sea."

"So you are a loyal German."

"Of course," he said.

"Have you noticed anything—ah, of interest since you've been employed here? They say that the Resistance is growing more active. This head housekeeper, for example. There have been hints that she might be involved in anti-German acts."

He hesitated before answering, putting it all together. The maid had been questioned by a woman.

This soft-looking woman? "Being German, madame, I would scarcely be told such things. Actually, I have seen no suspicious activity. I could voice no opinion one way or the other about anyone here."

"I see," she said. "Should you see anything interesting, you would, of course, report it to the proper authorities."

"Yes, madame," he said.

He had been told that they were everywhere, the Gestapo, the others who spied on their own, and that the atmosphere was especially tense after the attempt on Hitler's life a month ago. But to be questioned by two on the same day, within hours, was a bit much.

"I still don't quite understand why a good German is working a menial job in a French hotel," Silke said.

"One must admit, madame, that the French have developed a certain flair," he said. "The Swiss are famous as hoteliers, but I was told, by a man I respected very much, that the Ritz Hotel was the best of the luxury hotels. If I wanted to learn the business, he said, I could do no better than to serve here. I don't intend to be a steward forever."

"I see," she said. "Well, then. You may clear this away." She rose, swayed to stand before the window. It was evident that she wore no petticoat under the silken dress. Her long legs were outlined against the light through the translucent fabric. "If I should need anything, may I ask for you by name?"

"Of course, madame," Teddy said.

And then he got the hell out of there. That one, he thought, would be about as cuddly as a guntotin' rattlesnake.

*   *   *

The rest of the day was uneventful. He worked through the dinner hour, and it looked like another day with no contact with the Resistance leaders. Then, on the way to the room he shared with Blaise Deschaises, he saw Mady, in trim skirt and blouse, coming toward him. She said good evening as if they were merely passing strangers but, as she passed, she whispered, "Where the girl died. In half an hour."

Blaise was not in the room. He was relieved, because he had had about as much as he could take of the boy's sullen hatred. He bathed, put on his clean alternate uniform, checked his watch, and made his way through the service areas to the basement laundry room a few minutes early. The room was empty. He stood there a moment in the light of one bare bulb hanging from the ceiling. Then a side door opened and Mady beckoned to him.

There were three men with Mady in the inner room, a storeroom for linens. When Teddy entered, Mady said, "This is the man," and locked and bolted the door from the inside. The three men were dressed casually. There were no further introductions.

"I speak English or German," Teddy said to the men, who were eyeing him impassively.

"German," one of them said.

"You know why I am here?" Teddy asked.

"To tell us not to kill boches," said one of the men.

"Perhaps to reaffirm what we have suspected, that your General Eisenhower has decided to leave Paris in the jaws of the wolf rather than liberate her," said another.

"And," Teddy responded quietly, "to remind you that a direct march on Paris would result in tank and artillery battles in the boulevards. Is that what you want?''

"We are not here to answer questions," said one of the Resistance men sourly, "but to ask. What are the intentions of the Americans?"

"I can't speak for the generals," Teddy said. "I know only that there is great concern for Paris, and that the intention seems to be to avoid destruction if at all possible. The Resistance must remain quiet, must not provoke the Germans."

"They need no provoking," the largest of the men said. "They are, even now, mining all the public buildings, preparing to blow them up. Are we supposed to remain quiet while they reduce the historic landmarks of Paris to rubble?"

"Perhaps, if they are not provoked, they will not set off the charges," Teddy said. "Do you three speak for all of the Resistance?"

There was a snort of derision from two of the men together.

"I tried to get word to Colonel Rol," Mady said.

"So, the Communist Resistance is not represented here," Teddy said. "Will they move in spite of orders?"

"They take orders only from Moscow," Mady said.

"So we are here on a futile errand," Teddy said. "Am I right in thinking that this Colonel Rol could start a general uprising if he chose to?"

"Who knows?" One of the men shrugged. "My guess is, yes, he could put thousands into the streets. After that it would grow of its own accord."

"The tragedy is," said one of the men sadly, "the Americans could be here within days, and there is a French division within striking distance of the Seine at this moment. Once again, the generals are betraying France.''

Teddy debated his answer for a moment before he spoke, and he made his voice deliberately harsh. ''It was not American armor that sat safely behind the Maginot Line when Germany was most vulnerable,'' he said.

''Touché!'' A bearded man grinned. ''We are not ungrateful, my American friend. We are merely desperate. We have seen family and friends die. We have seen France bow and kiss the foot of the German while hundreds of thousands of Frenchmen were bundled into cattle cars and shipped to their death merely because of their religion. You see, we can't be too proud of ourselves, can we? Perhaps all this bloodthirsty talk of uprising, of throwing the boche out, is merely a way to try to regain our national honor, and, individually, our manhood.''

''And to prevent another *Commune*,'' said Mady.

''Yes, that is the most immediate danger, if one can forget that the bridges of the Seine are being mined for demolition by the Germans. My friend, what can we do?''

''Get me to Colonel Rol,'' Teddy said.

There was a silence. ''We can but try,'' said the man with the neat little beard. ''It will be dangerous for you.''

Teddy didn't answer.

''Now we must go, before the curfew,'' one man said. ''I have no desire to spend the night shining German boots.''

They left one at a time. At last Mady and Teddy were alone in the linen storeroom. She stood, turned toward the door indecisively. He seemed to feel a warmth radiating from her, felt a burning need to hold her. He moved toward her and she backed away.

"No, please," she said.

"It began of its own strength," he said, reaching to pull her into his arms. "I, for one, do not have the power to stop it."

"Not here," she said. "Please."

"Here," he said. "Now." He kissed her, and after a moment's stiffness she sighed deeply and came to him, leaning her softness against his body to accept his kiss and his caresses.

He put bedspreads on the hard floor, covered them with a pristine but worn sheet, and there, amid the linens of the august Ritz, they once again found escape from the war, from their concerns, from their own personal pain. And it was, he admitted to himself, as he made his way back to his room to find the woman's son sleeping, more than that. It was, in fact, more than he had bargained for, more than he had wanted. How stupid to become emotionally entangled with a woman at one of the more crucial and dangerous periods of his life.

13

THERE WAS ANOTHER candestine meeting
in the hotel that night. It took place in the Ritz Barn,
which was still open to the public. Alcohol was
served there only four days a week; the beverage
served on the other days was, mostly, an ersatz
coffee called *café national*, made from acorns and
chick-peas.

The man who waited at the bar was well dressed,
even though his business suit was a bit worn by
many cleanings. He was a tall man, regarded by
many as handsome, and he spoke, in addition to
French, German and English. The latter language
had had little use during the occupation.

Fortunately, he thought, he had received the rarely
heard code word on a day when it was possible to
find a bit of wine in the Ritz Bar. He sipped it
thoughtfully. Now and then, he had the urge to look
over his shoulder, for there were many German uniforms in the bar. He also looked carefully at the
faces of the women with the German officers—for

there would be a reckoning. The collaborationist whores would pay, and soon, for the years of fun and comfort they'd had as the cunts of the boches.

The message had come to him through the usual channels, via Switzerland. He was one of the few who knew that the origin of such messages was a small room well hidden in the Soviet embassy in Geneva. He hated blind meetings as much as he hated anything in his life, which had not been uneventful. The life of a dedicated Communist in France prior to the war had not been without its risks, but now he was about to stand exposed to someone he'd never seen before. He sipped his wine and waited.

When he had first entered and placed his order at the bar, standing, hoping that his wait would not be long, he had noticed a Luftwaffe corporal standing a few feet away drinking German beer. That seemed odd, for enlisted men usually did not have the means to frequent a place as expensive as the Ritz Bar. The corporal had looked at him, a hard, unblinking gaze. After that he'd paid no attention, standing there at the bar to order a second beer. People came and went, and the minute hands of his watch seem to freeze; then he checked again, and a quarter hour had passed. When he looked up, the German corporal had moved down toward him to give room to a group of three Luftwaffe officers, who glared at him and did not speak. Another officer joined the group, and the corporal was now at his elbow.

"We must give room to the brass," the corporal said, out of the corner of his mouth, with a twisted grin. The man nodded and gave a half smile. *Petit* boche, he was thinking.

"I know little of wine," the corporal said.

"Ummm," the man said, not interested in a conversation with any boche, unless it was an interrogation followed by a conversation of a type he liked to conduct, using a Luger for a tongue.

"They say it is a good year for wine in Aunis," the corporal commented.

The man felt himself freeze for a moment, then he relaxed and breathed again. "But it has been dry in Bordeaux," he answered. He had never made a more unlikely contact. A German Luftwaffe corporal? And yet the words were right, the mention of Aunis as a wine region just obscure enough to assure that it was not a casual remark. He sipped his wine and waited.

"Well, I suppose I will have to give my place to the brass," the corporal said, swilling the last of his beer. He reached into his pocket and withdrew a few francs. "It is my pleasure to treat you," he said, thrusting the bills in front of the man.

"Very generous." The man did not turn to watch the corporal leave. Instead, idly, he picked up the franc notes and put them into pocket. When he finished his wine he paid, being sure to use his own money, and left. At the end of the long corridor, he entered the lobby of the hotel and found a chair. There he began to arrange his franc notes, as if merely straightening them to place them into his wallet, and saw the penciled notation on the margin of one—a room number. He went to the desk to ask directions. He knew, from the look he got, that the room was in the section of the hotel reserved for Luftwaffe officers. Ah, well. If it was a trap, it was already too late.

He made his way to the room with long, confident strides, nodding cordially at the Luftwaffe officers he met in the hallways. One tap on the door brought the small corporal with the withered arm. When the door was closed behind them he looked around. The room had probably once housed the personal servant of one of the rich who had made the Ritz a semi-permanent home before the war.

With head slightly tilted, Wolf looked unblinkingly into the larger man's eyes. The man saw there something that he recognized, a challenge, a confidence that told him the man in the corporal's uniform was more than just that.

"An odd place," the Frenchman said.

Wolf laughed. "Where better than with Luftwaffe guards all around to keep us from being interrupted?"

"Ah," the man said.

"Please make yourself comfortable, comrade." Wolf suited action to words and sat down. "We have little time."

"Your authentication?" the man asked, before sitting.

Wolf gave it, and the man was surprised. Yes, indeed, the small corporal with the withered arm and short leg was damned well more than he seemed.

"Are you satisfied?" Wolf asked, unsmilingly.

"Yes, Colonel," the man said. "You have orders, I take it."

"It is imperative that the barricades go up," Wolf said.

"I suppose you know that there is opposition."

"There is always opposition, isn't there?" Wolf asked. "However, it is up to you and the others to see that it is done. De Gaulle is on the way to France. Leclerc and the Second Armored Division, Free French, are within a quick drive to the Seine. The next few hours, the next few days, will determine whether or not we lose France."

"De Gaulle." The Frenchman spat out the name in disgust.

"Yes," Wolf said. "Fortunately, the Allied generals and politicians feel the same way, if for other reasons. They don't want de Gaulle in control of France any more than we. The problem is, they have no alternative choice."

"There is a choice," the man said.

"Which is unacceptable to them, of course," Wolf said. "But, highly acceptable to us. When the Allied armor enters Paris it *must* find the key points under our control. Thus, we seize them. The time is short. How soon can Colonel Rol put men into the streets?"

"That is not the question." The man paused. "The question is, Colonel, *will* he put men into the streets? There is a growing feeling, even among the dedicated, that perhaps we should wait. No one wants to see Paris in flames."

"Would you rather see France under the control of the patricians, the de Gaulles?"

"It is a hard choice," the man said.

"Am I to understand that Colonel Rol might disobey orders?"

"It's possible. Possible."

Wolf's voice was calm, matter-of-fact. "Then you must kill him."

"I would rather kill de Gaulle. That, too, would solve the problem."

"That would only make him a martyr, gain the sympathies of the uncommitted, open the way for his followers, such as Leclerc. No, that is not the answer. The answer is to rise, comrade, to rise, to kill Germans, to seize the governmental apparatus of this city. Damn, do I have to remind you that he who holds Paris holds France?"

"No, Colonel," the man said.

"Perhaps a reminder would help," Wolf said. "You might tell the reluctant ones that the Gestapo is not the only organization that knows how to make a man sorry he has disobeyed orders."

"I understand." Yes, he had heard. The screams coming from the cellars of the KGB, in Moscow, would have the same quality as the screams coming from the basement rooms of the Gestapo.

"Yet, I can understand your problem," Wolf said. "I can understand the reluctance to sacrifice a hundred thousand lives or two and the glory of Paris. But we must not forget our purpose. We must see to it that Paris rises, before the Americans or the Free French arrive. We must present de Gaulle with a fait accompli. Once in control, not even he can displace us.

"So. I have been thinking. Through an odd coincidence, I think I have come up with something that might help convince the reluctant." Wolf smiled to himself in secret pleasure as the man waited. "Oh, I won't tell you now. Just tell your Colonel Rol that it is imperative that he proceed with the plans as ordered, that he must move no later than Saturday."

"So little time," the man said.

"You have been preparing for this day for years," Wolf said. "Now go. At ten minutes past one tomorrow afternoon, have Colonel Rol in the Place Maubert. Tell him it is vital. Tell him that he will meet a man there who will convince him that he has no choice but to do as he is ordered. Can you do this?"

"I can tell him," the man said.

Wolf waved a hand. "Don't worry. I'm not going to have him killed. You can come with him, if you're worried about that. Tell him to ride his bicycle to the café on the west side of the square. A man in the clothing of an industrial workman will be seated at the table nearest the large tree."

"He will come to no harm?" the man asked.

"Didn't I tell you he wouldn't?" Wolf asked impatiently.

"I will tell him."

"Have him there. Impress upon him that it is an order from the highest sources."

"I will do my best."

"It will, I'm sure, be good enough," Wolf said with finality.

The man stood. He knew that he was out of line when he said it, but his curiosity was too much for him. "Someday, sir, I'd like to how you've done it."

Wolf smiled. "Perhaps, someday."

He did not rise. The man left, closing the door behind him. Wolf's face became thoughtful. The strong, tall Frenchman had walked away as if it had been merely another meeting with another comrade. It was amusing to think that as soon as the man's role was fulfilled, he would die. Until the man had walked into Wolf's room, not one man in German territory knew that the Luftwaffe corporal, the general's valet, was anything more than a scarcely disguised watchdog, one of thousands placed in crucial areas so that the enforcement agencies of Hitler's police state could keep guard on the military men, who sometimes lost their dedication. One man who knew was one too many, at least for now. Soon it would change. When the Germans were driven out and finally defeated, when the men who had been carefully groomed were in control of France, then, and only then, would he emerge to take his just rewards. Then no one would laugh.

They had laughed when, as a young man, he had donned his brown shirt. They had called him cripple, degenerate, and once, in a beer hall in Berlin, he had taken on two of them, bloated with their pride in being members of the new elite, and with a swiftness and deadly skill belying his withered arm and his short leg, he had hospitalized both of them.

He had been born Bruno Lenk. During the terrible days of hunger in his native city of Berlin, when horse meat was at a premium and only the more fortunate had even that doubtful delicacy, he had fed himself from the garbage cans of those who had led Germany into the situation from which it seemed it would never emerge. He had seen his father die in the street fighting, and he had felt the blows of those who called him Bolshevik, because of his father's politics, and he'd seen his mother turn from a plump and pretty *hausfrau* into a woman who, to feed herself and her handicapped child, sold her body for scarcely enough money to buy a loaf of bread.

He'd been helpless then, a cripple. And one man had seen the fire deep down inside of him.

That man had changed his life forever, before being killed by the emerging Nazis. "Bruno," he had said, "we will lose this time. But there will be a next time, and we'll need men like you will be. Study. Hide yourself. Go with the tide. But deep inside of you, keep the belief that drove your father. Believe in the eventual victory of the proletariat, and it will come, someday."

So Bruno had studied. He had heard the speeches of Adolf Hitler, and he was astute enough to realize that Hitler was Germany's immediate destiny and that in the end he would lead the country to disaster. Then would come the real opportunity.

One advantage came of his malformed body. A charitable organization selected him for special treatment, and his education came as a result. Then, as a teen-ager, he had traveled secretly, on his own, to Russia; there, by the use of two names—his father's and the name of the man who had advised him to hide his beliefs—he had gained the notice of a minor party functionary. From then on, he had advanced. He returned to Germany in the early 1930s, in time to don the brown shirt and shout his approval of the man who would bring disaster for Germany and eventual victory for the Party. Flashing application of his secret knowledge of Oriental hand fighting had shown that he was no mere cripple, and he became a sort of mascot for the hearty Nazis, a showpiece.

And yet they laughed, because not even the special shoe could eliminate the limp entirely. Not even the fact that he was more man than most of them could eliminate the good-natured laughter. It was still laughter, and it still rankled.

He had his rewards, though. He had spoken, face to face, with Himmler himself. He had shaken the Führer's hand. And he showed no hesitation when he was offered a position in the dreaded Gestapo, when some wag thought it would be amusing to see a cripple make other cripples during the interrogations. Yes, he'd done that, too—to poor wretches who did not deserve it, to people who believed as he believed, but did not have the good sense to hide it, to wait for the time.

His assignment to France, as a scarcely disguised watchdog of the free-wheeling Luftwaffe command in Paris, had come as an unexpected opportunity, because the Party was weak in France, and needed a firm hand. His was that hand, for with all the resources of the Gestapo behind him, with the Luftwaffe as a front, he could learn things that were denied others. He was that unseen and unknown contact, with the route of his own orders coming through Switzerland, who laid down the Party line, who fostered the formation of the strong Communist Resistance by using German planes to smuggle arms to the comrades.

All his life people had laughed. And, thinking about it, as he sat alone, sipping fine French cognac, he knew that there was one more chore he had to perform before the fall of Paris, for one person too many had laughed. One woman too many had looked at him in contempt. He would allow himself one small indulgence. For that woman who had laughed, who had looked at him in surprise and contempt, had taken the tall and blond Werner into her bed the first night he was in the hotel. Mady Deschaises. Good Lord, what he could have given her, had she had the sense to see past his thin face and his handicaps. She could have been the mistress of one of the most powerful men in France, could have lived a good life during the occupation and a royal life afterward, when Paris and all of France was in Communist hands. But she'd laughed. She would find it hard to laugh when he had finished with her.

14

PARIS WAS QUIET on the evening of that August Wednesday. At the Moulin Rouge, Yves Montand entertained, and in the audience was a blond-haired pair of Aryan blood who heard the romantic songs with differing grades of sentiment and cynicism. The theaters of the city were open only in the late afternoon, and closed by dark. But there was no lack of audiences—even in these critical times there were plenty who wanted escape.

Otto Schellen had at last granted Silke's wish. Before darkness they toured the areas along the Seine, and saw the great cathedral, Notre Dame. Silke, impressed, had said, "It will be a shame." He knew what she was talking about. The splendid flying buttresses would crash down, and the work of centuries would die in minutes. But it had happened in German cities, where buildings equally great had been turned into rubble by the British and American super-bombers. Why, then, not here?

Silke and Otto rode in a super-velo, that odd

man-powered taxi pulled by four bicycle riders. He
had engaged them for the remainder of the evening.

The Metro ran only at rush hours and through the
evening. It was doing a big business that evening,
but at eleven it would close. And at twelve a still-
ness would descend on the city, the curfew.

Not all the movement in Paris was the traffic of
pleasure-seekers. All over the city, files were being
packed or burned, belongings were being stowed in
luggage. For the order had come down to non com-
batant units—the Gestapo, the SS, the staff officers—
to evacuate the city. It was said that the Vichy
government functionaries were also preparing to leave.

And yet there was a pervasive air of casual gai-
ety. Unlike other cities in Europe, Paris did not face
the nightly bombings, and, Paris being Paris and
always tending to overvalue itself somewhat, there
seemed to be no real concern among the gay crowd
at the Moulin Rouge. The party must go on. No
sense of desperation about it; only the blithe uncon-
cern.

Schellen could not understand it. He'd spent the
afternoon talking with various highly placed officers,
and he knew that the public buildings were being
readied for demolition. He knew that the still powerful Luftflotte 3 was ready to use all of its bombers in
a methodical razing of the city.

Back in the Ritz Hotel, the man known only as Wolf
waited in his room. When he heard the knock on the
door he walked, limping slightly, to open it.

"Ah, my friend, the General," he said, with
amusement in his voice.

The porter, Michel Skop, stood there uncertainly,
his hat in his hand. He had been going off duty, and

he was a bit put out by being ordered to the room of
the General's valet. He had an appointment of sorts,
at a certain house where a few francs would buy a
few minutes of the time of a woman whose time he
had purchased before, when he could afford it.

"Come in, come in," Wolf said, taking the porter's arm.

"Sir, I'm off duty, you know."

"Sure, sure. It will be all right," Wolf assured.
"Look what I have for you." He poured a generous
shot of cognac into a crystal glass and extended it.

Michel, leaned forward, his lips breaking into a
smile under his mustache. The fiery cognac hit his
palate well, and he smacked his lips and smiled.

"Sit down," Wolf said amiably. He had first seen
the fellow months ago. Like many, he had been
struck by the resemblance between this simple-minded
porter and de Gaulle.

Despite his dedication, his overall seriousness,
there was in Wolf a bit of whimsy. It pleased him to
think that he would use this double of the famous
general to assure that his orders were obeyed. It
would make a great story for the telling someday.
He would smile and tell how the brave and fierce
Resistance leaders were fooled by a child's ploy.
And there was a grimness to the joke, too, for the
brave and fierce Resistance leaders would not be
around to laugh. The tanks and automatic weapons
of the German garrison in Paris would account for
some of them, no doubt. As for the others, they
would have served their purpose. Their insubordin-
ation, their Gallic independence, would have to be
rewarded in various appropriate ways. One way might
be a working vacation in the mines of Siberia. That
would be among the more bearable rewards—at least

one had a chance of surviving for a time. Wolf never forgot a slight, and he'd had to crack the whip hard to keep the Frenchmen in line.

Michel Skop stretched his long legs out in front of him and relaxed. Wolf lit a cigarette for him, and poured more cognac.

"My friend," Wolf said, "I ask a favor of you."

"Certainly," Michel said expansively. "I like Germans, you know."

"Good, good. This favor is sort of a joke on a friend." Wolf laughed. "You like jokes, don't you?"

"I love them," Michel said, feeling the flow of warmth from the cognac.

"Of course, there will be a reward for you," Wolf said. "You could use a few extra francs, can you not?"

The vision of the lovely lady who sold her time occupied Michel for a moment before he nodded. Wolf reached into his pocket and withdrew a wad of francs, handed them over. "This is the down payment," he said. "You'll have more when we've played our little joke. And one of the requirements is that you do exactly as I tell you—no more no less—and that afterward you say nothing. To anybody. Do you understand?"

"Sure," Michel said, holding out his glass.

"No, my friend, no more right at the moment. Later. Now we must talk, and you must try hard to remember what I tell you."

He talked, slowly and easily. He listened, nodding in satisfaction, as Skop repeated the words he'd been told to say. They went through it several times before Wolf gave Skop another drink and sent him on his way. He would just have time for his visit to the lady before curfew.

Wolf was grinning in pleasure as he anticipated the expression on Colonel Rol's face. He called the night manager and said, "Tomorrow for two hours, I will require the personal service of the porter Michel Skop. He will be in my room at exactly eleven-thirty."

"Herr Wolf," the manager protested, "this is highly unusual. We are short-handed as it is."

"Shall I have General Schläfer call you personally on this matter?" Wolf asked imperiously.

After only an instant's hesitation, the night manager said, "He will be there."

"But of course," Wolf said. "I never doubted it for a moment."

15

ED RAINE RODE in the cab of a half-track as a reconnaissance unit of the French Second Armored Division moved out on Thursday morning. Among the officers was a palpable air of urgency. What lay ahead? How stiff would the German defenses be?

But Ed was more interested in the plans of the French. He put out feelers, asked questions, and got the same unsatisfactory answers. The division was merely following the commands from General Hodges's First Army headquarters. It would bypass Paris. The High Command had decided . . .

Ed wasn't buying that for a minute. He could read a map, and the lead elements of the French were arrowing straight toward the capital. There, ahead, lay Paris, the magnet.

He was with a young and brash captain who decided to move ahead. The captain knew the country, left the main column to take a side road, and drove like a maniac, hardly slowing at crossroads.

"I hope you know what you're doing," Ed said.
There were no others near them. Fortunately they
encountered no Germans. Ed estimated that the rest
of the unit was by now at least five miles off on their
right and, no doubt, behind them.

The small lane curved through farmlands and or-
chards, and there were many places where an 88-mm
gun could be concealed, where German outposts
could be lying in wait with machine guns at the
ready, but still the captain drove on.

"Hell," the Frenchman said, "we could be in
Paris in an hour or two."

"I think the others would be chagrined if we went
without them," Ed said. He tensed as he saw a
group of men on the road ahead, relaxed when he
saw that they wore civilian clothing.

The captain jerked the half-track to a stop. Enlisted men in the back leaped out. The civilians were
carrying arms, but when they saw the cross of
Lorraine, Joan of Arc's symbol, they began to em-
brace the soldiers and talk excitedly.

The leader of the Resistance group approached the
captain and saluted. His demeanor was unmilitary,
but he was trying, and he looked as if he knew how
to use the World War I rifle he carried.

"We must see Leclerc," he said. "It is of vital
importance."

Room was made in the half-track. The leader of
the Resistance group sat in front, with Ed and the
captain, who insisted on driving. Ed, sensing a story,
began to question the man as the half-track turned,
roared, and started back at breakneck speed to division HQ.

The man would not give his name. "It is not

important," he said. "Call me Jacquot. I am only one. If you are to write a story about the Paris Resistance, do not mention names, for all deserve equal credit. All have made a pact with death. Some say we are mystics, not rational, that we have done little and have had little hope. But we have lived in the belief that our country, no matter how hopeless it seemed, would be saved. And now you are here."

"How is it in Paris now?" Ed asked.

Jacquot shrugged. "The thugs are still there."

"Thugs?"

"The Vichy militia. They are sometimes worse than the Germans."

"Do you know," Ed asked, "that the Germans rate the French Resistance very low? They have said that it is nothing more than a nuisance, not a force like those in Yugoslavia and Russia."

The man shrugged. "Perhaps those Germans who are dead at Vercors feel differently. However, I agree. Most of us were content to wait. Most of us have collaborated, in one way or the other, if only in lining up for our small rations of food after most of it was sent to Germany, in riding bicycles, in wearing wooden shoes, and in paying high prices on the black market. Our reward has been hungry children and the deportation to Germany of many thousands to work in the war factories. We have suffered, but most were worried more about getting three meals a day than in fighting and killing Germans. We have not even killed men like this blind Scapini, the Minister for Prisoners. We listen to him read collaboration with his fingers feeling the Braille letters, telling us that we must work so that we will get our men, our soldiers who were captured in 1940, back. A million and a half have not come back."

"Is there much active collaboration?" Ed asked.

"Some. They will pay."

"And just what activities have the Resistance engaged in in Paris?"

The man cast him a baleful glance. "There isn't much to write about."

"There was the Vilde group, early in the war. They were imprisoned, or shot," Ed said. "Surely there were others."

"Yes. Many listen to the BBC and pass on the word of the truth. We circulate it by word of mouth. And some print underground newspapers. We have smuggled a few Allied airmen to safety, and have others in safe places now." He shrugged. "On the surface it does not seem like much. But there is Vercors, and there will be Paris."

"The Allied High Command wants the Resistance to remain quiet," Ed said. "Have you received such orders?"

"We have heard." The man paused. "I think it will not be possible."

"Why is that?"

"The Germans are planning to demolish Paris," the man said simply. "That is why I must speak to General Leclerc, to tell him to advance on Paris as swiftly as possible. When we strike, the Resistance, perhaps we can keep the Germans from completing their plans. They plan, for example, to demolish all the bridges over the Seine. There are demolition experts working all over the city at this very moment."

Ed felt a cold chill of dread.

"There is another danger," said Jacquot. "Already, this war has had the flavor of a civil war. De

Gaulle himself has fought against the Vichy French as much as he has fought against the Germans. And in Paris the two elements of the Resistance will throw the Germans out, then fight among themselves. Unless they are stopped." He mused for a moment. "But who can stop them?"

16

WOLF ALWAYS SLEPT well before a crisis. He attended his general in the early morning, asked for some free time, and returned to his own room. Skop was there a few minutes early. He dressed Skop in workman's clothing, including baggy, soiled visor cap which, when pulled low, hid most of Skop's face as he looked downward. There was time, on the way over to the rendezvous on the Left Bank in a velo-taxi, to have Skop repeat his lines again. They arrived near the Place Maubert well before the appointed time. Wolf knew that the Resistance would have the place staked out, so he left Skop several blocks away and took up his station in a sidewalk café where he had a clear view of the square. Now it was up to Skop. He was sure that the dull-witted man would carry out his part of the plan, for he'd found it amusing, in the past, to talk with Skop. He knew the man well. In a way, it was one cripple talking with another. Skop's handicap was from an injury and affected the mentality. Wolf's was congenital, and of the body. Yet there was in Wolf's subconscious, if nowhere else, the recognition of a common bond. He had no intention of having Skop killed, for example. It didn't even occur to him. If Skop told anyone about the little joke, he would not be able to make sense of it, would not know who it was he had spoken to, there on the Place Maubert. He was harmless, and likable. If he survived the coming cataclysm, Wolf would see to it that he had a job, a place to sleep, enough to eat.

The man called Colonel Rol rode his bicycle toward the square, fully aware of the time without looking at his watch. He had his eyes open for a trap, but the place looked normal. That, however, didn't mean that there were no Germans in mufti lurking nearby. Life was a risk. The orders had come from on high. The main reason he was entering the square shortly before one o'clock on Thursday was curiosity. He thought that perhaps he was at last going to meet the man whose connection went directly to the Kremlin. He wanted to know that man, for they'd be very much involved once the city was in their hands.

As soon as he was in the square, he spotted the man in workman's dress seated at a table by himself near the big tree. He slowed, leaned his bike against a storefront on the other side of the square, and sauntered slowly toward the café. The man was reading a newspaper, holding it close to his face, as if he had difficulty in seeing the print. Rol looked around, saw two of his men standing casually nearby, smoking, talking, acting as if things were quite normal. There was no signal of alarm. He approached the man's table and sat down at the next one; their chairs were only a foot or two apart. The man

lowered the paper for an instant. Rol saw only a
baggy visored cap and a glimpse of eyes, and then
the paper hid the face again.

There was a long silence. A girl came to get his
orders then returned to deliver a cup of the foul-
tasting *café national*. Rol sipped, waiting. The paper
did not move from before the face of the man across
the small table from him. There'd been no code word
set up. He had been given to understand that the man
would recognize him, and make himself known.

When, at last, his temper began to burn, he said,
"The news is bad, as usual?"

"It will get better, Henri," a voice said from behind
the paper. Rol started visibly. The number of people
who knew his real name could be numbered on the
fingers of one hand, not counting the thumb.

"Yes, my friend, Henri Tanguy, it will get better."

"Who the hell are you?" Rol asked, wanting to
reach out and rip the newspaper away.

"Be patient." The voice was soft, so it didn't
carry; it was barely intelligible from behind the paper.
"First, let me assure you that I know you, Henri. Do
you remember the Sierra de Caballos of Spain?"

He remembered well. There, fighting in the losing
cause in the Spanish Civil War, he had seen a man
die. The name of that man he had adopted as a *nom
de guerre*.

"Do you remember being thrown out of the Re-
nault plant when you tried to organize a trade union?"
the voice asked.

"I am convinced that you know me," Rol said,
having recovered his composure. "Now let me know
you."

"Patience," the whispering voice said. "You have
men watching, I assume."

"Of course."

"As do I. Let us not lose control, for we do not want to attract the attention of the Germans, do we?"

"Of course not."

"Well, then," the voice said, and the newspaper lowered with dramatic slowness.

Rol saw the baggy cap, the eyes shadowed underneath, a beak of a powerful nose, the mustache, the grim mouth that seemed never to smile. Somewhere out there, Rol heard his own voice saying, "My God."

"Do you think that you are the only man who has enough knowledge, enough support, to walk the Paris streets?" asked General Charles de Gaulle, twisting his lip with amusement.

"You," Rol said. "But how?"

"*How* is not important," said de Gaulle through the lips of the porter, Michel Skop. "*Why* is the important matter. I am led to understand that you intend to disobey orders from myself and from the Allied High Command, that you intend to put your men into the streets to fight Germans." He raised a hand. "No, let me finish. This is of vital importance. As you know, I am under a sentence of death. I would be killed immediately if I were captured. So it has to be of great importance, doesn't it, for me to risk myself to come into Paris to talk to you? I am here to make my order to you in person. You are not to fight. Do you understand?"

De Gaulle, Rol was thinking. Here. It was incredible—and yet he knew the man was a formidable opponent, and, although surprised, he could understand. All of France was at stake. De Gaulle was an ambitious man, a man who sometimes put his per-

sonal ambitions and his political goals ahead of the
welfare of Frenchmen, and seeing him there, on the
Place Maubert, with hundreds of thousands of Germans within a few miles, made it clear to Rol what
he had to do.

"I hear your words," Rol said.

"Will you fight me, as well as the Germans?"
Skop asked. His friend Wolf had coached him well.
He was proud of his performance.

"Frenchman should not fight Frenchman," Rol
said.

"Then you will not fight?"

Rol heard a certain sort of hurried cough. His eyes
jerked up. On the other side of the square he heard
the sound of an automobile engine. A German half-
track, with coal-scuttled soldiers seated in two rows,
was coming into the square. His man, seeing it first,
had given the warning cough.

"Do you have an escape route?" he asked de
Gaulle.

Skop had been expecting the vehicle. It was a part
of the plan. He rose without speaking, walked tall
and confidently toward the entrance to the café, and
disappeared. Rol, cool outside, a bit nervous inside,
drank his coffee. The German vehicle rounded the
square and drove directly in front of the sidewalk
café; he saw the soldiers in the rear looking at the
people at the tables. However, their eyes seemed to
be mainly directed toward two attractive young ladies. When the vehicle had passed, he paid for his
coffee, then walked to his bicycle.

For the man known as Colonel Rol, it had been an
incredible hour. The entire situation had changed. He
had been debating his orders from the Communist-
ruled Committee of Military Action, the command

for the Communist Resistance in the Paris area, and he had not been sure whether he could in conscience order the uprising. It would mean the certain destruction of Paris, for if he put his men in the streets, the German tanks would surely come, would use their powerful guns to destroy all that was Paris.

Now everything was changed. De Gaulle himself was in Paris. That had to mean, Rol felt, that the Gaullists were more powerful than he'd imagined. It could mean that the Allied armies were ready to thrust into the city.

It was time for a decision. As he rode his bicycle away from the most surprising moment of his life, he felt he knew what the decision had to be.

He had arranged a rendezvous with one of his most trusted comrades. He entered a narrow street, riding with a cigarette hanging loosely from his lips, his mind in turmoil. He saw his man ahead, leaning on his bicycle at a street corner, apparently looking into the window of a shop. Rol pulled up alongside.

"Tonight, at the headquarters," Rol said, lighting the cigarette with a large wooden match, covering his words with his hands as he puffed. "Everyone."

"Tonight," his comrade said. "And the meeting? What was it?"

"Not here," Rol said. "I will tell everyone, tonight."

"Another thing," his comrade said. "I was contacted by the Gaullists, by the man who is called Dejon."

"I too, have had a certain contact," Rol said, with a smile.

"There is one, an Englishman, who wants to see you, urgently. I told them I would consult you and contact them if you were interested."

"I don't have the time. Forget the contact." He sighed. "There is more important business at hand, my friend."

There were more contacts to be made. And there was a very important chore that, at the moment, had first priority. He left his contact, rode toward his home, making one stop in a little shop. Because of the shortages, it was almost barren of goods, but he bought a small bag of the ersatz coffee.

The shopkeeper ran one of the clandestine printing presses of the Resistance. Rol gave his orders. The type had long been set, waiting for the moment. He knew that in the sublevels of Paris—down there where the air was damp, and where openings extended into the maze of sewers, Métro tunnels, and catacombs wherein lay the skulls and bones of generations of Parisians—the press would run all night, and that the papers would be on the streets, being distributed, even as he and his men began their work.

His decision was made. Now to make history.

The man who had been instrumental in making that decision was laughing happily as he recounted the playing out of the joke to his friend, Wolf. He'd been given a glass of wine and he was pleased with himself. Wolf patted Michel Skop on the back and laughed with him.

"You may return to your work, my friend," Wolf said, giving Michel more money. "You have done well."

As Michel made his way to the Ritz he saw evidence of the Germans' haste to leave the city. He passed several areas where vehicles of all sorts—trucks, horsecarts, carriages, cars—were being loaded and men milled around shouting at each other in hoarse, guttural voices. Once he stopped to watch, fascinated by all the commotion. He gawked, almost hypnotized. By the time he came to his senses and remembered that he was due back at the hotel, he had pretty well forgotten where he had been.

Others were less pleased to see the abandonment of Paris by noncombat units. Schellen and Silke were strolling. As they crossed a wide boulevard, a truck carrying office equipment and clerical-looking types almost ran them down. Schellen yelled at the driver, only to be ignored as the truck sped away.

"So," he said, "it begins."

"Shameful," Silke said angrily. "Where is their manhood?"

"Oh, there'll be a few men left," Schellen said. "An army can function for a while without its noncombatants. Out there, beyond the Seine, there may be just a few tanks, a few men. But there are over ten thousand combat troops here in the city. If the Führer is running true to form, they have orders to hold each house, each street, to the death."

"You disapprove of that?" Silke asked sharply.

Schellen smiled at her. "It is not my function to approve or disapprove." He was holding her arm as they walked. "However, I think that the city is indefensible. If I were a military general, I think I'd want to consolidate my armies, draw back to a good position, and make the Allies pay dearly for each German life. I think it's wasteful to fight to the last man in terrain that is favorable to the enemy."

"I suppose that makes sense," Silke said.

A woman, meeting them, stared at them insolently,

spat at their feet just as she passed. "Boche," the woman said, from behind their backs.

Silke turned angrily.

"Don't excite yourself," Schellen said, gripping her arm. "Soon they will be spitting more deadly things at us."

"If it were left to me I'd kill them all," Silke said furiously. "Scum. They're all scum, subhuman!"

Schellen laughed. "It's been tried, my dear, and the sheer mechanics of handling so many dead bodies makes the task impossible." He patted her hand. "Let's forget the war for a while, for a few hours. Let's find a sidewalk café that has some wine and pretend that it's 1936 and we're in Paris for a vacation."

"You're the last man I'd have guessed to be a romantic," Silke said, but she was smiling.

"Ah, Paris makes romantics of us all. A glass of wine, a lungful of Paris air, and then dinner back at the hotel," Schellen said. "In our room?"

"Ummm," she said, putting both hands on his arm and clinging, brushing her full and firm breast against him. But inside, she was wondering. She didn't like the way this man made light of a serious situation. He was already conceding the loss of Paris. At that moment she wished, as she had many times before, that she had been born a man. God, if she were only a man—she'd show them. She'd be so strong, so determined, that with her leadership she'd stiffen the backbones of every German male. She'd put all those gutless office workers and Gestapo and SS military policemen on the front lines with rifles in their hands; and she'd hold them, the Americans and the British, throw them back into the sea. If only every German man could have the will, the fierce bravery of the Führer, then the situation would be much different.

There was one thing she could do. She had come to Paris for two reasons. One, because she was under orders to study and watch Otto Schellen, head of the foreign intelligence branch. Schellen was known to have been friendly, at one time, with Admiral Canaris, and Canaris had been pivotal in the plot—thank God unsuccessful—to blow the beloved Führer to bits. Schellen's record was excellent, but in these trying times, who could tell? Treason lurked in the most unsuspected places. Two, she was physically attracted to the man—with good reason, she now knew—and the trip was in the nature of a holiday.

But she could still do something—something to show that the Reich was not defeated yet. Paris was a hotbed of treason against the Reich; there was apparently a cell of the Resistance in the Ritz itself. It would be an exercise in her trade to see if, while she enjoyed herself, she could root out at least one of the terrorists.

The maid. The maid, perhaps, was the key. Silke Frager could not get it out of her mind that the maid had gone first, after her none-too-gentle questioning, to the head housekeeper. The woman's name, she had found out, was Mady Deschaises.

It was a case of hatred for Silke. Since she was helpless to vent her hatred effectively on the entire world, she had selected a smaller target.

17

MEANWHILE, MADY DESCHAISES had her own concerns. The American—this the man who had moved her emotions as no man had since her husband died—was being insistent. Twice that day, he had found excuses to see her, to insist that she continue to try to make her contact with Colonel Rol's Resistance group. She knew that it would seem suspicious to those who knew her to see her talking often with a man they knew as a German. It hurt her pride—and perhaps touched off a deep tremor of guilt in her—to think that they would assume she had, after so long, become one of those despised and hated women who sold themselves to the German conquerors for favors, for extra food, and wine, and gay times in a city where gay times were limited to Germans and collaborators.

"I have told you that I am trying," she said. "These things take time."

"Time is running out," Teddy said.

"Do you think you are the only one who is concerned?" she asked with a flash of anger.

"I must send out my report soon," Teddy said. "And before I do, I must talk with the Rol faction."

"I have sent a messenger," she said. "He delivered that message, at considerable risk."

"With no result."

"What do you want me to do, keep sending someone out until he is caught?"

"Keep sending someone out until you impress on Rol's men that the meeting is vital to all," Teddy said.

Men, she was thinking—How hard-headed they were! So sure of themselves, and yet they had failed so miserably at their feeble attempts to make the world a decent place. At times she felt that she hated all men—and yet, looking at this American, she could not hate. "So," she told herself, watching his broad shoulders as he walked away, "you have become the Frenchwoman of myth and legend. You have become the depraved woman of men's febrile imaginings." Love? The thought was not compatible with the state of things in Paris. It was no time for love. Soon the streets would explode. Soon the sewers would flow red with the blood of Germans and of French—of men, women, and children.

She sought out her sole contact in the Ritz, the only other member of the Gaullist Resistance she knew. "Have you heard anything?" she asked.

"Nothing. These things take time," her contact, a steward, said. "I delivered the message. I was told that Rol would be informed and that I would be contacted. That's all I can do."

"No," she said, "you can go to them again. Tell them that the American is risking his life in order to help Paris, to help France. Tell them that Allied action hinges on his report on the situation here. Tell them anything, but put the American in the same room with Rol.''

The steward looked exasperated. ''*Eh bien*. When I am off duty.''

''Now,'' she hissed. ''I'll cover for you. I'll tell Monsieur Alexandre you were suddenly taken ill. Now. You must go now.''

Mady Deschaises had a more direct means of reaching Colonel Rol, if only she had known. But she would not have been pleased to know that her son was a member of the Communist Resistance group. She had done all she could do to protect him, to see that nothing so horrible as seeing his beloved school destroyed by the Germans would happen to him again, and he always seemed to be so grateful. To keep him out of the war, she had gone to the Luftwaffe officers to explain that the fine foods they so enjoyed had to be prepared by skilled men, that the chefs were old, and that it was vital to train young men— so Blaise was designated a ''necessary worker,'' a designation that prevented his being selected for the labor battalions. Yet now he was in grave danger of a worse fate than life in the labor battalions, if the Germans caught him at his after-curfew activities.

Blaise had been notified of the meeting of his group and had made his way to headquarters well before the curfew. There was a trapdoor in the basement of the main building of the Paris Waters and Sewers Administration, and he was only one of several men who waited his chance and dropped through that trapdoor. There, down a flight of damp stone steps and behind a steel door, was Colonel Rol's headquarters.

Blaise had not come empty-handed. The pockets

sewn inside his coat were laden with thick glass
bottles. After he had greeted those he knew and had
shaken the hands of others whom he was seeing for
the first time, he set to work. He could feel his heart
beating fast, for the mere fact that so many of them
were together, exposing their identities to each other,
was proof that the time was near.

He rolled up his sleeves, uncapped his bottles,
and, with practiced skill, began to make Molotov
cocktails. The sulfuric acid and potassium chlorate
that went into the primitive grenades were from a
stockpile that, little by little, he'd helped carry to the
headquarters.

There was an air of excitement. From somewhere
nearby he could hear the rolling, bumping sound of a
printing press. He'd seen the products of that press,
newspapers that told the truth about German propaganda lies. He could imagine the headlines being
printed at that moment. When the time came, he
would help deliver those papers. And he would toss at
least one of the fiery cocktails into the open hatch of a
German Panther tank—that much he had promised
himself. The prospect of killing Germans soon again
excited him so much that his hands shook, and he
had to rest and calm his nerves with cigarette, lest he
spill the caustic acid.

When he had finished his job and the deadly glass
missiles were racked and waiting for use, he heard
his commander call for attention. The group of men
in the underground headquarters gathered around Rol.

"There has been a surprising development," Rol
said, "a development that requires us to speed up
our plans."

Blaise felt like whooping for joy.

"You know the situation," Rol said. "The papers

are being printed. When they are ready for distribution we will move. We will give the call. We will call the citizens of Paris to the streets. There is great risk, as you all know. Many of us will die. But we will fight to the end, and strive to keep the boches from doing terrible damage to our city.''

''When?'' Blaise asked, unable to contain his excitement.

''Patience,'' Rol said, with a fond smile.

''We are going out, then?'' asked Henri Morlaix, the Ritz chef.

''Yes,'' Rol said. ''To the streets.''

''Against orders?'' Morlaix asked. ''Is that wise? Won't it just give the Germans an excuse to destroy the city?''

Rol shrugged. ''They will destroy it, whatever we do.''

Blaise swallowed.

''The important thing,'' Rol said, ''is to get control of all key points. Whatever sacrifice is required, this is vital.''

Blaise had heard it all before. It grieved him to think of Paris in ruins, of the mighty Ritz a pile of rubble, of his mother, who might be killed in the destruction. But he was a man, and he agreed with Rol that France was the most important thing in his life.

''The way you speak, it is not today,'' Blaise said.

''No, my young friend,'' Rol said. ''Not today. I will tell you when.''

''And if the Gaullists have the same idea?''

''They will follow orders,'' Rol said. ''We must be prepared. Today we will remain here, working, readying ourselves.''

So it was to be the next day, Blaise thought.

"For at least two days," Rol said, "while we perfect our plans. Now I know that some of you have loved ones who will be concerned. You must not try to contact them. We can't risk having word get out before we're ready to act. There are cots if you need to sleep, but you must stay here, unless I send you out on an assignment."

For at least two days. While the Allied armies rolled closer. And the Gaullists. They would notice the disappearance of men from their jobs. They would suspect. Blaise didn't like it, but he was not in command.

Blaise awoke with a start, sat up on the edge of the cot, and rubbed his eyes. He glanced at his watch. Almost five—he'd slept three hours.

"Deschaises," Rol repeated, "come with me, please."

Rol led the way to a secluded corner. He took a package from a hiding place and held it before him.

"You are aware that I have asked the Allies and the Free French forces for funds," he said. Blaise nodded. "You are also aware that I have not received them. We need money."

"We need to fight." Blaise felt fully awake now, filled again with last night's impatience.

"We need money. There are things that must be done, my young friend. I have a chore for you. Take this package to your hotel—"

"You said we were to stay," Blaise said.

Rol ignored the protest. "Take this package to your hotel," he said, "and deliver it to a General Schläfer."

Blaise felt a quick surge of doubt. Why Schläfer?

Why the Ritz? As if seeing his hesitation, Rol said.
"You can come and go at the Ritz without arousing
suspicion. You are not to open this package, merely
deliver it. In return, Schläfer will deliver to you a
packet. Open it, to make sure it contains five hundred thousand francs. Do you understand?"

"Yes," Blaise said.

"Then bring the money here," Rol said, "where
we will put it to good use."

He took the package. It was a solid weight in his
hands as he left the headquarters, just before dawn.
It was safe to be in the streets at that hour, for early
risers were going to their jobs, but there was something about the situation that he didn't like. The
weight of the package in his hand was strange. The
whole transaction was strange. And then it hit him.
He had heard that Schläfer, like other Nazis, was an
art collector. Was this one of the treasures of France
that he was to deliver to a German general for mere
money? He stepped into an alley, squatted behind
garbage cans, and carefully opened the wrapped package. Then he knew, as he bared a leather case and
opened it to see a golden object lying on plush velvet,
why such a small package had so much weight.
There, barely gleaming in the predawn light, was the
Egyptian horse, the golden horse of Saumur. He
could not breathe for a moment. At first an unreasoning anger swept through him. When it calmed
slightly, he tried to reason it out. Rol had broken his
word, had retrieved the horse from the cave beside
the river. He was doing what Blaise had sworn he
would never see happen, deliver the treasure of the
school, the symbol of Saumur, into German hands.

But it was for the movement. It was for France.
What did it matter? Was it better to save the bauble

and see France fall into the hands of the patricians again? And did the fate of his country ride on what he did with the horse he'd carried away from that field of death? He was a confused young man as he rewrapped the package and set out, walking briskly, toward the Ritz. He entered the Place Vendôme before the sun rose, and there was the hotel. Somewhere up there was the German general who would carry the Saumur horse back to Germany with him.

He could not do it—not yet, at least. He had to have time to think. He left the square, wandered aimlessly through the streets, then along the guays of the Seine. Near the Hotel de Ville, the seat of the city's government, he crossed to the Ile de la Cité and stood in front of the Prefecture of the Police, gazing across the square at Notre Dame, as the sky grew light behind the cathedral towers. What was the golden horse compared to that treasure? No, that was not the way to consider it. He descended the steps to the river's edge and walked downstream with the flowing water to the point. He was alone at that early hour. Almost without seeing, he looked at the beautiful bridges that arched across the river. Along both sides of the river he could see the imposing buildings that would soon be blasted by the German tanks. He saw their façades crumble, saw the bridges explode into the sky, again and again. He felt like weeping.

18

TEDDY WERNER HAD made up his mind that he would wait no longer. It was Friday morning. If something had not occurred by that evening to show him that Mady and her friends were making a serious attempt to put him in contact with the Communist Resistance, he would have to take matters into his own hands. He would insist on being given the use of a radio transmitter and he would send out the word that the Resistance was not cooperating with him.

He told Mady as much when she came to the kitchen. "I will advise a cut-off of all aid to the Resistance," Teddy threatened. "I will tell them that the Resistance in Paris has decided to go on its own way, and advise them to go ahead with the plan to bypass Paris."

"Can't you see we're doing our best?" Mady snapped. She had been called to the kitchen to see if she could help solve a minor crisis. This one had arisen because a chef and an assistant chef had not

163

reported to work that morning. Since one of the missing workers was her son, and since Teddy said the boy had not been in his room all night, she was doubly worried.

There was no chance to talk further. Teddy was given a cart to be taken to the suite of rooms occupied by the blonde German girl who had asked him, not too seriously, to go with her to see the city. This time there was a man there, the German spymaster whom he'd seen in the General's rooms.

"You're late," Silke snapped, as she opened the door. Teddy pushed the cart inside and began to lay out their breakfast. "Is this the famous service of the Ritz?" Silke asked sullenly.

"I'm sorry, madame," Teddy said. "We're short-handed in the kitchen this morning. Something has happened to two of our chefs."

"Two men missing and the whole place falls apart?" Silke asked.

"I'm sorry, madame," Teddy repeated.

Schellen took his seat. "Come, Silke, the food smells delicious enough to do away with your foul mood."

True, she was in a foul mood. And it was his fault—Schellen had already been out once, and he had informed her that he'd be away most of the day. That meant another day alone in her room, since for the woman of a high-ranking German to go about the city unescorted was, given the mood of hostile unrest among the French, unthinkable. Silke sat and ate in silence, and glared as Teddy cleared away the dishes and left the room. When Schellen left immediately afterward, she tried to read, then threw the book down and paced the room. She showered, dressed in a flowing skirt and blouse, and paced some more. Then, with a sudden determination, she flung open the door and strode briskly down the hallway.

Any well-trained Gestapo agent would have quickly found out who the highest-ranking Luftwaffe officer in the hotel was, and Silke was no exception—she had learned his name, rank, room number, and much more in her first ten minutes alone the evening they'd arrived. Wolf opened the door when she knocked. She demanded to see General Schläfer and was told that he was away.

"Perhaps I can help you," Wolf said.

"Perhaps you can," Silke said. "You are the General's man?"

"You may call me that," Wolf said, with a sardonic grin.

"Two chefs did not report for work this morning," Silke said. "I want to know their names and why they are not at work."

"Ah," Wolf said. "That is interesting. May I ask why you are concerned?"

"No, you may not," Silke snapped. Wolf bowed and motioned her to enter. He soon had the director on the telephone.

"Monsieur Auzello," he said, "I understand that you are short-handed in the kitchen. Two chefs."

"You don't miss much, do you, Herr Wolf?" Auzello asked. "Yes. Perhaps they are ill. I'm sorry if your service has been slow this morning. We continue to strive to do our best under trying conditions. I wonder if you've had a chance to speak to the General and the other officers about our little plan?"

"Ah, your little plan," Wolf said. "And the answer is no, not yet. Now I want the names of the two chefs who are missing. Perhaps I can help. If, for example, they have been picked up for curfew violation I might be of some help in getting them released. We don't want the General's dinner to be late, do we?"

"Of course not," the director said. "I will inquire and call you back immediately."

Alone with Silke, Wolf permitted himself some frivolous thoughts. She was a true German woman, blonde and buxom, but there was a hardness to her, a quality that puzzled him. And her interest in the affairs of the Ritz was intriguing. While he waited for the call he offered coffee, which she accepted. She sat and balanced the cup on one well-formed knee, the flowing skirt making nice shapes around her legs. It reminded Wolf of something he had to do. It reminded him of Mady Deschaises. He tried to make conversation and was answered in words of one syllable. When the phone rang he answered, took down two names, and turned to Silke.

"The chefs—or to be more accurate, one chef and one assistant—are, in order of rank, one Henri Morlaix and one Blaise Deschaises. Does that mean anything to you?"

"Perhaps," Silke said. The name kept cropping up. Deschaises. "Would this assistant chef have any connection to the head housekeeper, Mady Deschaises?"

"I believe so, as a matter of fact," Wolf said. "Her son, as I recall."

She was silent. It was too much of a coincidence. "Have you heard of any Resistance activity during the night?" she asked.

"No," he said. "That very matter was discussed when your friend, Herr Schellen, had coffee quite early with General Schläfer. Things have been very quiet."

"I have something I must do," Silke said. "Are you prepared to follow my orders, Corporal?"

"I bow to your wishes, madame," Wolf said, "but as to orders, I fear that I take my orders from General Schläfer."

"Yes, of course," she said. She dug briefly into her handbag and produced a delicate wallet. "Will you please examine these credentials?"

He bowed and took the opened wallet. The picture did not do her justice, but he knew the identification well. He had one exactly like it. "Ah," he said. "In that case, madame, I will do as you say. I'm sure the General would wish it."

But he was thinking fast. What the hell was another Gestapo agent doing in the Ritz without his knowledge? The Ritz was his territory. For a moment he considered exposing his own Gestapo standing so that he could question this woman, but decided to hold his tongue.

"I want you to get this Deschaises woman up here, to my suite."

"May I inquire why?"

"No, you may not. Do as I say. If possible, do it without others knowing, but if you must, let them know. I want her in my room within the next half hour. Is that understood?"

"I understand," Wolf said.

After she left, he considered the situation for a moment before carrying out her commands. He'd been in the hotel for over a year and he'd seen no suspicious activity. Oh, no doubt there were radio receivers hidden in the building. There were radio receivers all over occupied France. They did no real harm. The French Resistance did no real and lasting harm, as a whole. He could not understand why the female agent was suspicious of Mady Deschaises. He decided that he would obey the woman's orders, if only to find out what was going on.

He went down to the service areas and found Mady in her office. She looked up, her distaste for him evident. Once again he felt that quick anger. Soon he'd wipe that look off her face and replace it with a look of pure fear. His anger made his voice brusque.

"You are to come with me," he said.

"That's impossible at the moment," she said, looking back down to the papers she had been examining.

"It is in regard to your son," he said. She looked up quickly, her face going white.

"Blaise? Has something happened?"

"There's nothing to worry about, at the moment," he said. "Not if you come with me."

She rose, smoothing down her skirt with hands that were suddenly moist with nervous perspiration, and followed him.

He did not speak as they made their way up to the suite occupied by Schellen and Silke. When he paused and knocked on the door, she asked, "Is Blaise here?"

"You will see," he said.

Silke had pulled her hair back and tied it in a businesslike bun. She wore a blue skirt of heavy, durable material and a loose-fitting light sweater. Wolf took Mady's arm and pushed her into the room. Silke regarded the soft-looking woman with eyes that were unblinking and cold.

"Sit down," she said.

"You said it was about my son," Mady said, lowering herself into the chair.

"You are the woman known as Mady Deschaises?" Silke asked.

"Yes, of course."

"And your son is Blaise Deschaises?"

"Yes, please. Tell me what's wrong."

"Do you know where your son is at this moment?" Silke asked.

"No. I thought—Wolf said—"

Silke moved swiftly; the two slaps, backhand and forehand, rang through the room. Mady's head jerked and she cried out, half rose from the chair but was pushed back by Silke. Wolf let a little smile of amusement cross his face.

"Tell me where he is," Silke said.

"Wolf, will you please call the director?" Mady said, her voice quivering a bit.

"It's out of my hands, Madame Deschaises," Wolf said.

"The General, then," Mady said, as Silke let her lips curl and slapped Mady again.

When Mady spoke again, the quiver was gone from her voice. "Please don't do that again."

"Take off your clothes, you French bitch," Silke said, jerking Mady to her feet.

"I will do no such thing," Mady said. "Wolf, I ask you for the last time, will you please call either the General or the director?"

Wolf laughed. Silke's dire frown wasn't scaring this one at all. He was interested now. He just wanted to see what would happen next. He saw Silke tense.

"I said take off your clothes," Silke said. Mady merely stared. Silke hissed and drew back her hand to slap Mady again—and the next move came so quickly Wolf almost missed it. Before Silke's hand finished its arc, Mady had taken a quick step backward and had buried the toe of her heavy work shoe in Silke's soft stomach. The blonde woman sat down, both hands going to her midriff, gasping, trying to suck the air back into her lungs. The sounds she was making were not pretty.

"I will see to it that this is reported to the director, the General, and the police," Mady said, calmly stepping over Silke's legs and moving toward the door. Wolfe made no move to stop her. She turned at the door. "Please. Do you know where my son is? He didn't come to work this morning."

"I don't know," Wolf said.

When the door slammed behind her, he looked at Silke. She was able to breathe, but she was still holding her stomach.

"I'll kill her," she gasped.

"Perhaps next time you'd better call on someone for help." Wolf chuckled, going to her to lift her to her feet. She jerked her arm away.

"And you," she said. "I'll see to it that you suffer for this."

"Good Lord, what are they turning out these days?" Wolf asked. "Amateurs. Dilettantes. Didn't they teach you anything? I saw that kick coming a mile away, and you let her sucker you."

"Yes," Silke hissed. "You will suffer. Get out of here."

"At your pleasure." Wolf bowed mockingly. "If

you wish to mention my name in your report, please
spell it right. They're familiar with it in Berlin.''

"What do you mean?'' Silke asked.

''Amateurs,'' Wolf sniffed, leaving the room.

But he would remember that the woman who
laughed at him had also bested a German woman,
and, pitifully inadequate as she was, she was still
German. Merely because a man believed in international Communism didn't mean that he had lost all
pride in race. The Deschaises woman would pay for
that, as well as for other things.

Mady, meanwhile, was not as calm as she'd seemed
to be. Inside, she was shaking. She hurried down to
her office and made one telephone call, then sought
out Teddy.

"I have fallen under suspicion,'' she said. ''I
must go into hiding.''

"Where?''

"It is best that you don't know,'' Mady said.

"Listen, damn it, you can't just run away and
leave me. Who can I talk with? Who is my contact?''

"God, can't you just go away?'' she asked. ''No.
I know that you can't. The contact is a man whom
you have met. Be careful when you approach him.
Find some excuse. It isn't usual that a mere steward
goes to the director's office.''

"Auzello?'' Teddy asked.

"Yes. I have informed him that I am going to
hide,'' she said. Then her face softened. ''Be careful. It is only a matter of days now. Then, perhaps—''
She couldn't finish. She left him. The last he saw
of her was her back, shoulders straight, back stiff.
And he felt a quick pang of regret.

Although he went about his work, his mind wasn't

on it. Things were changed now. Auzello—perhaps the director was more important in the movement than Mady. Perhaps he could do something. The time for caution was past. Teddy went directly to the director's office.

Once there he did not stand at attention, but put his finger to his ear and looked around, asking silently if it were all right to talk. The director nodded.

"You knew all along, didn't you?" Teddy asked, in English.

Auzello showed no surprise. But he knew that something had happened or Mady would not have gone underground, or revealed that he was a part of the Resistance. "Mady?" he asked.

"She was questioned by a woman agent of the Gestapo," Teddy said. "She is going into hiding."

Auzello nodded. "She told me."

"It's up to you," Teddy said, repeating to Auzello what he'd told Mady earlier.

"That is a recipe for disaster," Auzello said. "It will give them a free hand. We will be forced to obey orders. They will start the uprising."

"Tonight I will use a radio," Teddy said.

"No," Auzello said. "I have tried. I will try again. You must give me time. Give me the night. Nothing can be accomplished by day."

Teddy hesitated. "Tomorrow, then. I see them tomorrow or I wash my hands of it."

"Yes, yes."

"Can you tell me where she is?"

"Who?"

"Mady," Teddy said.

"One of several places," Auzello said. "For her safety you should not know. In case—" He shrugged.

"Go now. Don't come here again. I'll reach you when I have found out something."

It was surprising how empty the place seemed. He went to his work, but there was in him the knowledge that *she* was no longer in the hotel. Therefore it was empty.

19

HE WAS, AFTER ALL, only eighteen. He was alone, and he carried something that was very dear to him. He could not make the decision alone. He was torn between his promise to his dying teacher, there at Saumur when the Germans were almost on him, and his belief that Colonel Rol's beliefs were best for his country. He was young, and for most of his life he'd gone to one person when he was troubled.

He went into the service entrance of the Ritz, hiding his face as best he could beneath his cap, turning it when he passed someone. His mother's office was empty. He went inside, closed the door, and waited for a half hour. When a maid came, he asked if she'd seen Madame Deschaises.

"Not in the last hour or two," she answered.

"Find her," he said. "Tell her I must see her."

He waited another half hour. When the door opened again he froze, for there stood the very German bastard he hated most of all.

174

"What are you doing here?" Blaise asked, when the German had closed the door behind him.

"I heard you were looking for your mother. Now you answer a question for me," he responded. "Why didn't you report for work this morning? Your mother was worried."

The fact that he knew his mother's feelings was a knife in Blaise's guts. He shifted his weight, as if to move forward, but remained grimly silent. Teddy was blocking the door. Blaise moved toward him, after a moment's silence, pausing to look up at the larger man.

"Get out of my way," Blaise said, his German rather fractured. In four years he'd made an attempt to learn the language, out of necessity, but his heart had never been in it.

"You won't find her," Teddy said.

Blaise looked up quickly. "What have you done to her?" he asked.

"She was questioned by the Gestapo," Teddy said.

Blaise felt his stomach turn over. "You—" he began, and then fell silent.

Teddy was about fed up with the petulant boy. "No," he said, his voice low and serious, "you. Because of you. Because you didn't show up for work. Because you share a name, if not the same intelligence."

"I don't have to take this from you," Blaise said, stepping back.

"Think of *her*, damn you," Teddy said. "Have you done something to cast suspicion on her?"

Blaise opened his mouth, closed it. "I simply got drunk, that's all. I was too drunk to come to work."

"And was Henri Morlaix drunk with you?"

Blaise felt a cold chill of dread. After all, the man was a German. He told himself to hold his temper, to be cool. Why hadn't he suspected the German in the first place? It was so unlikely that a German would be content to work as a mere steward, just to learn something about the hotel business. The man was a plant, and, under the guise of concern for his mother, he was trying to make Blaise confess his involvement in the Resistance.

"I don't know about that old man," he said. "I know only about myself, and the person with whom I was drinking was certainly not an old man."

Teddy noted the quick change. The boy was now on the defensive. "All right," he said. "You were drinking with a girl. It's nothing to me. I did, however, want to warn you that your absence from your job has brought you, apparently, to the attention of someone. If I were you I'd walk carefully."

"Thank you for your concern," Blaise said. "I can take care of myself."

"Yes, I can see great wisdom in your eyes," Teddy said, still a bit angry. "So smart that you have caused your mother to have to go underground."

"How do you know that?" Blaised asked.

"I know."

"Because you have shared her bed?" Blaise blurted, not thinking of where it would lead.

Teddy felt his fist clench involuntarily. "That is between me and Mady," he said.

"Boche," Blaise spat. "My mother playing the whore—"

He was not allowed to finish. Teddy's hand—open, hard, big—slashed against the side of his face. Blaise almost went down, his anger blazing, his hand darting to his pocket and emerging with a knife which, with one swift motion, was opened and exposed. Blaise assumed the classic knife-fighter's crouch, his hand making small circles aimed at Teddy's middle.

Back in Texas, as a boy, he'd seen a knife fight in a roadside honkeytonk once, and he'd seen what a knife can do. His first impulse was to leap backward, to open the door and gain room to move. The office was small, with most of the space taken up by Mady's desk and filing cabinets.

Blaise was moving forward, his intention clear. Teddy knew, then, that he shouldn't have slapped the boy. He should have used his fists. To slap him had been more of an insult than a knockout blow would have been. And Blaise looked as if he knew what he was going to do with the long-bladed knife. Teddy cast his eyes around. He leaned quickly, seized the wire letter basket from Mady's desk, letting papers fly as he used it as a shield, holding it in front of him, backing around the desk as Blaise advanced.

"Blaise, put it down," he said.

The boy did not speak, moving forward, balanced, ready to lunge. He made a feint and Teddy jerked the wire basket to block the slash that didn't come. Teddy backed around the desk, past the chair, thought to pick it up but was afraid to make the move, which would give Blaise the chance to lunge. He kicked something on the floor—the package Blaise had put there while he waited. As his heel struck it, he lost his balance for a split second, but regained it in time to hear the knifeblade clang against the basket. Blaise jerked to pull the knife free, but the guard caught on the wire basket, pulling Teddy forward. The knife was entangled just long enough for Teddy to swing from his shoulder with a left that caught the boy directly on the point of the chin and made Teddy

think that he'd broken a knuckle or two. Blaise went
down as if his legs had suddenly become rubber; the
knife fell out of the basket and clattered to the floor.
Teddy moved swiftly to pick it up. He stood there
looking down at Blaise.

"Crazy little bastard," he muttered, in English,
forgetting himself. Then he thought, well, this is
Mady's son. Kneeling, he put his hand to Blaise's
throat. The pulse was beating steadily and the boy
was breathing regularly. He'd have one hell of a
headache, but he'd be all right. Squatting there,
Teddy saw the package, picked it up and hefted it.
Curious, he opened it. The golden gleam answered
no questions—posed more, as a matter of fact. He
rewrapped the package and sat on the edge of the
desk until Blaise moaned and tried to sit up.

"Just take it easy," he said. "You're going to be
a little dizzy for a while."

Blaise's head weighed a ton, but he managed to
lift it and then to struggle into a sitting position.

"You are a dead man," Blaise said.

"Wonderful," Teddy said. "Just wonderful." He
prodded the package with his toe. "I'd like to hear
you talk a little bit about what's in the package," he
said.

Blaise knew that all was lost. There was no way
he could explain. "You opened it?" His head was
still a bit cloudy.

"I did," Teddy said. "Tell me about it."

"It—it's a family heirloom," Blaise said. "I was
going to give it to my mother for safekeeping."

"So with a treasure worth thousands, Mady has
worked as a maid and housekeeper for all these
years?" Teddy smiled. "Try again."

"It is true. It is of great sentimental value. She

didn't want to sell it.'' God, he needed help. He needed help to kill this Gestapo agent and escape, to go underground, as this liar said his mother had done.

What should he do with the boy? For Mady's sake Teddy didn't want him to get into trouble, but that object he was carrying was worth enough money to get many men into trouble. But what could he do?

"Take it and go," he said.

"Huh?" Blaise asked.

"Look, I don't give a good goddamn about you," Teddy said. "You're a punk. As far as I know you've stolen that thing. For your mother's sake, I hope not. Just take it and get out of here. Remember that Mady's gone. She's hiding. I don't know why they questioned her. As I said, probably because of something you've done. And if that's the case, I'd advise you to do the same thing—hide."

"You're telling me to go, just like that?" Blaise asked, not believing.

"I will set you an example," Teddy said. Taking the knife from his pocket, he tossed it into Blaise's lap and turned to go out the door. He didn't look back to see what the boy did. Punk. How could someone as admirable as Mady have a son like that?

In the office, Blaise stood, holding his sore chin gingerly. Yes, he had to go. But he had his orders: to deliver the horse to the German general. The hallway was empty. He walked swiftly, to get the deed over with as fast as possible.

Had he looked behind, he might have seen Teddy following him, at a distance. When it became evident that Blaise was heading for the Luftwaffe officers' quarters, Teddy felt a great sadness. He could only guess that Mady's son was a collaborator. Why else was he delivering so valuable an object to a German officer? He noted that Blaise was heading directly toward General Schläfer's room, and his impulse was to let him, to forget him. But there was Mady. Maybe the kid was just making a mistake, wanting some quick money. He stepped into the open and called softly. "Blaise!"

Blaise froze, turned slowly. Teddy raised his hand and beckoned.

This time, Blaise thought, he would be more careful. This time he would kill the German. He walked toward Teddy, hand in pocket.

"If you pull that knife again, kid," Teddy said, "you're going to find it difficult to walk with your balls kicked off. I'm tired of playing with you."

There was a bit of doubt in Blaise's mind. At any moment a door could open and a German officer could emerge, to ask questions, to call the guards. He took his hand from his pocket.

"What do you *want*?" he whispered, coming close.

"Are you selling it to the Germans?" Teddy asked. "Selling an art treasure would be one of the more serious kinds of collaboration, wouldn't it?"

"Damn you, it's none of your business."

"Because of Mady, I'm making it my business," Teddy said. "Come with me."

He had little choice. A fight in the hallway would be disaster.

Teddy led the way to the room they had so uneasily shared, motioned Blaise in first. Inside, he held out his hand. "I think I'd better keep that."

"You will have to kill me first," Blaise said.

"God in Heaven," Teddy said, rolling his eyes. "If you people had fought the Germans with as much stubbornness." Whoa, he thought. But he'd said it, and Blaise was looking at him strangely.

"Just who are you?" Blaise asked. "Where did you know my mother before?"

He thought it over. Something was going on with the boy, that was for sure, and he couldn't quite buy the idea that Mady's son would collaborate with the Germans.

"Mady told me you were at Saumur," he said. "When the cadets held up an entire Panzer division for three days."

"That was long ago," Blaise said.

"Did you fight or run?" Teddy asked.

"That is my affair."

"You know, I think you fought," Teddy said. "I think there's more to you than meets the eye. Whose side are you on?"

"I am not political," Blaise said.

"Like hell," Teddy said. "You're into it, aren't you?" He moved closer. "You weren't out drinking with a girl last night. It has something to do with that bauble you're clutching so tightly, doesn't it? What's the deal? Selling it to the General? I've seen the art and jewelry he has in his suite. Selling it for what? Not for yourself. For the cause? What cause?"

"It's a family heirloom. We need the money," Blaise said.

"Blaise, this is no time for silly lies. Are you aware of what's going to happen here?" Teddy asked. "Do you realize that there are certain elements who have so much political ambition that they're willing to see Paris in ruins to achieve their aims?" He knew that he was doing something dangerous, but he was thinking of Mady. For her sake, he didn't want the boy to get into trouble. "They're saying that two hundred thousand lives is a small price to pay for Paris, and the control of France. Do you know that?''

''I am not political,'' Blaise said, but he was wondering how this German knew.

''Your mother thinks you are not political. I hope she's right. I hope you're not mixed up with those who are willing to tear Paris down in order to build a new colonialism with a fancy name.''

Blaise could not speak.

''Because what they want to do is trade one set of tyrants for another,'' Teddy said. ''To trade occupation by the Nazis for the rule from Moscow of another tyranny.''

It dawned on Blaise that this tall, blond man was not talking like a German, but more like a Gaullist. He was puzzled.

''I'm saying these things because of Mady,'' Teddy said. ''I will tell you this. If you do anything to hurt her or to bring shame to her, I'll personally look you up and give you more of what you got in the office.''

''I can get rid of you simply by reporting what you have said to the Germans,'' Blaise said. ''You must know that.''

''Yes.''

''Then why are you saying it? You're not French. I don't think you're German. Just what in hell are you?''

''A man who does not want to see Paris burned,'' Teddy said. ''And you?''

Blaise was trying to puzzle it out. He knew only a bit of English. He used it. ''When will the Allies come to Paris?'' he asked.

Teddy didn't answer. To speak would be to put it all on the table, to admit that he was not what he seemed. He weighed it. He put his life on the bet when he said, in English. "They will bypass the city and avoid battles."

"Ah," Blaise said. "You knew her, then, before the war." Because it all came back to knowing that this man had shared his mother's bed.

"Yes," Teddy said, knowing that would be easier for the boy to accept than the rather unexpected thing which had happened between him and Mady.

"Your secret is safe with me," Blaise said. "I must tell you that I'm sorry. I had no idea."

"Want to tell me about that horse now?"

Blaise shook his head. "No. Not just yet."

"Can you take me to Colonel Rol?" Teddy asked, taking a shot in the dark. The boy had too much fight in him to merely hide away in a kitchen.

Blaise jerked a look at him. "Why?" he asked, putting his cards on the table, too.

"To save Paris."

"We don't want to see Paris destroyed, either," Blaise said.

"Ah, so it's on the line, at last," Teddy said. "You know what I am and I know what you are. Are you aware that the Allies have ordered the Resistance to be quiet, not to start fighting?"

"We understand that motive there. It is to make it easy for de Gaulle to walk in and take over."

"Better de Gaulle in a whole Paris than someone else in the ruins," Teddy said.

"That is a matter of opinion."

"Yes, you're a Frenchman," Teddy said, "stupid, hard-headed, self-centered, totally devoid of logic—"

"I am French," Blaise said, bristling.

"Your mother has no idea, does she?"

"No."

"Do you think she'd approve of street battles in Paris?"

"She is a woman. Women don't understand these things."

"And you do." Teddy shrugged. "Well, I've done all I can do. I risk my ass coming in here to talk to Parisians about a way to save their city, and I find a bunch of radicals who want to rule a pile of rubble. Goddamn it, I think I'll just leave you to it. If I knew where Mady was I'd join her, forget the whole damned thing. You can tell your Colonel Rol that it's his decision. He holds the fate of the city in his hands. If he wants the Germans to blast it to the ground, tell him simply to start killing Germans. The planes of Luftflotte Three are standing by for orders at this moment. They have enough bombs to make ten bomb runs each. They'll start in the northeast and then move to the Champs Élysées and the buildings along the river. Obviously there are no ground guns to stop them. They'll bomb at night so that there will be no Allied fighters to harass them."

"How do you know this?" Blaise asked.

"I make it my business to know," Teddy said.

"This is true?"

"When you hear a hundred and fifty planes coming, look up, then find yourself a hole."

"We know nothing of this."

"They're planting charges on the bridges and in public buildings. Do you at least know about that?"

"Yes." Blaise seemed to be holding his breath.

"And you're willing to let it happen? Think, Blaise! You're talking about Paris. Do you really want to see it blown up from within and blasted from the air and pounded with tank guns and artillery? If you do,

OK. If not, tell Rol I want to talk with him, and soon, because something is going to happen soon.''

Blaise let his breath out in a slow sigh. ''I will tell him.''

Teddy nodded, pressed further. ''The golden horse?''

Yes, it was the horse. Rol had so little regard for it, for its traditions, that he was willing to sell it for mere money. Was the English agent right? Was Rol equally unconcerned about the fate of Paris, just so long as the Communists ruled after the war? He was silent.

''You'd better get out of here,'' Teddy said. ''But before you go, do you know where Mady might be?''

He thought for a moment. ''Yes,'' he said.

''I'd like to see her.''

''Do you love her?'' Blaise asked. The question sounded so full of innocence that Teddy wanted to blush.

''Yes,'' he said. And it had come quickly, without thought. *Yes.* He had felt that he would never be able to say that again, but it came out without thought. ''Yes.''

''She will be here, in the hotel.''

''Here?''

''Others have hidden here. The Gaullists kept a British flyer here for weeks before they could move him out.''

''Where?''

Blaise told him. The hidden room opened off the same linen storeroom where they had made love using bedspreads for a pallet on the floor. ''Be very careful,'' Blaise said.

''That horse,'' Teddy said. ''I'm still curious.''

"It is the property of the Cavalry School, sort of a mascot, a symbol."

"And you were going to sell it to finance the Resistance?"

Blaise did not answer. "I must think," he said.

Carrying the horse, he walked into the growing twilight, the package heavy under one arm. With each step he seemed to be able to see it, to see it as it should be, in the dining hall, on the mantle, under its glass case, where each cadet could see it and remember that once that very school had trained officers for Napoleon. And all around him Paris was golden in the fading light, a living, breathing city, which he loved, which he sometimes took for granted, but loved to the bottom of his heart.

"Whatever it takes," Colonel Rol had said. "If it costs two hundred thousand lives, if Paris is a battlefield, it is worth it."

And the man in the hotel who was not a German had said that it would be an exchange of one kind of tyranny for another.

Oh, damn, damn, damn. All he wanted to do was kill Germans. And to talk to his mother. He had to talk to his mother.

20

THE GESTAPO, WITH armed men in the black uniforms of the SS, swarmed into the Ritz. They went first to the office of the director, the grim and silent men in civilian clothing, while the SS guarded the entrances. Auzello played the fawning, frightened collaborator, citing his good relationship with the Luftwaffe, proclaiming his innocence of any wrongdoing, saying almost tearfully that he did not know where the woman Mady Deschaises was.

Teddy was in the kitchen when the SS guards burst in, automatic weapons at the ready. He answered questions in crisp German, showed his identification, and, aside from a couple of insulting remarks from an SS officer about a German, even a Swiss-German, being content to work with subhuman French, there was nothing to it. The Ritz, a relatively small hotel, was still a complicated place to search, and the hotel's routine was knocked to hell by the search. Then it was over. At least the overt signs of it were over, but there was no doubt in anyone's mind that the Ritz was now marked, that it would be watched.

That saddened Claude Auzello, for he had sincerely hoped to be able to make the senior Luftwaffe officers actual stockholders in the hotel. It would have been a small price to pay, the logic being that since the officers had a financial stake in the hotel, they would do all they could to keep it from destruction. After the search for Mady, Auzello didn't know where to turn, but he could only try. He tried to contact General Schläfer, but was put off again. Wolf, it appeared, was doing nothing to help.

Auzello sat in his office, staring bleakly at the file folder holding his outline of the stockholder plan. Disgusted, he dropped it into the wastebasket, then sat motionless, staring at it. Finally, sighing deeply, he retrieved it from the wastebasket, opened the bottom drawer of the desk, and slipped it in. After closing the drawer he folded his hands, placed them on the desk, and stared at them, long and hard. Nothing.

And so another day was wasted. Friday had come and gone; the Allied armor was rolling closer and closer. Late in the day, Teddy made it a point to visit the director's office. Auzello looked angry to see him, but soon calmed under Teddy's insistent questioning. Yes, he had tried, once again, to arrange a meeting with Rol. No, there had been no concrete result. "They say that they will contact me tomorrow," he said.

Frustrated, Teddy went to his room, lay down, knowing he could not sleep. He left the room and went to the basement. The laundry rooms were deserted at that time of night and he walked toward the linen room. He had no idea where the entrance to the

secret room was, but he was determined to find it.
At least he could talk with Mady. He was in the
linen room, looking around, moving stacks of clean
and ironed sheets, when, hearing a sound behind
him, he moved swiftly. The pile of sheets he had just
held was thwacked solidly by a piece of lead pipe in
the hands of a man he's seen around the hotel once
or twice, one of the maintenance crew. He rolled
away from the blow and came up on his toes,
dodged another attempt to brain him, and landed one
good blow with his sore fist, saying, ''Ouch'' as it
hit. The man went down—not, however, all the way
out. Teddy held the pipe now, though; he said,
''Move and I'll flatten your skull.''

Mady, having heard movement in the linen room
and then the scuffle, recognized the voice. She opened
the small door, down near the floor. Her voice was
calm but firm. ''Don't hit him, Teddy.''

He turned swiftly, a smile coming automatically.

''Jean,'' Mady said, to the dazed man. ''It is all
right. He is one of us.''

The man shook his head ruefully. ''I wish someone had told me that,'' he said, gingerly fingering
his chin. He left the linen room.

''Come in, Theo,'' Mady said. ''You should not
be here, but since you are, come in.''

The room was tiny, but a makeshift ventilation
shaft provided fresh air, a small mattress lay on the
floor, some nonperishable food was stacked on a
little table. Mady closed the door behind them. The
room was lit by a bare bulb hanging from the ceiling, casting harsh shadows on Mady's face, making
her look somewhat haggard. He pulled her into his
arms and kissed her, then released her.

"They came to look for you this afternoon," he said.

"I heard them."

"Blaise was here earlier."

She gasped.

"He's with the Communists, Mady. Did you know?"

"Oh, God, no!"

"We had a little trouble, he and I," Teddy said. Her face blanched. "No one was hurt. We came to an understanding. I asked him to arrange a meeting for me with Rol."

"I asked him, I *begged* him not to get involved," Mady said.

"We're all involved, Mady," he said. "There's no escaping that. I think we have a little time before Rol's men start something. They're trying to raise money, so they must not be ready to hit the streets. But time's running out and there's nothing I can do. And quite frankly, I just had to see you."

"Oh, my darling," she said, coming to him. "Oh, I wish it were over."

He closed her mouth with his, and the world out there ceased to exist for a while as he slowly lowered her to the mattress on the floor and began to adore the smoothness and roundness and warmth and humanness of her. He had no idea how long they escaped in their mutual love, but he was lying by her side, drowsy, content, filled with wonder at the sweetness of her, and it was dark, for they'd turned out the light. Then he heard the sound—a scratching, a click, a movement. He rolled off the mattress and saw the gleam of light as the door was being opened, as a crack appeared. Mady was sleeping. He tensed, readied himself. He would take at least one of them with him. He would not live to see another woman he loved dead.

"Mother," the voice said, whispering. Mady's head moved in her sleep. "Mother?"

"Blaise?" Teddy whispered back.

"Who?"

"Werner."

The door opened. Blaise crawled in. Teddy turned on the light, squinting at the sudden glare. Mady put her hand over her eyes and moaned in her sleep.

Blaise was looking back and forth. The sheet had slipped and was exposing the top part of Mady's breasts. Teddy leaned and covered her. Then, realizing he was naked, he pulled on his trousers. Mady sat up suddenly, saw Blaise and reached out for him, then clutched the sheet to her.

"Very cozy," Blaise said, shocked to think what had been going on.

"Grow up," Teddy growled. "Why are you here?"

"I have to talk. To my mother."

"Where have you been?" Mady asked.

"If you two can get your mind on to important things—"

"Did you see Rol?" Teddy asked harshly.

He had. He had, indeed. He had told Rol that the General had not been available. The horse was hidden again, and this time only he knew where. He had told Rol that the General would be back late that night and that he had made an appointment. He had lied. And then he had told Rol that there was an English agent who wanted to talk and Rol had said that the English agent seemed to have knowledge of more people in the movement than was healthy, for everyone had been after him to meet with the agent.

"He thinks it is important," Blaise had said.

"It is too late," he was told. "Now we don't need their help. Now we are ready to help ourselves."

"The Allies are concerned about saving Paris," Blaise had said, and Rol, angry, had shouted at him, telling him that he'd heard all he wanted to hear about saving Paris, for the problem was in saving France. And then he'd sent Blaise away, to get the money.

"He will not see you," Blaise told Teddy.

"To me that means one thing," Teddy said. "He's almost ready, isn't he?"

Blaise was silent. Mady reached out and pulled him down to sit beside her on the mattress. "Your father fought for France," she said. "We all fight for France. Don't you know what you're doing? Don't you know that by helping Rol and the Communists you are doing your best to deliver France into the hands of a new set of masters?"

"The people," Blaise said.

"Damn it, can't you read?" Teddy almost shouted. "Don't you know that the Russians are going to be sitting on top of half of Europe when this is over? They're going to be in control of everything not occupied by the United States and Great Britain. Do you want France to be a part of a new Russian empire under a fancy name? Do you know how many people Joe Stalin has killed to stay in power?"

"The people," Blaise said. "It is the people who matter."

"Jesus Christ," Teddy said. "You Frogs. You damned French. We've come over here twice now to pull your chestnuts out of the fire. Let me tell you one thing for sure, Blaise. We won't come again. We won't come to save you from control by the Politburo, from taking orders from Moscow. Right

THE FIRES OF PARIS   193

now we're doing our best to keep Paris from being a battleground and all you people can think of is grabbing power. Your mother has been risking her life as a member of the Resistance—''

"You?" Blaise asked, looking startled.

"I have done what I could," Mady said. "Perhaps I should have told you. I wanted you to stay out of it altogether, to survive, to be able to be a free man in a liberated France."

"You are willing to turn France over to de Gaulle?" Blaise asked.

"At least he has fought," Mady said. "He has fought both the Germans and the Vichy French. At least he will not make France a Communist concentration camp. He will allow the citizens of France to vote. Can you say the same for your people?"

"De Gaulle—" Blaise said.

"Is a symbol, a man. He will not live forever," Teddy said. "But he will reestablish the Republic. The public offices will be occupied by Frenchmen, not by appointed foreign commissars. Is that what you want?"

Blaise was confused. All this time. All this time his mother had been a part of the Resistance, risking her life, risking torture in the cellars of the Gestapo. And in his male pride he'd thought that he was the only one who cared. And outside there was Paris and only one more day before Rol called the people to the streets.

It was the horse. Rol wanted to sell the horse. France was a nation that valued tradition, and Rol was willing to throw it away. He was willing to see Paris and all of its monuments and buildings and bridges under the bombs of the Luftwaffe.

"Oh, God," he said.

"Tell us what you know," Teddy said.

"I can't. I can't betray them."

"Aren't they going to betray Paris?" Mady asked.

"Blaise, we're not asking you to change your beliefs in one moment," Teddy said. "We're asking you only to give us time, give us time to save Paris. Then, when the Allies have driven out the Germans, the political questions can be decided as they should be decided, at the ballot box. Doesn't that make sense?"

"Day after tomorrow," Blaise said dully.

"Sunday?" Teddy asked. "He's going to the streets?"

"Yes. It is all in readiness."

"Theo, please turn out the light," Mady said. Teddy did, and she found her clothing in the darkness, then turned the light back on. Teddy had also finished dressing.

"What time is it?" Mady asked. She and Teddy were both amazed to find that it was not yet midnight. "There is time," she said. "Before the curfew. You must go with us, Blaise."

"You can't go out," Teddy said. "They're looking for you."

"I must," she said. "Come."

They left the hotel singly, met in the darkness of a street corner and set off. It was a long walk and the curfew hour was coming near. They saw a few Germans patrolling the streets, which were emptying fast. At an old building off the Avenue de Clichy, they were admitted, after some confusion, to a room in which sat one of the men who had talked with Teddy in the linen room at the Ritz. Blaise seemed to have become more certain that he was right. He told his story readily.

"You have done the right thing, my son," the Gaullist leader said. "Now you will fight with us."

Blaise shook his head sadly. "I will join my comrades," he said. "If there is to be fighting, I will betray them no further by fighting against them."

"A man must do as he feels," the Gaullist said.

"What will you do?" Teddy asked.

"We do what is necessary," the Gaullist said. "We will not have another Commune."

"Crazy," Teddy said, for he knew by the grimness in the faces of the men in the room that Paris was lost. They were all crazy. All he had done had accomplished exactly the opposite of what was intended.

"You two," the Gaullist said, indicating Teddy and Mady, "can stay here." He shook Blaise's hand. "Good luck."

"And to you," Blaise said, looking briefly at his mother before he left.

Soon they were alone in the shabby room. The blackout curtains were in place. The room was dimly lit by one lamp. Teddy took her hand. "Don't worry about him," he said.

"It's not only about him I worry."

"We should be safe here," he said. "If worse comes to worst, we can try to make our way out of the city and move toward the American lines."

"No," she said. "I won't leave."

He held her close. "Well," he said, in English, "where you go I go, baby."

"*Pardon?*" she asked.

"That means that I'm with you," he said. She squeezed him, but she was, he knew, preoccupied. He found the terrible imitation coffee and brewed a pot. It was growing late. The city seemed quiet. Once he heard the distant roar of aircraft engines—multi-engine jobs, probably British, headed for some target in Germany. He shuddered. The aircraft of Luftflotte 3 would boon be flying over Paris, much lower.

After a long, long time, she lay down in a rumpled bed, leaving Teddy smoking moodily, wondering what the next few days would bring. He reviewed the situation. He didn't like it. He didn't like being in a position where he had no control over events. As a fighter pilot he had always been in sole control of his own destiny once he was in the air. Then, alone in the cockpit of a Spitfire, it was up to him, to him and him alone. Now vast forces were being unleashed, forces over which he had no control at all. And he was helpless. Or was he?

In his brief service at the Ritz, he had become so much a part of the scenery—for example, in General Schläfer's rooms—that the Germans often talked openly in his presence. He had heard the plans for the bombing of Paris. He could be of much greater value at the Ritz than hiding out in this small room.

He thought Mady was asleep, but she was not. Her eyes opened immediately when he touched her shoulder.

"I have to go back," he said.

She accepted it. She seemed to understand. She stood, began to neaten her hair.

"No, you stay here," he said. "There's too much risk in your going back."

"You said it," she told him, with a smile. "I'm with you."

At least, he felt, he would know where she was if she were hidden away in the little room in the basement. He didn't like it, but there was, also, a practical consideration. Without her, he might very well get lost merely trying to get back to the hotel in the darkness.

They kept to the shadows and twice had to hide to avoid German patrols. He knew that it would be disaster to be picked up as curfew violators. Mady was already being sought by the Gestapo, and he didn't want to test his cover by the serious questioning that would go on if he were caught out after midnight with a known anti-German woman. So they moved from shadow to shadow and Mady, knowing the city well, kept to narrow streets and hidden alleys.

The arrived at the hotel before the first light of day and got Mady into the hidden room without incident.

He had two hours sleep before he was awakened by another steward. Serving breakfast to the General in his room, he heard talk of the American advance. The German armies in Normandy were about to be eliminated from the war by destruction or capture. Most noncombatants had already left Paris. There was no mention of Resistance activities or of the plans to destroy Paris.

None of the men in the room knew that on that island in the Seine, almost in the shadows of Notre Dame, hundreds of men were moving. It was approaching seven in the morning. The silent men were converging on the Préfecture of Police, the main headquarters for the Paris police force.

Only a few others saw a brightly colored piece of cloth unfurl in the early-morning breeze from the top of the building. It was only a piece of cloth, but it was the French tricolor, and it had not flown over any building in Paris in over four years.

21

THE MAN WHO called himself Colonel Rol
left his headquarters quite early on Saturday morning. All was in readiness. His plans were complete.
His men were moving into position all over the city
for the sudden thrust that would come on Sunday
morning—a quiet day usually, a day on which the
Germans would be more or less relaxed. He wanted
to see for himself the situation in the city, to take a
look at some of his prime targets. He rode his bicycle across the Seine, noting that a German demolition team was at work setting a massive charge on
the bridge supports. He made a mental note. Men to
try to prevent the charge from being detonated.

It was going to be a muggy day. Already there
was a hint of warmth in the air and it felt good to
pedal strongly and to think that within twenty-four
hours the early-morning hush would be broken by
the sound of fire fights and the screams of dying
Germans.

He slowed down and noted that a sense of peace

seemed to hang over the island in the Seine, that all was quiet. And then he shook his head, for, from a distance, he heard something he could not be hearing. He turned his head to catch it, and as he moved toward the sound he felt astonishment. The sound he was hearing was male voices, many of them, singing. And most astonishing of all, the song they were singing was a song with vast significance to all of France, the national anthem, the "Marseillaise." He stopped under the imposing walls of the Préfecture of Police. There were hundreds of them, and they were singing, and the sound, although magnificant, was a terrible surprise to him. The building that housed police headquarters was one of the most important targets on his list, and they, those inside, were definitely not his men.

He left his bicycle and went to the front door. Armed men in civilian clothing told him to move along. He rode away, knowing great anger. The Gaullists had moved. Somehow they had known and they had moved ahead of him and they held the Prefecture. The Préfecture and what else?

It was only Saturday, August 19. His men had orders to move on Sunday morning.

De Gaulle, he thought. De Gaulle had been in Paris. He had seen him with his own eyes. It was de Gaulle who had ordered the uprising to begin. Fortunately, his own orders had already been distributed. It was only a matter of implementing them immediately, instead of waiting until Sunday morning. He made his way to a friendly place and began.

It started quietly. Posters went up calling for a general mobilization of all patriotic Frenchmen. Rol's orders spread. In the telephone exchanges his agents destroyed German listening equipment.

Blaise Deschaises heard the orders with a vast
sense of relief. He was still hurting inside because he
had betrayed his comrades, but that no longer
mattered. Now all Frenchmen would fight. He told
his own squad of men to get ready. He struck first at
a passing German half-track, lofting the Molotov
cocktail, which he himself had made, to go arching
down into the vehicle. Burning German infantrymen
poured out, fell, rolled, trying to beat out the flames,
and the guns of Blaise's group opened up, killing the
Germans as they burned.

But there was more involved than killing Germans. All over the city the race was on. The Gaullists, realizing that the fight was underway and could
not be stopped, took to the streets and raced to seize
police stations, town halls, all public buildings. The
battles were small and isolated, Germans being killed
wherever they were found. They had not yet had
time to react, and many died under the guns of men
like Blaise Deschaises.

At the Ritz, Teddy Werner was serving late breakfast
to two of his steady patrons, Otto Schellen and Silke
Frager, when the telephone rang. Schellen answered,
and came back to the table grim-faced. "It has
begun," he told Silke.

Teddy felt a chill of dread. He waited to hear
more, but Schellen took a bite and chewed thoughtfully. "I think, my dear Silke," he said, "that it is
time for you and me to make our way back to
Berlin."

"You're going to let the swine drive you out?"
Silke snarled.

Schellen laughed. "The dogs bark, but the cara-
van moves on," he said. "We have our own con-

cerns. I, for example, have not been trained in door-to-door infantry fighting and I don't care to begin at this late date. If you'd like to stay, you have my permission.''

Teddy had to know. ''Herr Schellen,'' he said, ''excuse me. Am I to understand that there is fighting here in Paris?''

''I'm afraid so,'' Schellen said. ''So far it's in isolated pockets. It will spread, however. I do hope you have a comfortable hole picked out.''

''Yes, thank you, sir,'' Teddy said.

He could not wait to get away, but had to pretend to be the dutiful waiter until they had finished their breakfast. Then he bolted for the kitchen. In his excitement, a waiter there didn't even bother to stop talking when Teddy approached; he was telling his audience, gloating, smiling, that the Allied tanks were now in Chartres, that the Paris uprising was underway. He saw Teddy and smirked. ''I would think that some among us would be thinking of finding safer places,'' he said.

All over the hotel, electric excitement permeated the air. Although the communication between the Luftwaffe in the Ritz and the office of Berlin's commanding general was not of the best, there was still enough to let the officers in the hotel know that the uprising had begun. Everyone had expected it. When it came there was no real surprise, and although there was fighting all over the city, the Germans were not panicked. Their attitude brought a hidden and sardonic smile to the face of Wolf. He listened as his general spoke with the head of Amt VI, Otto Schellen, and explained the plans of General von Choltitz.

Only one thing puzzled Wolf. He knew that the

Communist Resistance had planned to strike on Sunday morning, and he was a bit angry when he first heard the news of the takeover of the Préfecture a day early. He assumed, however, that some unexpected event had precipitated the action. Since it had gone well, since the men of Paris were pouring into the streets armed with whatever weapons they'd been able to hide, Wolf was pleased.

He was pleased, too, to find that von Choltitz was vacillating. According to what Schläfer had been told, there would be no immediate destruction of the city, merely an attack on the Préfecture, which seemed to be the main point of resistance. Already German tanks were moving toward the square in front of Notre Dame.

Wolf regretted the past need for secrecy, for his lack of contact with the Resistance. He would have loved to be with them, directing them. But they seemed to be doing all right without him—and in fact it was considerably less dangerous in the hotel.

Upon hearing that von Choltitz was going to fight the rebellion with limited means, instead of beginning the ordered demolition of the city, Otto Schellen said, "I must remind you, General, of your orders."

"Yes, yes." Schläfer looked uncomfortable. "There is time. The bombers are at the ready."

It was Silke, of course, who had called for the Gestapo search of the hotel, and she was displeased when the search failed to turn up the Deschaises woman. God, she wanted that bitch, wanted to see her cringe under torture, to beg forgiveness for that kick, to change from the proud and sleek French bitch into a whining, bleeding, haggard old woman.

Silke was unhappy, too, because Schellen had

spent so much time with the Luftwaffe and had not taken advantage of the chance to see Paris before it was in ruins. Admittedly her reasons were selfish, but she even felt a bit of regret for the city. Too bad, she thought, that she didn't get to see more of it. However, she was in total agreement that the city should not fall into Allied hands intact. While Schellen talked with the Luftwaffe, she looked out a window, almost hoping to be able to see some of the fighting. But the Place Vendôme was quiet. Looking out that window one would not guess that somewhere in the city men were dying.

She was bored, and it was inadvisable to go out into the city. She was a woman of few pleasures. She loved her work and she loved love. And when she was not working, her thoughts often turned to her other favorite subject, so that, for some reason, she kept thinking of the tall, handsome German steward.

The Panther tanks were moving across the Pont Saint-Michel and the Pont-Neuf to the Ile de la Cité.

Blaise Deschaises was conducting a hit-and-run type of warfare, moving his small band here and there, hitting wherever there was a target, experiencing a fierce joy. At last he was once again killing Germans. The honor of France was riding on his young shoulders. It did not seem a heavy burden.

Dirctor Claude Auzello had made one last attempt to contact General Schläfer. Reaching him on the telephone, he said, "My dear General, there is a matter of uncompleted business between us."

Schläfer chuckled dryly. "I would advise you to

step outside. I think there you will hear the sound of tank cannon.''

Auzello hung up with a sigh. Now the hotel was in the hands of God. He expected at any moment to hear the sounds of fighting close at hand, and he could almost feel, as if they were tearing into his own skin, the burst of shells against the facade of the Ritz.

Late at night, when the activity in the hotel was at an ebb, Teddy made his way to Mady's hiding place to hold her close and tell her that it had begun. Knowing that her son was out there in the city, somewhere, she clung to the only person she had—to the strange man who had come into her life so unexpectedly, to the man who, for the first time in years, made her feel like a woman.

Sunday morning was a mixed light, with broken clouds dimming the sun. The humidity was high. If one could have looked down upon the city in safety from a height, the peace would have been deceptive. Couples strolled along the Seine. In the parks, bicycle riders and pedestrians paraded in their Sunday best. It was almost as if the city, the country, the whole world was holding its breath.

With von Choltitz's approval, the Swedish Consul had arranged a cease-fire. The BBC broadcast appeals from Free French leaders to ignore calls for rebellion.

Only a few fought to break the truce. A furious Colonel Rol was sending out orders to one and all. ''Fight,'' he told them. ''Fight as long as there is a single German in Paris.''

Posters went up all over the city on that quiet

Sunday, saying that the cease-fire was merely a ploy by the Germans to give them a chance to organize and eliminate the working class in Paris. The Sunday sightseers suddenly found themselves caught in a fire fight, as men like Blaise Deschaises obeyed Rol's orders. By afternoon, the truce was forgotten.

The news, of course, had gone out of the city and had been received with varying degrees of anger by the various members of the Allied High Command. When Rol used a clandestine radio to call for help, for arms, that plea brought, from a number of nostrils, a snort of derision. The general attitude was that the Paris Resistance had started their insurrection, let them be the ones to finish it. The Allied generals, with a couple of notable exceptions, had their eyes on the Rhine, not on Paris. They knew that Paris would fall, like a ripe plum from the tree, once it was encircled.

One of the generals who disagreed was Charles de Gaulle, who had just arrived at Cherbourge, his return to France. Upon hearing of the beginning of fighting in Paris, he sent an urgent message to General Eisenhower insisting that Allied forces be diverted to Paris. And he sent a command to an encampment in an apple orchard near the town of Écouché.

In the dark hours after midnight, a slim man pushed his cane into the soft sod of the orchard and shook the hands of a colonel who stood beside a staff car. Then the colonel got into the car, which drove quietly away with its lights off, followed by three dozen tanks and trucks. The colonel had his orders. He was the first to lead French soldiers toward Paris. This was not reconnaissance; this was liberation. His orders were to represent the Free French in the capital city, and he was named by the man with the cane to be the first French military governor of Paris.

The man with the cane was Philippe de Hautecloque, General Jacques Leclerc. He was disobeying orders from the Allied command. He was prepared to further disobey them, and to obey the French commander only. The Allied leaders felt that the French Second Armored could not move into Paris without their help. In that, Leclerc knew, they were wrong. He has seen to that. The division had enough supplies stockpiled to move independently. He had just made his first move, sending a small contingent on the road to the city he had sworn to liberate.

Now there were precautions to take. At his command trailer, he called to an aide.

"The two Americans," he said, referring to the American liaison officers, Captain Hoye and Lieutenant Rifkind, "take them on a little sight-seeing trip."

His aide saluted and turned to go.

"You might also distract the American correspondent, Raine," Leclerc added.

That, he felt, as he prepared to sleep, would take care of the three men who might report strange happenings to the American command of V Corps. Leclerc was in total agreement with de Gaulle. At all costs, Paris must be liberated by Free French forces. At all costs the Communist Resistance leaders were to be kept from being seated, in control of the city, when the Allied troops arrived.

And in Paris on Monday morning, the papers printed by Rol's hidden presses were on the streets. They contained one message: AUX BARRICADES! "To the barricades''—the old revolutionary rallying cry of Paris, of the Commune.

Soon everything light enough to by hauled, lifted, or rolled was being piled in the streets of Paris. The barricades went up in the industrial districts and in the Latin Quarter and in Montmartre.

Paris had risen. There was no going back now.

22

ANY PLACE WHERE one is forced to stay becomes a prison. The small room hidden behind the walls of the linen closet in the Ritz was growing smaller and smaller for Mady on that Monday. Already she had spent three nights there. Counting the nights was possible, because Teddy came at night. She tried various methods of passing the time— remembering her life, with emphasis on the pleasant things; doing mental exercises, such as reciting the multiplication tables up to twelve-by-twelve; humming all the songs she knew, trying to fill in the missing lyrics. She was amazed to find that with such intense concentration, she could remember many things.

Her thoughts went often to Teddy Werner. She had not, until then, thought of the future. For four years of German occupation the future had been bleak, and not at all guaranteed. For the first time she began to think, to hope, that there might be a future for her, and she conjured up variations on it. Perhaps she would see America. Perhaps she would marry the tall man from that faraway Texas. Then, in gloom, another alternative. Perhaps, like most men, he had merely taken what was offered so freely and would forget her as soon as his own troops came to the city and he was safe.

She spent a good half hour trying to will him to come to her. And so intent was she on the wish that she thought she heard a sound at the little doorway to the hidden room, but it was only a maid in the linen room.

Mady had always hated small, dark places. Even with the bare lightbulb turned on, the walls of the small room seemed to close in on her. She paced a few steps and turned, paced again. And there came to her ears a series of quick, dull thuds, sounds so powerful they sifted through all the intervening masonry and walls of the hotel.

Oh, God, the fighting was moving closer. She had trouble breathing. The windowless room was buried far down in the basement of the hotel. If the hotel were hit by shells or bombs, all of those tons of stone and wood and plaster would come crushing down. She put her hands over her ears and stood very, very still. She told herself to be calm.

When the light went out she screamed. Total darkness engulfed her. They had hit the hotel. They had hit the hotel and all the lights were out and she was going to be trapped there, far down under the rubble. She fell to her hands and knees and began a frantic search. God, why hadn't she foreseen such an eventuality? Why had she not asked for matches and a candle? Perhaps there was one and hadn't noticed it. She broke a fingernail digging frantically through the food supplies and then, wanting to scream, made her decision. She crawled to the wall, felt along it, found the small door to the linen room. She dug at it with her fingernails and finally had it cracked—and there was blessed light, a beam of it.

She lay there, breathing in gasps. It was only the naked bulb in her room. The bulb had burned out. She would wait. The maintenance man who had revealed himself to be a member of the Resistance would come, and she would ask him for another bulb. It was as simple as that.

She lay there for what seemed to be hours and no one came. Not even a maid. And now and then she'd hear the distant explosions. She could only guess what was going on in the streets, but she could imagine that the Germans were systematically destroying the city, coming closer and closer. She had no watch. Behind her the darkness of the room seemed to take on a personality, seemed to fill itself with all her old childhood horrors—things unseen but felt, a presence, a nameless evil. And she kept telling herself that she was an adult, that it was only darkness, that there was light, that sliver of light coming in the crack around the door that led out of the dark, close place to freedom—and danger.

But what if everyone had fled the hotel? What if the fighting was close and, for safety, they'd all gone?

Oh, Teddy. He'd never leave her. Unless he'd been killed. Or unless the hotel itself was now occupied by German soldiers.

It was, quite simply, the terrors that can seize the mind in a dark, closed, small space that caused her to open the small door, to peek fearfully out to see an empty storeroom, and then to crawl out and close the door behind her.

THE FIRES OF PARIS 211

The laundry room was also empty; there she could heard the sounds of the distant fight a bit more clearly. She did not know that the guns were attacking the Préfecture of Police, in the middle of the river, and trying to displace with blast and fire the barricades that had been thrown up all over the city. She knew only that she was alone and that the fighting had started and that she had to know.

She chose not to go near the kitchen. A small stairwell led upward to a corridor near her own room. She crept upward, listening, hearing only the sounds of the fighting, muffled, distant. It was as if the hotel was completely deserted and she was the last one left alive, and that haunting feeling pushed her onward. She opened the door into the corridor. There was no sound, no movement. She crept out and started down the corridor and still there was no one.

There are times when life hangs on coincidence. And many situations in life are brought about because of a force built into the human body, stronger more often in the male, but present in females, too, if it is more controlled.

It was the libido of one woman that put the life of another woman in danger. Silke Frager, alone in her suite, hearing the sounds of distant battle, had become more and more bored. More and more her thoughts turned to that tall, blond, handsome German steward.

She considered calling room service and asking for him by name. In the end, she decided to take a walk through the hotel. She knew that she should not risk her relationship with Otto Schellen for a casual affair with a hotel employee, and so she made a whimsical deal with fate. If, during her walk, she encountered the steward, she would tell him to come to her rooms, or she would go to his. If not, then she would have gained a bit of exercise.

She made her way to the lower levels, strolled through the lobby, down the long corridor to the Ritz Bar. There were men there, a few, mostly Germans in uniform. The sight of them angered her. Why were they not out fighting the rebelling French? She turned and walked aimlessly and angled back toward the service areas, helping fate just a little bit, thinking that it would be more likely to encounter Werner there. She turned a corner and halted in midstride— for there, dead center in the hallway, not thirty feet away, was Mady Deschaises.

For a moment, neither woman moved. "You," Silke gasped, leaping forward.

Mady considered making a stand, but it quickly came to her that any commotion would bring others. She ran. Using her advantage of knowing the hotel well, she ran back down the hall, opened a door to the stairs, running down for her life, hearing the footsteps of the other woman behind her. She gained the laundry room and took complicated little hallways through the basement, avoiding the kitchens, thinking that her best chance, now that she'd been seen, was to get out of the hotel.

Opening a little-used door, she stepped into a service court where there were refuse bins and some loose trash moving sluggishly in a soft, humid, breeze. As she reached an alleyway, she looked over her shoulder to see that she was not followed.

Now she could hear the sounds of battle well. The air was filled with them, and as she looked up she could see smoke rising from different areas of the city. The sad destruction was underway.

She realized that she had to move toward the sounds of the guns. There she would find the Resistance and, past the Germans, she would be safe. How to get past them was the question. As she gained a street she threw herself back into a doorway and cowered there as two tanks rumbled past, their turrets open, tank commanders looking out, guns at the ready. If she followed the tanks they would lead her to the Resistance. She moved from shelter to shelter, but the tanks outdistanced her and she followed them by the sound of the firing, which came closer and closer as she walked.

The German tank commanders knew that they were moving against men armed only with light weapons. They moved forward arrogantly, waiting to blast their enemies—ragged men in civilian clothing, with World War I rifles—to bits. The sight of the mighty barricade thrown up at an intersection caused them to slow, then halt. Mady came up behind them, turning a corner to almost walk into the treads of one of the tanks. The man in the turret looked down, smiled. Mady ran for the building at the side of the street, expecting to feel the burst of machine-gun bullets across her back, but she gained a doorway in safety.

The tanks, turrets still open, moved down toward the barricade, their big guns blasting, shells lofting debris from the barricade. She had a grandstand view as an object arched out from a window and went directly down the open turret of the lead tank. There came a whooshing explosion; flames and flesh and smoke poured upward, and the tank slewed and ran into a lightpost, crushing it, then crashed into the wall of a building.

The second tank backed furiously, halting near Mady. She could not move from the doorway in which she had sheltered. A hail of small-arms fire came from the barricade. The tank backed around a corner and the firing continued. She was waiting her chance when, unheard in the din of firing, unseen until he grabbed her, a German tank crewman leaped into the recessed doorway with her.

"Come with me," he said. She had no choice. They ran, bullets making thunking sounds on the air around them, to gain the cover of the corner where the German tank waited. She was lifted by two of the Germans, lifted roughly. She felt the hot metal of the tank on her bare legs, was lashed, quickly and tightly, to the turret of the tank, sitting straddling the hot barrel of the cannon. The engine of the tank roared and the tank was moved and she prayed. For the tank was turning the corner, and as it appeared to the men behind the barricade the firing began again— and stopped suddenly. The tank sat in the middle of the street, and the huge cannon between her legs bucked and roared.

"Kill them," she screamed, as the cannon blasted again. "Kill them!" But no one heard.

23

BLAISE DESCHAISES, AFTER conducting in-
dependent German hunts, had joined in the defense
of a barricade. He knew it was only a matter of time
before the tanks came, and he had made ready. His
personal squad, still intact, was equipped with at
least two each of the potent Molotov cocktails. In
anticipation of a tank attack, he had stationed himself and his men in the second-story windows of the
buildings on the street in front of the barricade. It
was one of his men who gave just the right arc to a
cocktail to send it down the foolishly open turret of
the lead German tank. The second tank retreated too
quickly to be caught. Blaise readied his own two
bottles and waited. The tank would be back, turret
closed this time. The best method of attack then
would be to shower the tank with cocktails, start
flames licking the entire tank, making it too hot for
the men inside. When he heard the engine roar and
heard the clank of the treads he yelled out to be
ready.

"Oh, the boche bastards," he said, when he saw the woman tied to the turret. "Hold it, hold it," he yelled to his men, some of whom were close enough to hear, some not.

The tank sat there in the middle of the street like a fat, obscene metal monster and slowly and methodically began to blow the barricade apart. Blaise knew that sooner or later the men there would have to fire, that sooner or later he'd have to give the signal to kill the Frenchwoman tied to the tank, killing the tank along with her. But how does a man give an order to kill a countrywoman?

He told the man who was with him in the room to stand ready. He took one of the deadly cocktails and ran down the stairs. He was in a doorway slightly behind the tank, and the sound of the cannon, firing a measured intervals, was a sort of whooshing, clanking explosion in his ears, making him want to put his hands up to cut off the sound.

He measured the distance from the doorway to the tank. The soldiers in the tank were giving their full attention to the barricade, using its machine gun in between cannon shots. And, in a moment of silence, he heard the woman's voice. She was not screaming. She was yelling, "Kill them, kill them!"

He felt a moment of admiration, and then, lest more hesitation cause him to yield to the terrible fear, he ran, crouching, toward the side of the tank, praying that he would not be seen. With a quick swiveling of the turret, machine-gun bullets could sweep him away. But he'd seen death before, and he knew that it comes to all—sometimes even to an eighteen-year-old man taking on a German Panzer single-handed.

He was beside the treads now, and the boom of

the cannon almost deafened him. His knife was in one hand, the cocktail in the other. Upward he leaped, using the sprocketed wheel for a step. He could feel the vibration of the idling motor, felt the entire vehicle quiver in sympathy with a round of machine-gun fire, and then he was beside the woman and looking into her startled face.

Blaise felt like screaming. His hands shook as he ripped the lashing, jerked her down and off the tank, lacerating himself and her as they rolled, fell. He somehow protected the bottle and rose, the tank gun once again causing that sharp, painful blast in his ears, to slam the cocktail up and over, directly in front of the turret. Pushing the woman who was his mother ahead of him, feeling the searing blast of the explosive liquids, he ran, feeling the hair on his neck singe, hearing, from the barricade, the cheers and the beginning of fire, the bullets clanging and whining off the steel of the tank.

From a window another cocktail arched down, and the German vehicle was wrapped in flame. It backed, tried to turn; but the chemical fires heated it, made it unbearable inside. The turret was flung open and a man climbed to the lip, tried to leap past the flames, was hit in midair by a hail of fire from the barricade. One crewman made it, somehow, leaping clear of the flames, landing on his hands and knees to scramble directly toward Blaise.

The German was in the clear, protected from the firing from the barricade by a decorative pier on the building, on his hands and knees still, panting, his skin scorched and peeling. He looked up into the muzzle of Blaise's pistol.

"No, Blaise," Mady said, when she realized what he was going to do, but his name was lost in the

spitting bark of the German weapon, a 9-mm automatic taken from a dead German officer. The tank
crewman fell, not to move, the bullet taking him
directly in the top of the skull and emerging at the
base of his neck.

"He was hurt," Mady said.

Blaise looked at her coldly. "What in hell are you
doing here?"

"I was discovered," she said. "I had to run. I
was trying to make my way to the Resistance."

"Well, you're here," Blaise said.

He walked directly in the center of the street,
holding his mother's hand, walking cockily toward
the barricade. There was cheering. Two tanks smoldered behind him. Men clapped him on the back,
shook his hand, looked in admiration at the attractive
if rumpled woman by his side. They were welcomed.
They were kissed.

"There will be other tanks," Blaise said. "Let's
save our celebration until after we have killed them."

"Ah, the young tiger," an older man said.

"Blaise, I must talk with you," Mady said. She
pulled him to one side. "Theo Werner is alone in the
hotel. Only you and I know that he's not German.
We've got to get him out."

"He's a big boy," Blaise said. "He can take care
of himself."

"He came to help us."

"We're helping ourselves," Blaise said proudly.

"Blaise, he's important to me."

He looked at her sullenly. "Then you go get him
out."

She nodded grimly. "If I must." She started toward the barricade.

"All right, all right," Blaise said, catching her by the arm. "I'll send someone."

"No. Go yourself. He knows you. You know the hotel. You can get him out."

He shrugged. Hell, maybe he could kill a German or two on the way. Maybe the French people in the hotel had already killed Werner and the other Germans. If so, that would be a blessing, and it would save him a lot of trouble.

"For you, and for you alone," he said. He checked his weapons, the pistol and the submachine gun he'd just requisitioned from a German who was in no position to object. And then he remembered.

"Mother?"

"Yes."

"If anything should happen to me—"

"No, no," she said. "Don't say it."

"Wait. Listen. Remember that ventilation area, that small space off the kitchen where I used to hide from you when I was a child?"

"Yes, I remember."

"In the third ventilation shaft to the left of the entrance, there is a certain package. I want you to take it to Saumur, if I'm not around to do it myself."

"You will be," Mady said. "You will be."

"Now," he said, all business. "There is a place of safety near here—at least as safe as anywhere in Paris. You know it. It is the apartment on the Avenue de Clichy. You were there before. Go there and wait for me. I'll bring you your precious Werner."

"Thank you, son," she said simply.

As she made her way to the apartment, she heard sounds of sporadic fighting from all around the city. The apartment was empty. Once again she was alone, with only her concern for the two men in her life to keep her company.

Blaise took only two young men with him, near his own age. They had to dodge a strong force of armor moving toward the fighting, and Blaise almost went back, because he knew his comrades behind the barricades were in for a tough fight. But he had made a promise and, although he resented the man who had crept into his mother's affections, he did recognize the man's bravery, to come into a strange country as an underground agent. Yes, France owned him his safety, even if his trip to Paris was a gesture in futility.

The area around the Place Vendôme was quiet. Blaise left his two comrades in hiding with his automatic weapon, and, carrying the concealed Luger, entered the kitchens of the Ritz. Immediately he saw that they were very short-handed—his friend Henri Morlaix was behind a barricade somewhere in the city, and others were also missing. A chambermaid he knew said, yes, she'd seen the steward Theo Werner. He had just left the kitchen, taking an order to the Luftwaffe suites.

Fortunately, Blaise did not have long to wait. He saw Teddy wheeling the service cart down the corridor and intercepted him.

"You are to come with me," he said.

"Why?"

"You're not safe here," Blaise said.

"I can't leave, not just yet," Teddy said. "First there's Mady—"

"She's with us, now," Blaise said. Teddy looked at him in surprise, waiting for an explanation. "The female Gestapo agent saw her—"

"In the hidden room?"

"She came out. She panicked when a lightbulb burned out," Blaise said, shrugging as if to say, "Well, you know women."

"When did this happen?" Teddy asked. He had not had a chance to see Mady that day.

"Never mind. She wishes you to come. When the Resistance reaches the hotel, they'll kill you as a German."

"You're sure Mady's all right?"

"Yes, damn it, she's all right." He gave the address.

"Look, Blaise," Teddy said. "I can be of more use here. I just came from serving coffee and cakes in General Schläfer's room. They talk quite openly in front of me. I told you that the bombers of Luftflotte Three are standing by to level Paris. Here, very possibly, I can know when the order is given."

"So, we know when the city is to be reduced to rubble. What does it matter?"

"It matters a lot if you'll listen. If you can organize a force. The plan is to have German troops mark the targets with flares. Does that give you any ideas?"

Blaise nodded grimly. "If we knew where, and when, we could at least see to it that there were no flares," he said.

"Exactly," Teddy said. "When things get tough, I'll make a run for it. I'll need to know how to get in touch with you or someone who can move fast."

"That's a problem," Blaise said. "We can't predict the Germans. I think it would be best, if you have news of importance, for you to go to the apartment on Clichy, where my mother will be. She will know how to reach someone. Meanwhile, I will tell

my officers that we must be ready to move instantly
when we hear from you.''

    ''Be careful,'' Teddy said.

    ''And you,'' Blaise said, only somewhat reluctantly.

24

As GENERAL LECLERC had planned, Ed Raine was very successfully diverted on Monday—all day. Not until he returned to headquarters at sundown did he learn that a contingent of the Second Armored Division was on its way to Paris—with a twelve-hour lead. He cursed himself for being made a fool of, and he roundly cursed the cherubically innocent French press officer who had taken him sight-seeing.

He vowed to be more vigilant in the future, to keep the story from escaping. Normally any army unit wants to have its reporters aware of all developments, so long as future strategy didn't get to the enemy. But clearly Leclerc was up to something cute, and he was treating the Americans as if they were the enemy from whom secrets would be kept.

The secret itself was no secret, of course. It was Paris. But when? By what route? And would Leclerc actually directly disobey orders from his Allied superiors?

The next morning, Ed comandeered a jeep and driver, and set out on the trail of the advance contingent. Unbelievably, the three dozen tanks and trucks had disappeared without a trace—or so the driver would have Ed believe. And Ed's French wasn't up to following the rapid exchanges in provincial dialect between the driver and his none-too-forthcoming informants. Without doubt the man was telling the natives to play dumb.

Defeated by the friendly French duplicity, Ed returned to the orchard near Écouché well before noon. He was greeted by a French officer who asked him if he'd found the enemy.

"No. Just a bunch of peasants who'd never seen a soldier in their lives."

"Pity. They should have looked here. They'd have seen a fine soldier—your bearded American friend. He was looking for you."

"Fortunately he didn't find me," Ed said. Hemingway had rejoined the headquarters contingent only a day or so before. He was having the time of his life these days. He was always going out and playing soldier, instead of newsman, and he had bet anyone who would listen that he was going to be the first correspondent into Paris—even if it meant organizing his own army of FFI and going into the city without the armor. He was the man to try it, too, and Ed wasn't that brave.

"He set off on the road to Paris," the officer said.

"Yeah, so what else is new?" Ed asked.

"Pardon?"

"What's the scoop from group?" Hell, even the Frenchies knew that bit of American slang.

The officer shrugged. "I shouldn't tell you this, but the General has been away."

"Yeah?" His interest was aroused. "Where?"

"I can't say."

That was a noncommital answer. Ed didn't know whether the officer couldn't say because he didn't know, or because he didn't care to say, but it was worth looking into. Ed grabbed a bite of SOS and then went general-hunting. He didn't find Leclerc immediately, but he got some interesting news. The American Fourth was only thirty or forty miles from Paris, still planning to bypass the city. The High Command had yielded just a bit, enough to authorize an air drop of arms and supplies into the squares and parks of embattled Paris. Ed thought this was significant. He knew that de Gaulle and Leclerc were willing to run the terrible risk of battles in the beautiful interior of the city, but his last information from American sources was that everyone from Ike on down, and especially Bradley and Patton, were dead set against sending an army into the city.

But something was going on. There was a general air of expectancy in the headquarters, with officers drinking coffee, talking on field telephones, getting up to walk around nervously, looking and waving as the tanks and vehicles moved out.

There was an unconfirmed report that there was heavy fighting in Paris, that tanks were on the move. It was hot and still and the division was moving, probing, lancing forward, finding only light German opposition. The headquarters staff seemed to wilt under the strain, to become more and more irritable as the afternoon wore on and Leclerc did not appear.

"Major," Ed asked Leclerc's G3, "just where the hell is the General?"

The Major shrugged.

"Has he gone to see the Americans?" Ed asked.

"You said it, not I," Major André Gribius said, smiling at Ed. "Should you send it out with your dispatches, it would be an unconfirmed rumor."

So that was it. Ed knew that de Gaulle and Leclerc has been putting the pressure on. He knew that the Second Armored had enough supplies and gas stored up to hit the high road for Paris without further support. Had Leclerc gone to see the high brass—maybe Ike, maybe Omar Bradley—to deliver an ultimatum? Give us the order to liberate Paris, or we do it on our own. That would be one hell of a story, if he could only dig it out.

Ed spent most of the day hanging around headquarters. Then, finally, in the early evening, there was a telephone call, which he could not manage to overhear. One by one the members of the headquarters staff were given the word, some word. The sense of anticipation grew as the staff headed for the jeeps and trucks parked nearby.

"Look, you fellows," Ed said. "You know damned well I'll find out sooner or later. What's going on?"

Major Gribius merely smiled and said, "Come along, then."

They loaded into the vehicles and drove to a little airstrip that had been cleared nearby. There they waited, smoking, standing in small groups, scanning the sky. It was almost dark when a distant buzz floated in, the sound of a light aircraft engine. An olive-drab Piper with French markings circled in, made a quick landing, taxied toward the waiting group of officers. Out leaped Leclerc, almost before the plane stopped rolling.

Ed knew, then—for the usually dour general was smiling. He returned the salutes with a snappy gesture, and the words came in a happy shout. "Major, let's go to Paris!"

It was after midnight before the complicated job of turning the division could be planned, the orders relayed, with attention called to Omar Bradley's direct order to Leclerc to avoid heavy fighting in Paris. But the news spread, and every now and then, from distant units just getting the word, one could hear the cheers.

The Second began its move toward the city on the morning of August 23, a Wednesday. By evening of that day, the number of dead in the city would have mounted to near a thousand French men and women, and the Grand Palais, one of the prides of Paris, would be a gutted ruin. At dawn, in a summer rain that muddied the road and drove down relentlessly to blind the tank drivers, the Second, moving in twin columns as fast as the Detroit-made power plants could move its vehicles, slipped and slithered along narrow roads, past quiet farmhouses, in a race to save a city.

25

IT SEEMED INCREDIBLE to Teddy Werner
that life continued to be more or less normal in the
luxurious hotel. The Luftwaffe officers, apparently
without any real duties, ordered what the kitchens
could provide, complained about the lack of favorite
foods, seemed to be in no hurry to give serious
thought to the sounds of battle, which did penetrate
even the walls of the Ritz. If they noticed the pall of
smoke hanging over Paris, they seemed to consider
it only a temporary condition.

Teddy, being of German blood himself, knew
Germans as an obstinate and confident people. Perhaps they thought that the fighting was merely a
nuisance, that the French Resistance, so ineffective
during the years of occupation, could not possibly be
a serious threat. And, as General Schläfer said, there
was a considerable German army out there in front of
Paris and a strong garrison within the city. No one,
it seemed—at least not the Germans—could believe
that the end was near, that soon Paris would cease to
be a German city.

Another German, Wolf, could not understand why von Choltitz was waiting. He knew, from his own general, that von Choltitz was under strict orders to destroy the bridges, the telephone system, the factories, Paris itself. Why was the man waiting? The Americans were near. It would take only a swift dash, a smashing, quick run, through the meager defenses and into the city proper for the nearest elements of the Fourth Division.

However, it suited Wolf's purpose for the Germans to withold destruction. If his Resistance leaders could save the city, while holding it, he had no objections. He'd become quite fond of the old town, and to have Paris intact, or more or less, would put the Communist leaders in an even more powerful position. But Wolf, like Teddy Werner, had heard the same plans, the same orders, and both knew that the bombers of Luftflotte 3 would do the job, even if von Choltitz, for some unfathomed reason, failed.

Wednesday was a long and terrible day for Teddy. He was concerned for Mady, for the fighting was widespread. He heard Schläfer talking with another officer, who suggested that the bombers take out points of resistance.

"They would have to bomb the whole city," Schläfer said, "and kill as many German soldiers as French."

There was no hint as to when the orders would go out, and now there was a possibility that the original plan, to begin in the northeast factory districts when the bombers did come, would be changed. It seemed more important than ever to stay in the Ritz.

"General," Teddy said, after serving lunch to Schläfer, "may I speak?"

"Go ahead," Schläfer said, not really paying attention.

"I have decided," Teddy said, "that I should ask you to give me some aid in getting out of Paris."

"Yes, good idea, since you're German," Schläfer said.

"If, sir, it becomes necessary, that is," Teddy said.

When the General didn't speak, he continued. "I have confidence that the defensive forces will stop the Allied advance, sir. I merely thought it provident to plan, in case the worst should happen."

"I'll keep you in mind," the General said.

So there was no information, or the General didn't care to give it. Or he, too, felt in his mind that the defenses would hold, that Paris would not fall.

Elsewhere in the hotel, Otto Schellen was receiving a caller. The man was in the black uniform of the SS, and he held the rank of *obersturmbannführer*. He had flown in during the night. He had just come from the command post of Generaloberst Alfred Jodl, the man entrusted with seeing to it that Hitler's orders to raze Paris were carried out.

"If you will ask the *fräulein* to leave us," the SS man said, not being too polite about it.

Schellen nodded to Silke, who pouted a bit, and then left the sitting room to slam the door of the bedroom.

"I will tell General Jodl that I don't like what I see here," the SS officer said.

"I can't say that I do, either," Schellen said, easily, smiling disarmingly. He had little use for the SS.

"I am here on direct orders of the Führer," the SS officer said.

"Strange, so am I," Schellen said.

"The High Command suspects treason."

"Man, the High Command always suspects treason," Schellen said, with a sigh, bringing a frown to the SS man's face. "But tell me about it."

"You are to—"

"I *am to?*" Schellen snapped. "I am *not* to be ordered by a mere SS *obersturmbannführer.*"

"I am merely transmitting orders from high up. You are to visit von Choltitz, to observe. He continues to postpone starting the reduction of the Paris factories—factories that will, if they fall into enemy hands, be used against us. You are to make a report to General Jodl as soon as possible."

Schellen shrugged. "Why can't the SS handle that?" He sighed again. "I think the General feels that he can hold Paris, that it is too soon to knock it to the ground."

"Be that as it may, General Jodl wants a report. That is all I have to say." With that, and a bow, the black-uniformed man left.

"Well, my silken confederate," Schellan said, "it seems we have a social call to make before we leave this peaceful city."

Silke had been listening at the door. She had heard Schellen's comments. She did not like his flippant attitude about orders from a *generaloberst*, and from the Führer himself. She was making mental notes. She'd had about all of the man's light cynicism that she could take. Good Lord, no wonder things were going badly, with men like this weakling in high places.

"Put on something sexy," Schellen said. "The General might appreciate a bit of vicarious escape."

To spite him, she dressed in a two-piece suit and

blouse, and he merely smiled. The trip across the embattled city was not without incident. Once, the armored vehicle which Schellen had borrowed from his Luftwaffe friends narrowly missed being fried by a near miss from a Molotov cocktail and more than once light-arms fire bounced off its steel sides. Silke, in spite of her bravery, was white-faced and shaking when they reached von Choltitz's headquarters and were told to wait.

"So this is our destroyer of cities," Schellen thought, as he and Silke were ushered into the General's office. Von Choltitz was looking out the window, his hands behind his back. To Schellen, he looked more the *bügermeister* than the general who had devastated Sebastopol. He was short, rather stout, and, without his hat, his hair was thin and slicked back. He had a small mouth, and serious eyes behind wire-rimmed glasses.

He was polite, shook hands with Schellen, planted a continental kiss on Silke's hand. "We had a rather adventurous trip across the city," Schellen said.

Von Choltitz smiled thinly.

"The head of Amt VI has not come merely on a social call," Von Choltitz said.

"No. No," Schellen said. "There are certain people, General, who wonder what's going on here in Paris."

"Ah," von Choltitz said.

"Although it is not normally my function, I am sort of a messenger, Schellen said.

"I see. And the message?"

"Get on with it, General," Schellen said. He smiled. And may God help you."

"The message. From Jodl?"

"And up," Schellen said.

"And do you agree with the orders, Herr Schellen?"

"Agree? It is not for me to agree or disagree," Schellen said. "I think, however, of centuries of culture."

"As do we all," von Choltitz said.

Silke had held her tongue as long as possible. "Think of the burning cities in Germany," she said.

"They are always the more fierce," Schellen said, smiling at Silke.

"I will do my duty," von Choltitz said, with a touch of sadness. "I thank you, Schellen, for coming to me. I know what is happening. Do you?"

"Yes," Schellen said. "I know."

"We will need transportation," Silke said. "Don't forget that, Otto."

"You're not going to stay to see the final act in our little drama?" von Choltitz asked. Then he smiled. "But no. It is no place for a lovely German lady. I will see to it that you have safe conduct. I'd suggest the airport. A man of your influence should be able to arrange air transport."

"Exactly what I had in mind, General," Schellen said. He shook the short man's hand, warmly. "I would not exchange places with you."

"Tell them I will do my duty," von Choltitz said.

"Your problem, Silke," Schellen said, lightly, as they rolled through the streets, a tank before them and behind them, "is that you have no sensitivity."

"Oh, shut up," Silke said, just as the lead tank burst into flames and a hail of fire began to clank off the sides of the armored car. She screamed. Through a viewport, Schellen saw them, the men of Paris, with a girl in a flowered dress dashing forward, arm drawn back. He saw the girl stagger, then regain her

balance long enough to throw the bottle she carried.
And he thought, as he saw the bottle arc upward and
then downward, that it would be his last memory on
earth. However, the cocktail missed. The girl who
had thrown it fell as it shattered nearby, on the
pavement, and a burst of machine-gun fire from the
other tank lifted her body and made it dance obscenely.

Then he heard and felt the concussion. He guessed
it to be a grenade. The vehicle rocked and began to
smell of smoke.

"I think we'd better abandon ship, my dear," he
said calmly. So it was to end like this, on a Paris
street, with a woman, perhaps, pulling the trigger.
There were flames. He heard screaming. Silke was
silent and eager to follow orders. He lifted the hatch
and she, suddenly in panic, crawled up his body,
climbing past, to emerge first. He heard a burst of
fire and she fell back into his arms. She was bleeding from two wounds, each of them fatal, one in the
head, one in the heart. The warm blood flowed
down his arms, onto his chest, wet and sticky. He
looked into her face and saw Germany—fair, often
beautiful, but, like Silke, marred inside, serving more
than one master, but in the end knowing only one:
death.

Tears came to his eyes, not because of Silke, but
because of Germany. In that moment he knew that if
by some miracle he escaped the burning armored
car, he could never again serve the present government of his homeland with sincerity.

He held Silke Frager's body, feeling it twitch. The
acrid smoke was adding to his tears, and the heat
was growing. Thrusting the body before him, he
climbed out the hatch, emerged with her in his arms,
expecting to feel the bite of bullets, saw out of the

corner of his eye that the following tank was also disabled, ablaze. The Resistance men were in the open now, standing along the building fronts, weapons at the ready. Schellen made his way to the pavement, still holding Silke. Her long blonde hair cascaded downward, blood still dripped. Two men approached.

"Congratulations," Schellen said, in his accented French, "you have killed two tanks, an armored car, and a woman. Will you kill me now?"

There was no answer. One of the men was young, handsome; Schellen looked him directly in the eye, waiting for him to raise the Luger and kill.

Blaise Deschaises had led the attack on the column of two tanks and the car, and he was proud of the way his force, to which he'd added several non-Communist fighters, had handled it. He was, however, saddened to see the beautiful blonde girl dead. He didn't know exactly what to do. The man in civilian clothing was obviously German. He killed Germans. No, he killed German soldiers. This one had the look of a diplomat.

But he'd seen the girl in the flowered skirt throw her Molotov cocktail and die.

"You are here by your choice, not ours," he said.

Schellen, cool, having already accepted death, smiled. "Do I leave by my choice, my friend?"

"Kill the boche," a voice muttered.

"Shut up," Blaise said. "Take the girl."

Two men lifted Silke's body from Schellen's arms.

"Your papers," Blaise said.

The papers Schellen carried identified him as a businessman, a dealer in office supplies. "My crime is selling paper clips and pencils to the Army," he said. Actually, he didn't really care. However, he had been trained, had made a career of being cool in sticky situations.

Blaise read the papers. "Where will you go?" he asked.

"I have been promised transportation if I reach Le Bourget," Schellen said.

"Go, then," Blaise said.

"Is it far?" Schellen asked.

"Far enough." An unhelpful comment, but he was, at least giving the man a chance.

"Could you give me directions, please?" Schellen asked. He knew the way. He made it a point to know his escape routes, but the man was young, and he was face to face with death and, he thought wryly, didn't give a shit. He was playing a game.

"Get out of here," Blaise said, "before I change my mind."

"And the girl?"

"She will receive the same treatment as that one," Blaise said, pointing to the dead Frenchwoman.

"That is fair enough, I suppose," Schellen said.

He made his way carefully, dodging the sound of battle. It was a long walk and it lasted far into the night. He contacted a German signal unit and convinced a junior officer of his identity.

As he left the airfield in a bomber—one of those that would later bomb the city—he made his way to the cockpit. Two young men were there.

"Will you fly over the city?" he asked.

"We can make it a practice run," the pilot said.

"Target?" asked his copilot, willing to play the game.

"May I suggest the target?" Schellen asked.

"Our pleasure," the pilot said.

"The Préfecture of Police."

"Good choice," the pilot said. He got on the intercom, his voice vibrant, young. "My fearless crewmen," he said, happy, joking, "we are going to make a practice run. Let's do it as if it were the real thing. The target—" He consulted a chart, obviously newly mimeographed. "—L-33. Got it?"

They came up the Seine low, unworried, for there were no guns; and on the ground, in the city, there were those who heard the snarling twin engines of the low-flying plane and dived for cover. Thinking that it had begun.

Schellen could see dimly. There was a moon. There were isolated fires. Once he thought he caught a whiff of smoke. And there, not mistakable, even in the darkness, even in the dim light of the moon, was the great cathedral, across the square from what was, for the moment, a mock target.

"Steady, steady," came the bombardier's voice. "Bombs away."

"Did you hit it?" Schellen asked.

"Of course," the pilot said happily.

"Or did you hit the cathedral?" Schellen asked.

The pilot cleared his throat. "Yes, there is that, isn't there?"

Schellen went back and found an uncomfortable perch. It was a short flight. The Allied bombers had been finding the flight to Berlin to be shorter and shorter, too.

So there was Germany, a blonde girl with a flawed heart, her beautiful hair hanging, brushing the cement on which had been mixed blood, gasoline, burning chemicals. And he knew that it was over. He had known for some time that it was over. And there was in him a vast sadness for Germany and for the girl, the girl he'd taken to Paris for his own pleasure. He had killed her. But had not the fact that she was a Gestapo agent been a contributing factor?

No matter. She was dead and there would be many more dead and he was sick of it. There remained only a decision as to what to do. To be a good German? To fight on until the end as the Führer ordered scorched earth and a battle to the death for each foot of German soil?

Well, Otto, he told himself, it will be an interesting period of time, this time coming up. Very interesting.

Behind him Paris bled.

26

MADY STOOD ON a balcony. It was a small wrought-iron balcony, and to stand on it she had to press her back against the stone of the building. A sound had brought her there, from inside the apartment where she'd spent a lonely three nights. The sound was a low thunder in the distance and there were no clouds to produce it. She knew, although she'd never heard it before, that it was the sound of guns, of the guns of the approaching Allies.

There were sharper and more immediate sounds. Paris was undergoing her agony, and the fighting was savage. From the direction of the Place de la République, she could hear it, and she knew that men were dying there. Her heart hurt for her son.

With that worry there was another. Teddy. He had not come. He was, as far as she knew, still at the Ritz, and he would be in deadly danger when the Resistance took the hotel, for there were many there who knew him as a German.

For years the Germans had enforced their occupation by terror, with public executions. A tired young man, coming to the Clichy apartment to rest, had told her that some of the Resistance were taking no prisoners, but, remembering the German brutality, were killing those who had surrendered. It was a bloodbath—and it would engulf Teddy Werner; he would not be able, in the heat of it, to convince them that he was not German.

She was only a woman, but women had died on the streets since Paris rose up. If she stood idly by, while her son fought, and while the man she had come to love was endangered, she did not care to live.

She prepared herself for the trip across the city by eating the last piece of bread in the place, and then she set out. She managed to avoid areas of fighting.

She felt great urgency, because in the hour and a half it took her to walk to the Place Vendôme, the sound of the distant guns came closer.

At the Ritz, the seriousness of the situation had finally penetrated the complacency of the Luftwaffe staff officers. In fireplaces all over the German portion of the hotel papers burned, bags were being packed.

Teddy had served the best breakfast he could arrange to the General: two slices of bread, a small pat of butter, a container of jam.

The General had eaten calmly, although Wolf was, at that moment, packing his bags. "You're leaving, sir?" Teddy asked.

The General merely nodded.

Teddy's concern was still the bombers of Luftflotte 3. "And the bombing?" he asked. He knew it was impertinent, but he had to know.

THE FIRES OF PARIS   241

"I have talked with von Choltitz. He says that it is impossible. We would kill our own men."

"The guns are near," Teddy said. "Outside, one can hear them quite clearly."

"There is still time," Schläfer said. "There is still Aulock."

Teddy had heard the name; Generalmajor Hubertus von Aulock was in charge of the defenses around Paris. He had no idea how stiff a defense Aulock would be able to make.

While Teddy was still in the room, clearing away the remains of the meager breakfast, the General had a call from von Choltitz's headquarters and relayed the information to his aide. The entire German garrison of Paris was embattled. The seemingly overwhelming force was hard put to withstand the attacks of unorganized street fighters. The men stationed near the Place de la République were trying to break out, and were having a hard go of it.

"Well, Wolf," General Schläfer said, "the time has come. Is there anyone you are looking forward to seeing back home?"

Wolf smiled. "Yes, sir," he said. "Your things are ready, General. I have sent the trunks and boxes on ahead."

"Good, good. I'm going in a few minutes. You will remain, to see to it that the baggage is handled properly. You may join me at your convenience." He put on his cap and snugged it down firmly. "See what you can do for Werner, here."

"Yes, sir," Wolf said. Alone with Teddy he looked at him with thinly disguised contempt. "I'd suggest that you attach yourself to one of the departing units of enlisted men, Werner."

"Yes, thank you," Teddy said.

He could not, of course, go with the Germans. That would merely put him deeper into trouble. He thought of the hidden room, down below, wondered if he could merely secrete himself there and wait for Mady or Blaise to come. But others in the Resistance knew about that room, and if someone thought to check it—

He had not accomplished his purpose. He had no idea whether or not orders had been drawn to bomb the city. And he had no place to go. He would be in grave danger on the streets, not only from the fighting itself, but from being stopped and questioned by any Frenchmen.

Wolf, too, had left something undone, but through no fault of his own. The woman had simply disappeared. He regretted it. But, like Teddy, he had no intention of going to Germany. It was time, Wolf felt, to begin to claim some of the rewards for his long years of living a double life. The men he considered his own, although none of them knew him, were in control of most of the important points in Paris.

There were, he knew, some trouble points. The Gaullists had the Préfecture of Police, for example, but all the Gaullists had going for them was patriotism and fervor. The Communists were organized and would complete the takeover before the nearing Allied armor came into the city.

Somewhere in the city Wolf had a safe haven. All he had to do was make a contact, long prearranged, and he would be safe. He hoped, however, that the hidden cell of Communists with whom he would make contact had possessed the foresight to choose a location with a damned good bomb shelter.

*   *   *

Some of the departing Luftwaffe showed signs of undignified haste, the growing roar of the guns acting as a goad. The hotel was emptying rapidly. General Schläfer was one of the last to go, entering an armored vehicle in the Place Vendôme.

"I will join you at the airport, sir," Wolf told him, "after I make sure that your possessions are safely shipped."

Schläfer nodded. He almost hoped that the French would catch the man who had been a thinly disguised Gestapo spy in his headquarters for over a year, but, on the other hand, he hoped it wouldn't happen before Wolf got his collection of art objects safely aboard a plane.

With the Germans gone, Teddy had no further reason to stay at the Ritz. He went to his room, changed into worn civilian clothing, and left the hotel without being seen. With a street map of Paris, he intended to go to the apartment where Mady awaited. Unarmed, speaking but little French, he knew that his safety depended on not being stopped by any of the scattered and vindictive Resistance units which, it seemed, controlled most of the streets.

As Wolf reentered the Ritz, he had a moment of uneasiness. He was very much alone. He hurried to the suite just vacated by the General and made his telephone call. Amazingly, the entire Paris telephone system was still functioning, and he knew from that that the Germans had failed in their avowed intent to paralyze the city and begin its destruction. He felt mixed emotions. It was weakness on the part of von Choltitz, a contemptible weakness. But it worked to his advantage, for he made his contact easily and was told to wait; in the evening men would come for him. He dressed in civilian clothing, donned a blond wig which had been secreted, altered the look of his face with a false blond mustache. He looked so different that he was sure he could walk safely past anyone who had known him as a Luftwaffe corporal. Except for that damned limp.

The people who worked at the Ritz were too interested in trying to hear the latest news about the location of the Allied armor to concern themselves about one corporal. There was an air of expectancy, of no longer hidden elation, all overlaid with the very real possiblity that the worst was yet to come. When Mady entered the service areas she was met with excited greetings and the assurance that the Germans were gone. She got a kiss on both cheeks from an excited cook, and when she asked the where-abouts of Theo Werner there were shrugs. Finally a steward said that he'd last seen Werner taking food to the Luftwaffe suites.

It was pleasant to be back home, Mady felt, for the hotel had been her home for many years. She felt safe there. She walked the familiar corridors, went confidently into the part of the hotel that had been Luftwaffe territory. Empty. In the crisis not even the maids were working. She was beginning to be very anxious. She opened the door to the suite that had been the ranking general's and went inside. The place was a mess, a fire smoldered in the fireplace, the heat of it having made the room too warm. Papers were scattered over the carpet. It was so quiet that she did not have the courage to call out, to ask if anyone was there. Instead, she took a deep breath, walked to the bedroom door, and threw it open. The bed was rumpled and unmade. Silly to think that this was a disgrace, that some maid should have been there already, to worry about the day-to-day work when the entire city might come under the bombers at any moment, but there it was, that resentment for her maid force, allowing a mere war to interfere with the service of the Ritz.

Mady stepped inside and tried to scream as arms went around her, a hand went to her mouth. She recovered quickly, let her entire body go lax, trying to drop out of the grasp of the unseen person behind her. She almost made it, but was held at the last possible split second, for the man holding her knew the tricks, too.

"Be still," Wolf said in a grating voice. "I don't intend to hurt you."

She stood still.

"I'm going to turn you loose," Wolf said. "If you try to scream I'll have to knock you unconscious." She nodded affirmative, felt the hand over her face relax. She took a deep breath as she was released and turned slowly, not making any sudden moves.

Wolf's eyes widened. He had not recognized her from the rear as he seized her. "Well, well," he said, with a smile under the false blond mustache, which hid his identity from Mady for a moment.

"Corporal Wolf?" she asked, after she saw the eyes.

"What an unexpected pleasure." Wolf grinned.

"You didn't go with the others?" Mady asked, although the answer was obvious. Her mind was working rapidly, trying to find reason for the German to be in civilian clothing, disguised with wig and false mustache. She could find no answer.

But one of Wolf's secret desires had been answered. She was there, alone with him in a part of the hotel that was otherwise deserted. Oh, it was good, fine, wonderful. Too many people had laughed at him in his lifetime. And this one, although she had not laughed openly, had treated him with contempt. He had made gentlemanly advances toward her, knowing in his heart that he was not her enemy, but one who had the best interests of all the French people at heart. He was to be an important instrument in bringing a new way of life to them, to all the workers. And she had treated him with that coldness which told him that, inside, she was laughing. She had, he felt, committed the final sin when she so quickly leaped into bed with the tall, blond, handsome Werner. That was an insult he would now avenge.

"I could not leave without saying good-bye to the charming head housekeeper," Wolf said, with a little bow. He straightened and moved at the same time, catching Mady completely off guard. His fist hit just the right button on the side of her chin and she sank limply to the floor.

She wanted to put her hand on her face, for it hurt. She tried to move her arm and it weighed as much as a world. She shook her head and that made the hurt worse. Then she began to see. A Ritz chandelier, the ceiling, an afternoon light coming in the window. She realized, then, why she could not move her hand. She was spreadeagled on the bed, her arms and legs tied with strips of toweling. She was not frightened at first, not until she saw Wolf. He came up beside the bed and looked down.

"How do you feel?" he asked.

"I have a headache," she said.

He went away, came back with a glass of water and aspirin. She lifted her head and took the two tablets and swallowed.

"Better?" he asked.

"It will help," she said. She was able to think. Why had he done this to her? But she was not aware that her head was not as clear as it seemed, for she was thinking that, perhaps, he was merely deserting the Germans, had been discovered, and wanted only to immobilize her until he could get away. That possibility gave her hope and she said. "Corporal, if you're in trouble, I might be able to help."

He sat on the side of the bed, grinning. "You will help a great deal," he said. And his hand went out and for the first time she realized that her clothing had been removed. A flush of shock colored her face as his hand closed rather roughly on a full breast.

Only a woman can understand rape for what it really is. Mady Deschaises was no virgin. She had lived a long and happily married life with a man who retained his fabled French sensuality until days before his death. She had known Teddy Werner, two men total, in her life. Since rape was always a possibility under German occupation, she had talked about the subject with other women, and the consensus was that if it happened, the best thing to do was relax, not to fight, for a woman's strength does not match that of a man. If the worst happened and one became pregnant, there were doctors who would help, and old-fashioned midwives who knew how to use a goose quill to abort the product of rape. Before that moment, she would have said that she would do as women agreed it was advisable—take it, take the rape, go home and take a bath, and call it one of the misfortunes of war.

But when she faced the possibility—when she realized she was naked, helpless, her legs spread open by the bonds and saw Wolf rise, begin to take off his clothing slowly—it was different. First, as Wolf undressed, she was angry. How dare he? He was obviously bent on invading the very core of her privacy. He was going to go into her very body without her consent, and it was her body, her all. Then there came a sense of deep regret. Even inside the room, she could hear the sounds of fighting and the ever-nearing roar of the battle for Paris. To have this happen at the last moment, just before deliverance, was unbearable.

He was nude, now. He knelt on the foot of the bed, his eyes squinted, a smile on his face.

"Please don't do this," she said.

"Ah, such politeness," he said softly.

"We can help you," she said. "You obviously want to leave the Germans. Please, let us help you. If you do this someone will come and they'll kill you."

"We?" he asked.

"Me. I can help you."

"Just how can you help me?"

"I have friends," she said. "We can hide you until the Allies come. Then you can surrender and—"

"That is not exactly my plan," Wolf said, "but you interest me. When I have shown you what a real man is, we will discuss your friends, and what you can do to help me."

It was going to happen. She couldn't stop it. She struggled against her bonds, her body arching up, but the movement stopped when, calmly, smilingly, he slapped her—very hard, the sound sharp, cruel. She fell back.

"If you scream I shall have to hurt you," Wolf said.

It happened.

And then her ordeal began. He went about it methodically. It does not take fancy instruments to give pain to a soft, frail human body. The fingers can do things which are so painful that a scream is merely an addition. A small pocket knife, used for cleaning a man's fingernails, can, without inducing fatal injury or heavy bleeding, inflict a pain so severe that the whole being rebels and nature brings sweet blackness. She came back from blackness again and again and it was incredible that, in the midst of it, he violated her again with lunges and grunts and words so filthy that, even in her pain, she was shamed beyond all belief.

"Who are your friends?" he asked.

"The workers of the hotel," she gasped. "They could hide you."

"The Resistance," he said. "Who are your friends in the Resistance?"

He didn't really care. He was surprised at himself. When the Nazis had begun to make him a Gestapo agent specializing in interrogation he had felt his stomach turn during the first few sessions, but he'd done it. And now he found that he enjoyed it. Perhaps, through this woman who had rejected him, he was taking his revenge on the world. It was an exercise in pure pleasure to stuff her mouth so that her screams were muffled and to touch, prick, strike the vulnerable areas of her body that were the most sensitive and to see every muscle go stiff in straining protest and to see her body lift off the bed and to hear the coughing, muffled screams. And he had all afternoon. The thing aroused him. Once again he used her, and this time she actually seemed grateful, for, while he was satisfying that lust which had resurged twice, three times, there was at least no pain.

Never had he enjoyed such complete dominance over another. The power he felt sent him into spasms of joy and he lay there panting.

"Do you have any idea who I am?" he asked her, as he removed the stuffing from her mouth so that she could speak.

"No," she gasped.

"You suspected that I was Gestapo?"

"Yes, we suspected."

"But what else?" he gloated.

She would not live to tell his secret, and, somehow, it increased his power over her to tell her. He talked as he lay there atop her, told her of his youth, of his Gestapo work, and then he surprised her. He would be one of the most powerful men in France. At that very moment men, his men, were in control of Paris.

She began to hope again. The man was simply mad. Perhaps, by humoring him, she could convince him to let her live, for she was sure in her mind that he intended to kill her. She spoke to him, promised him help. He laughed.

"You help me? I don't need help."

"The Allies," she said. "And the French. De Gaulle will come—"

"We hope he will," Wolf said. "We hope he will come while there is still confusion. There is a special squad of sharpshooters who hope he will come."

"You're going to kill him?" she asked.

"Of course," he said.

It was time to get back to the fun. He used thumb and fingers to find a certain nerve in her neck which, when punished, caused her entire head to jerk. She managed just one scream before he put the stuffing back in her mouth.

27

THE GIRL WAS about eighteen, Ed Raine
guessed. She wore a red, blossoming skirt and a sort
of peasant blouse. The flaring skirt showed a spread
of hips from a tiny waist and the blouse, one strap
threatening to come off a smooth, suntanned shoulder in the girl's excitement, showed more, a healthy,
blooming bosom hinted at by the soft, smooth mounds
as she ran alongside the jeep, a joyous smile showing young and healthy teeth and a pink tongue as she
cried, "Vive la France! Vive l'Amerique!"

Ed had managed to sneak a jeep all to himself for
the triumphant push toward Paris. Up ahead the tanks
rattled and thundered along and the populace was
going mad, clambering up on the iron monsters to
shake the hands of the crew members peering out of
the turret or the hatches, girls throwing their arms
around the men, delighted that the troops which had
come were French.

The young girl was still running beside Ed's
slow-moving jeep. "Darling," he said, grinning, feel-

ing fine, "you're going to tire yourself out." He
slowed even more and put out his hand. She vaulted
into the vehicle, and he had a soft and agitated girl in
his lap for a moment until, with a swirl of skirts and
a show of fine young leg, she crawled over him into
the passenger's seat. There she sat, proudly waving,
leaning now and then to plant wet kisses on the
cheek of the conquering newsman.

Elements of the Second were far ahead, possibly
approaching the limits of Paris itself. Ed had never
quite believed that Leclerc intended to follow orders
and bypass Paris. And his gut feeling that de Gaulle
and Leclerc intended to move on Paris, with or
without the consent of the High Command, had been
correct. He'd staked his reputation on the Free French
being allowed to enter Paris first. It made sense. It
was good politics, and even if F.D.R. and Eisenhower thought that de Gaulle was an egotistic, selfish troublemaker, having the capital of France liberated
by French troops would make great propaganda. It
would lift the morale of the entire country and,
maybe, just maybe, buy the active participation of
more Frenchmen in the final assault, when the Nazi
bear was driven to his den behind the Western Wall
and became even more fanatic in defense of the
sacred fatherland.

And yesterday the division had, with Ike's reluctant blessings, openly set off for Paris. En route it
had made a show, a patriotic parade through the
countryside, villages, and towns. At Chartres, as
everywhere along the route, the people had turned
out to cheer, to weep, to wave the tricolor. After
a night at Rambouillet, the parade had continued,
as three columns converged on the southern flank
of Paris. Every village along the way produced

its populace, who handed food and wine to the conquerors.

Then, suddenly, though predictably, the party was interrupted. At Massy-Palaiseau and on the fringes of Arpajon and at Trappes, with Paris only a dozen miles away, the three columns ran head-on into the 88-mm cannon of Generalmajor Hubertus von Aulock's defense forces. One by one the leading Sherman tanks flamed and smoldered under the fire of over two hundred cannon. The fighting was fierce at spots, but slowly, one by one, the guns were silenced, and the columns moved forward.

Ed Raine had for a while managed to be near the lead, but a half-track he was riding in had been disabled, and he had lost place in the procession, until he'd commandeered this unattended jeep. Back here, a mile or two behind the spearhead of the column, the celebration was in full cry in the late afternoon. And there was a deliriously happy and quite luscious girl in the jeep with him, skirt hiked up, nice knees exposed.

Ed's personal life always seemed to be in a mess. For four years now he'd been more or less in love with a dizzy Limey broad. His girl. The girl he'd asked to join him in more or less holy wedlock so many times he'd lost count, a girl who just could not make up her mind. Bea. He thought of her as he looked at the smiling, waving girl.

"What's your name, darling?" he asked.

"Monique," she said, blazing a smile at him.

In English he said, "I would have been damned disappointed if I'd come to France without meeting at least one girl named Monique."

"I fight Germans," she said, also in English.

Then, in French. "I listen to the BBC. I distribute newspapers."

"Good for you, darling," Ed said. "What else do you do?" Dirty old man, he was thinking. To the victor belongs the spoils? Want a chocolate bar, darling? Jesus. But, holy smokes, what legs on that girl! She gave him a look that told him she knew he was flirting. She seemed not to mind.

Ed had never been a womanizer. To him, a man and a woman together were, had to be, something special. Perhaps it was because he seemed to make a habit of losing women. He had found the right one early in his life, and he'd seen her body mangled in a wreck in the States. In Berlin, before Hitler defied the world by attacking Poland, there's been a woman, and she'd died at the hands of the Gestapo. And Bea. There were times when he thought it best if he should lose her—nonviolently, of course—but he could not get her out of his system. Dizzy little blonde Brit broad. Had the power to make him feel like a teen-age stud again. Had the power to make him angry enough to wring her peaches-and-cream Limey neck.

So you ride along with a gay, conquering, liberating Army and you sneak looks at a little French girl who's climbed in the jeep with you and you remember all the stories. Girls like soldiers, especially liberating soldiers, soldiers of a friendly country. There were a lot of theories, if one cared to explore them. One stated that the girls knew they'd never see the foreign soldiers again and knew that a brief fling would never come back to haunt them. And there was, of course, the power of American food, cigarettes, candy, chewing gum. In deprived France one could buy a woman's time for a pack of cigarettes.

Ed was not inclined to do so. He was not even inclined, although it *was* tempting, to take advantage of the hysterical happiness of the French women and girls upon seeing the liberating troops.

There was sheer happiness on this Monique's face. It was a day she would remember all her life, and she would tell her grandchildren and her great-grandchildren about it if she was lucky.

"Why are you, an American, with the Free French?" Monique asked, as the jeep passed a crowd and entered a relatively empty street.

"It's a good story," Ed said.

"Story?"

He told her about his work, about being a newsman.

"Hey, you will write about our town? You will mention me?"

He smiled. She was just an overgrown child. "Yes, darling, I'll mention you."

"I'll tell you all about myself," she said. "I'll tell you about the years of the boche."

"Sure. I'd like to hear," Ed said.

"Take the next turn to the left," she said.

Why not? He knew the command had been given to camp that night in the outskirts of the city; Paris wouldn't be liberated until tomorrow. Anxious as the troops were to be in Paris, they didn't want to walk into German traps at dusk.

He took the turn. Now they were away from the tanks and the crowds. He had taken the turn without really thinking.

"Where are we going?" he asked, when she directed him to take another turn.

"Where we can talk," she said.

OK, he thought. Maybe a feature story about how a young girl felt on Liberation Day. He followed her directions into an old residential district, halted the jeep in front of a narrow house in a line of houses, followed the bouncing red skirt to the door and into a neat room with furniture which looked as if, sometime in the dim, distant past, it had been made by some semiskilled craftsman.

"You make yourself comfortable," she said. "I have wine and cheese."

"Hey, that's not necessary," he said. He knew how scarce food was. But she went out of the room and came back with a bottle of good, red wine and some delicious cheese.

He'd carried his bag in with him. It wasn't a good idea to leave anything loose in a jeep, even in a so-called friendly country. The shortages were too severe, and the temptation too great. He opened it, took out C-ration cake, cigarettes, two Hershey bars. Monique acted as if he'd uncovered the national treasury.

She oh-ed and ah-ed and had to be coaxed to open one of the chocolate bars, but when she did the quickness with which she devoured it showed her pleasure. Then she smiled at him with chocolate on her lips and leaned forward to put her hand on his. "Thank you. I should not have been a pig and eaten it all, but it's been so long."

"I have more," he said. "I'll leave you some."

She burst into tears with a suddenness that shocked him. "Oh, you Americans are so wonderful," she said.

"Come on now," he said. "Come on." She wiped her eyes, sunny again. In her emotional state, he knew, she was capable of quick extremes. He drank the wine and nibbled the delicious cheese.

She talked. She told him how, as a young girl of

fourteen, she'd seen the boche come, how she'd cried, how the men had gradually disappeared from the town—some to fight with the Free French, some deported, some killed. Ed listened and began to get the feel of it, the horror of it, and he felt a wave of sympathy for her. He wondered if she'd escaped the attentions of the German soldiers, for she was a choice morsel. He almost asked, but didn't, for if she had been forced, in order to survive, to submit to a German's advance, it was her business, and she could forget and outgrow it. He made mental notes. Yes, there was a story there. And she talked and talked and the wine bottle was empty and there was another.

"We have been saving them," she smiled, "for just this occasion."

"We?" he asked.

"My mother and I," she said.

"Where is your mother?"

She looked away, shrugged.

"Dead?" he asked.

"In the winter," she said.

"What do you do?" he asked.

"I survive," she said. "I have a job."

"Tell me about it."

"It isn't much of a job," she said. "There is little to sell in the store, but there are some things. I am a clerk. It's a woman store, you know? Dresses and—" She giggled girlishly. "—things which women wear under the dresses."

"And a young man?" Ed asked.

She smiled. "Yes. He had to go away."

"Is he all right, then?"

"I pray that he is. He was warned in advance that he was to be deported to Germany to work in the factories. He said he would go into the Vercors. I had one letter from him, before the fighting began there.''

"He'll come back," Ed said.

"Yes." She lapsed into silence. He drank another sip of wine.

"Well, darling, I think I'd better go see what the Army is doing.''

She put her hand on his arm. "No."

She was looking at him with a gentle smile.

"No?" he asked, feeling a little stir, a quite un-Ed-like glow inside.

"This day, this night, they are too wonderful to spend alone.''

Just like that. Maybe she wasn't so innocent. Maybe she had survived in ways that women learn during wartime.

He told himself that the thought of being able to sleep in a bed was what made him smile and say, "If that's what you want.''

"Wonderful," she beamed, rising. "Now, you are dusty and sweaty. You need a bath. Your clothing needs a good wash. You go in there. You will find a tub. Undress. I will have the water for you in a moment; it has been heating while we talked. Rest, relax.''

"Hey," he said. "The service sounds great, but you don't have to—''

"I *want* to do it," she said. "I want to show that we are grateful.''

Well, he could use a bath. He went into the small room. An odd, high-backed, old-fashioned tub was there. Monique came in a moment or two later with a steaming kettle of water. "You are not undressed," she said.

"Well, if you don't mind," he said. "I'll wait.''

"Ah, you are modest," she smiled, going for more water. When the tub was full enough, and she'd poured in cold water to temper it, she looked at him and backed from the room. "Take off your uniform and hand it to me," she said.

He undressed. The GI shorts seemed capable of standing alone, and he was ashamed to include them, but they, especially, needed a wash. He handed the whole bundle through a partially opened door. Then he climbed into the tub. Ahhhh. Only a man who had been through the North African campaign knew the sheer luxury of a hot bath. He leaned back, soaked himself, used a rough, strong soap to lather. He was covered in the lather when the door was flung back and a businesslike Monique came into the room, ignoring his protests, and knelt behind him.

"Don't fuss," she said, taking the soap and cloth and doing a thorough job on his back. He relaxed. It did feel good. He hadn't had his back washed in a long time.

"OK," she said, giving the slang affirmative a charming French twist. "I pronounced you clean. Stand up."

"Go away," Ed said. "As you noted, I'm modest."

"Nonsense," she said. "We are going to sleep together, so what is this modesty?"

He gulped. "We are?

There was a pause. "Unless you find me not desirable."

Whee. He turned his head. What the hell. To the victor. "Darling, I find you very, very desirable."

Her smile was lovely. "Then stand and let me rinse the soap from you." He stood. He was surprised and a bit self-conscious, because her matter-of-fact statement had aroused the man in him, and there was quick evidence of it. She laved water over the evidence, caressed the evidence briefly, and laughed. Then he was stepping out of the tub and she was drying his back and rubbing briskly with a worn but rough towel and then, in front of him, looking up at him with an impish grin, she whispered, "Since we are not sleeping together to sleep, we don't have to wait until it is dark."

She had a lovely fragrance, a hint of something, perhaps a bit of cologne which she had hoarded through the long years of occupation, and mixed with it was her natural girl smell, her fragrant, clean hair, a smoothness of body which was a delight that occupied him for a long, long time before, as they both gasped in the glory of it, they were united.

He could always catch up with the division. He'd leave her early enough to join the troops before they got on the road again. Meanwhile, here was Ed Raine lying in a deep, soft bed, with a bit of French heaven in his arms. He didn't care where she'd learned, didn't question her knowledge, knew only that this girl was doing a kind and wonderful and exciting thing for him, knew that he wished that time could be stopped and he could spend an untroubled eternity there. He lay there while she went to the other room to iron his uniform, then welcomed her back to the bed for more closeness, more heaven. And when it was near darkness, the soft color of her skin blending with the shadows of the room—when, laughing, sated, they lay side by side and she told him of her dreams for the future when the world would be free again and her man would return and she'd be married and have a dozen children—Ed was suddenly ravenously hungry.

He got up and began to pull on his clothes.

"You're not going to leave?" she asked.

"I'll be back in half hour or so," he said.

"You won't."

"I will. I promise."

He found an Army kitchen on the outskirts of Lonjumeau and did some fast talking. He came back with enough food in a basket to feed Monique for a week or so, and they feasted. Monique ate with pure delight, seated cross-legged on the bed, naked and happy at being naked, talking, laughing, washing food down with good American beer.

So, he thought, in the late hours. So, I have become like the rest. I am the conqueror claiming the spoils. But it wasn't quite like that. It was two people together. It was something he would always remember.

After they'd eaten, after she had playfully aroused him to make love again, they had talked some more. She'd told him that he was the second man she'd known, that she had slept only with the young man she had promised to marry, that it was the least she could do to show her gratitude to the American nation. She had a sense of humor, all right.

"I can't quite manage to show my thanks, at least in this manner, to all of you, so I have chosen you."

He laughed. "But why not one of the French soldiers?"

"Pah," she said. "They are brave heroes now. They fled in 1940. Now, with American guns and tanks they come back. The ones who stayed, who have done what they could do to make it uncomfortable for the boche, they are the heroes, not those little men who ride the American tanks as if they built them themselves."

So he took it, her gratitude, and he was sorry

there wasn't more, for her youth, her vitality, her happiness, was so much a contrast to his own tiredness of war, his own doubt that it would ever be over. He would be leaving the front after Paris, his mission completed, to go back to his new job in Washington.

He had seen enough war. And he almost dreaded going back to London to see the indecisive Bea. She'd kept him on an emotional yo-yo for four years; perhaps if he merely went straight back to Washington and put an ocean between them the thing would work itself out.

So he took the gift from the young French girl and he savored it and when he awoke, with the early dawn, and saw her, sweet, young, sleeping so peacefully, he knew that it would be best to leave her that way. He dressed quietly in his freshly washed and ironed uniform. If nothing else, he'd be the neatest and cleanest man in the correspondent corps.

28

THE APARTMENT WAS EMPTY. He thought he caught just a hint of the fragrance Mady wore. He had narrowly escaped being taken by a group of armed French civilians in getting there, but his relief at having reached safety was colored by Mady's absence. He was at a loss as to what to do. He sat down and lit his last cigarette and tried to imagine where she could be. Had she, in her zeal, joined the street fighters? If so, he was helpless. He didn't dare go back into the streets without someone who knew him.

He rose, paced. He was just about ready to risk everything when he heard footsteps outside the door and heard them pause, then the door began to open. He looked for a hiding place, but it was too late. He prepared to try to explain, to fight if necessary. The door was flung open and he felt an immense relief when he heard Blaise's voice calling for his mother. When Blaise saw Teddy his submachine gun jerked up quickly, then he relaxed.

"She's not here," Teddy said. "I got here just a few minutes ago."

"Damn all women," Blaise said. "She was probably worried about you and went to the hotel."

"We've got to find her," Teddy said.

"I will find her," Blaise told him. "You would only be in the way."

"Well, go then," Teddy said. "Don't waste time."

"Don't give me orders," Blaise said.

"Goddamn it," Teddy shouted, "we're talking about your mother."

Blaise started to speak. But the man was right. He should go. There was one other problem, however. He took enough time to tear a piece of paper from a brown sack and write hurriedly.

"Keep this on you," he said. "If someone comes, show it to them, hopefully before they shoot you. It identifies you as a friend."

"I appreciate it, Blaise," Teddy said. "Now get the hell out of here and find her."

Blaise resented it. Why the hell couldn't she have stayed put? He had Germans to kill. He was glorying in it. But he went, as fast as he could, delayed as a fire fight broke out in front of him and he had to skirt it, wanting to be in it. It was growing dark before he reached the Ritz. He could see the glow of fires. A small observation plane was circling along the river and the sound of the Allied guns was very near. He could almost feel them out there, and he knew that the night and the day ahead would be crucial to the fate of Paris. He, among others, could not understand why the Germans had not started the destruction of the city.

He asked for his mother in the kitchen. Yes, she

had returned, that afternoon. In the excitement, however, no one remembered having seen her since.

He went to her office, her room. He stopped a maid and inquired. By luck, the maid has seen Mady going toward the former Luftwaffe headquarters section. He frowned, went instead to the lobby, to the director's officer, where Clause Auzello, still worried lest his beloved hotel be ruined at the last moment, assured him that he had not seen Madame Deschaises.

The corridors were empty and there were only a few lights burning. There was a feeling of loneliness there in the now-vacant section. He hurried along the halls, not wanting to take time to look in every room, calling out her name now and then. There was a light coming from under a door. He went in to find an empty suite, and then continued down the hall, made his way up to another floor. This section of the hotel wasn't familiar, and he didn't know that he was approaching the suite of the German general. But there, too, was light. Opening the door, he moved quietly not through intent, but from recently acquired habit. The office and sitting areas were a mess, and empty.

He heard a muffled sound from the bedroom and moved toward it. He was in the Ritz. The Germans were gone. There was no danger. He made no real attempt to be quiet and, inside, Wolf heard the bump as Blaise's thigh hit against a chair. Wolf left his pleasure for a moment and seized his Luger, had it pointed at the door when it opened.

Blaise's eyes were drawn to the bed as the door opened in front of him and he felt a deep shock when he saw the distorted face of his mother, saw traces of blood on her nude body. Then he saw the naked little man kneeling on the bed and started to raise his weapon when the first of three bullets from Wolf's Luger took him in the chest. He died even as he fell, but his muscles were moving and the German submachine gun was rising, rising, and his death spasm sent a burst that took Wolf low in the stomach and stitched upward, the force of it knocking him violently off the bed.

"Thank God, thank God," Mady was saying to herself. She could not speak. He had gagged her thoroughly, stuffing toweling into her mouth and tying a strip over it. But she was saved. She could not see the man who had opened the door, but she had seen the violent storm of bullets knock Wolf bodily off the bed, had seen the blood begin to spurt.

She moved her head. All she could see was the open door, and the top of a man's head. The man lay on his face, a beret covering his hair.

"Help me," she begged, the sounds meaningless through the gag. She had had things done to her which had threatened her very sanity. She felt ill. And as she waited, and waited, and no one came, she knew that if the sickness in her stomach came up she would drown in her own vomit. She prayed and willed her heaving stomach to be still.

29

FROM THE SECOND story of a battered house Ed Raine could see Paris. Orly Field was just ahead. The French Second Armored, having paid a heavy price to Generalmajor Hubertus von Aulock's guns, faced Friday morning, August 25, with mixed emotions. Exhausted by the heavy fighting, they were like sleepwalkers; their dream was Paris, so tantalizing close. And there was a new and disturbing development. Many of the Second's officers knew that the High Command had sent the American Fourth Division on the road to Paris. It would be heartbreaking, with the city so near, to have it liberated by the Americans, while a French division languished near Orly.

"Go," was the order. "Go, damn it."

The first tanks of the Second entered the city via the Italian Gate and shortly after nine o'clock the American-built Shermans were in front of the Hôtel de Ville.

Ed Raine, lucky for once, had picked the right

unit. He was just behind the tanks in a half-track and he saw the people of Paris pour out in joyous waves to greet the return of men who had left their homes over four years ago. It was, he felt, quite a moment. He felt a bit awed by it, and had trouble trying to think of just how he would describe it. He decided that words were inadequate.

"I think this calls for a drink," he said, to his companion, a British correspondent who had hitched a ride with him and the staff officer who commanded the half-track.

Ed poked the happy officer on the shoulder. "How about borrowing your vehicle?" he asked. The officer was in the process of getting out of the half-track and took no notice. The driver and the others in the vehicle poured out, too, to join the delirious crowds, to take their well-deserved praise from the people of Paris.

Ed climbed into the driver's seat, the Britisher joining him. "You're sure you know how to drive this thing?"

"We'll soon find out," Ed said. He felt a little giddy. Four years of it! It was the excitement, he guessed, the joy of Paris, and the relief to see it still intact. He managed to get the half-track moving, blowing the horn to make a way through the growing crowds.

"Just where do we get this drink, old man?" the British correspondent asked.

"We're going to beat that son of a bitch to the Ritz bar," Ed said, for it had come to him that that would be a just reward for having lived through four years of war, to beat the boastful Hemingway to his declared objective in Paris. Papa had disappeared, going off with his accumulated personal Army of

Resistance fighters toward Paris. With luck, the dash of the tanks to the heart of the city would have put Ed near the Ritz first. Hemingway made a habit of liberating famous bars. It would be fun to beat him to the most famous one in all of Paris.

He had a map, got on the wrong street only once, was delayed by crowds of excited French people who wanted to climb onto the vehicle to kiss and shake hands.

And there it was. He'd never seen it, only in pictures. But he knew it. He parked the half-track in front and entered the lobby, to be swarmed by hotel employees. His uniform was GI, and they could not know that his insignia was merely that of a war correspondent. He inquired for the bar and was directed there, led there by two beaming woman in maids' uniforms, followed by many of the staff. He had only entered the long corridor leading to the bar when he heard the sound of male voices singing the French national anthem. And when he went in the first face he saw was the beaming, round, bearded face of Papa Hemingway. Hemingway leaned his back and elbows on the bar and sang at the top of his lusty voice, and all around, filling the room, with his army, the FFI fighters.

"Shit," Ed said.

But what the hell? He shook Hemingway's hand and congratulated him on another victory. Someone had found some booze. The singing went on, and it was a good day, a fine day, a day to be remembered until he felt a touch on his arm and looked down to see a frightened hotel maid.

"Excuse me, could you tell me if there is a doctor here?" the maid asked.

"No," Ed said. "Is there anything I can do?"

He followed the girl through the hotel, up flights of stairs, taking time to admire the beauty of the place, to give thanks that it had not been destroyed.

There were two dead men on the floor in the messy suite. He stepped over one, a young boy. The other one was naked. But the thing that hurt was a woman, naked, her body bruised and bleeding, lying in a fetal position on the bed, her eyes wide open and unblinking, her breathing so soft that he almost could not detect it. Jesus, he thought, try to write a story to match the situation here.

"Madame Deschaises," the maid was whispering. "Please, there is an American here. He will help you."

She heard the words, but they had no meaning. They seemed to come from far away. She wanted only to be dead. The things Wolf had done to her had taken the last of her pride, her ability to face life. She wanted to die, willed herself to die, but kept hearing the words, "American." And there was something nagging at her. She clutched her knees with her arms and felt the aches in her body. She'd lain there, tied, afraid that she was going to vomit and die, throughout the long night, and her sanity had crawled away back somewhere to hide. Yet something nagged at her, something vital.

"Get some water," Ed told the maid. "Clean her up a little."

She felt the warmth, the gentle touch. She was covered. And she could still not speak.

"You'll be all right now," Ed told her, kneeling beside the bed.

She shrank away from him, as if fearful of his touch. Her eyes blinked, then, and it all came back and she screamed, just once, before thrusting her knuckle into her mouth.

"We'll find a doctor for you as soon as we can," Ed said.

"The General," Mady whispered.

"Who?" Ed asked.

"De Gaulle."

"Yes, he'll be here soon, I'm sure," Ed said. "The French Second Armored is in the city. The Americans are coming. It's all over."

"No," she said. "De Gaulle."

"What about him?" he asked.

"They're going to kill him."

There was something about her that made him doubt that her words were merely the ramblings of a tortured woman. There was a seriousness about her, a new look in those previously blank eyes. She tried to rise and he put his hand on her shoulder and pushed her back.

"They're going to kill him," she repeated.

"Who? How do you know?"

She was still confused. She tried to think. "Wolf," she said. and the memories came and they were too much. "The Communists," she said, and then she was sinking, sinking, sinking down into the nightmare that never ended.

Ed could not get it out of his mind. Even after a doctor came and administered to the woman on the bed, he heard the words. He knew a little bit about the situation in Paris, and, from the officers of the Second Armored, knew that there was a rivalry between the Gaullist and Communists elements of the Resistance. But to kill de Gaulle? It would be senseless. It would merely make the man a martyr, and insure that his followers had the sympathy of France. The Communists would be mad to do it.

But he'd already made up his mind to be there when the tall and grim-faced man came to Paris. He went back to the bar. His British friend decided to stay and enjoy the hospitality of the grateful Ritz. Ed set out alone in the half-track. He was on hand, having called in some debts from Second Armored officers and getting a tip, when an armored car led a small motorcade past the Hôtel de Ville, where, among others, Colonel Rol awaited de Gaulle, and on to Second Armored Headquarters at the Gare Montparnasse. There he watched Leclerc hand de Gaulle a copy of the surrender document signed by the destroyer of cities, General von Choltitz. In the end, von Choltitz had spared Paris. For some reason, the document made de Gaulle angry. It was not until later that Ed found out why. It was signed, among others, by the Communist leader, Colonel Rol.

"The General thinks that the Communists are trying to take the credit for the liberation of the city," a staff officer told him. "In some respects, the hostilities have just begun."

And Ed was one of the first to know that Leclerc had violated still another standing Allied High Command order. He had accepted the surrender of Paris not in the name of the Allies, but in the name of the French Republic.

But there was no attempt on de Gaulle's life. Ed made his way back to the Ritz, was lucky enough to find an empty room. He had felt tired, but, alone, he changed his mind.

Someone, from somewhere, had found more booze, good brandy, good wine. The Ritz Bar was jumping. Papa Hemingway was still holding court, although most of his ragtag army had faded away. Now there were more correspondents, some French military, some civilians. Hemingway saw Ed and pulled up another chair at his table. The big man was in a foul mood, and the two men who'd been sitting with him seized the opportunity to leave. Ed knew Hemingway only slightly, but he knew enough about him to know that he was suffering a letdown after the excitement of being the first Allied correspondent into Paris.

"I just came from de Gaulle's headquarters," Ed said. Hemingway shrugged. "He's giving a cold shoulder to all the Communists who fought in the uprising."

The answer was another shrug.

"Nice to see that the city is relatively undamaged," Ed said. "After what we feared."

"Not even the Germans," Hemingway said.

"Some damage down around the Place de la Concorde. Slight. A few fires. Not like London."

"Still time," Hemingway said, pointing upward with one finger. Ed looked up, half expecting to hear the sound of the air-raid sirens and the faraway buzz of heavy aircraft engines. There was a long silence.

"Hemingway," he said, "you've talked to a lot of FFI. Would the Communists elements gain by killing de Gaulle?"

There was a light of quick interest in Hemingway's eyes. "They might gain a civil war." He sipped. "No, I don't think they're that stupid. He's already a symbol of Free France. Dead, he'd be a second Joan of Arc."

"There was a woman here in the hotel," Ed said. "Some sadistic bastard had tortured her. Two dead men in the room with her. She said they were going to kill de Gaulle, the Communists.''

The subject interested the big man. He leaned forward. ''You say de Gaulle is giving the Reds the cold shoulder?''

''His staff people say he's damned angry, that he's declared war on the Communist elements.''

''Revenge, maybe. Some of the FFI with me were Rol's men. They said the Rol faction fought most of the bloody actions. I don't know.''

''I think,'' Ed said, ''that I'm going to stick pretty close to the General for the next couple of days.''

Hemingway laughed. ''Ike and the rest might welcome it. The chickens started coming home to roost when Leclerc snubbed the Brits and Americans in taking the surrender.''

Ed didn't ask how Hemingway knew. The man had uncanny sources of information.

''The old boy's still unhappy because Churchill didn't decimate the RAF in the battle of France, because we sank the French fleet, because he wasn't accorded the status of Roosevelt, Stalin, Winnie. Maybe it would be a good thing if the Reds did get him. At least we'd be sure then, maybe, whether France would be an ally after the war or an enemy.'' He drank. ''Yep, if I were you I'd stick with him.''

But first, there was a night of blessed sleep in one of the fine huge beds of the Ritz. He was placed in a suite in the part of the hotel that had been occupied by the Luftwaffe, and he spent a few minutes going through a pile of documents left by the departing Germans. Nothing exciting, dull reading. He did not hear the activity in the hallway as the bodies were removed, after hotel employees had identified them as a German corporal named Wolf and the son of the woman who had been tortured.

There were still isolated fights going on in the city and, in the confusion, the doctor who finally came decided against trying to move Mady to a hospital. Her physical injuries were painful, but slight. It was her spirit, her sanity, that concerned the doctor. He gave her a sedative, left some with the maids who would look after her.

Teddy Werner, identified to a suspicious Resistance group by Blaise's hasty note, arrived at the hotel well after dark. He was escorted by two well-armed FFI, who explained to a hostile group of employees that M. Werner was, indeed, an American who had come to help. He received a few handshakes and a few kisses on the cheeks and a wet smack from a pretty little maid before he could ask about Mady. The silence that fell told him that something was terribly wrong. And then he was in her small room where, one night that seemed to be ages ago and less than two weeks, he had loved her, had known her silken softness. She was sleeping. Her face was puffy with bruises. There were small bandages here and there.

He wanted, more than anything else, merely to stay by her side, to watch through the night until she wakened, but there was another concern. He knew Germans. He knew that the Luftwaffe had been under orders to bomb Paris. And there was no reason to believe that simply because the city was now under Allied control that the orders would not be carried out. He had talked, on the way to the hotel, with the FFI men, and had been promised a meeting with one of the Gaullist leaders. He left Mady's room sadly and followed the two men through the streets.

It was Jacques Chaban-Delmas who awaited them, and he spoke English. It was a pleasure to use his own language as he told Delmas of what he'd heard in the Luftwaffe General's quarters.

"We must inform the Allies and get fighter cover," one of the men said. Delmas shrugged.

"Not at night," Teddy said. "If they come at all they'll come at night."

The men in the room looked up as if awaiting the sounds. "They were told that German soldiers would place flares," Teddy said. "I don't know if they know, yet, that the city is no longer under German control. It's a chance."

"Ah," Delmas said. "We place the flares outside the city, in the countryside, and the bombs kill a few cows."

"It won't work," Teddy said. "They'll be able to see that they're not over a city. No."

Delmas looked at him. "What you are saying, my friend, is that we must make a decision as to which part of Paris dies."

Teddy nodded grimly. "They were to make the factories in the northeast their primary target, and then strike at the heart of the city, for maximum damage to the most valuable and the oldest monuments and buildings."

"I won't make that choice," Delmas said. "We will let them come. We will take our chances. I will not mark my countrymen for death."

"I know how you feel," Teddy said. "But, think, man. The war isn't over just because Paris is liberated. It's going to be long and hard. We'll need those factories. And I don't even like to think of Notre

Dame and the Tuileries, and the Hôtel de Ville and all the rest.''

A tear rolled down Delmas's cheek. ''Yes, yes. God forgive us, but yes.''

He positioned his men in the northeast. The location of the flares would put bombs into poor residential districts, and people would die, but the factories would be saved, and, perhaps, just perhaps, the Germans would be content with bombing the industrial targets. There was no way to lead them away from the Seine and the historic buildings along its banks.

That night the bombers did not come.

30

CHARLES DE GAULLE'S victory parade was against all logic, and against orders from V Corps. Ed Raine saw it from the beginning, from the Arc de Triomphe. The man was regal. He had, Ed thought, balls. He'd pulled the Second Armored into the city as a security guard, and to show the people of Paris that it was Free French troops who had liberated them. He had a country to win or lose, and he wasn't worried at all that his rash action left only a regiment of Yanks and a French combat team between Paris and the German rear guard.

He told Leclerc and the Resistance chiefs to walk one step behind him. He set off alone, following four Second Division Shermans down the Champs-Élysées, and the sun shone on France and on her future.

Ed knew only one other man who could have carried it off, and that man would have had to do it in a wheelchair. War, he felt, as he watched six feet four of lanky, arrogant, splendidly regal Frenchman

279

win the hearts of a city and a nation, has a way of
bringing the cream to the top. Or, to put it another
way, desperate times seem to generate their own
leaders. And Charles de Gaulle was taking his place
with the Big Four. FDR, Churchill, Stalin, de Gaulle.
Never mind Chiang Kai-shek. And the magnificence
of the bastard showed for the world when the snip-
ers, not yet cleared from the city, began to fire and
he strode proudly on, while others ducked for cover.

Behind him the parade was a disorganized mass of
joy, and that, Ed knew, was the way he wanted it.
He wanted no gleaming and orderly rows of tanks
and men to detract attention from the star of that
show.

"De Gaulle!" the crowds screamed. "De Gaulle!
De Gaulle!"

Into the Place de la Concorde, past the slender
Egyptian needle.

Ed took a quick route, driving his jeep through
deserted streets, for the crowds lined the parade
route. And there was his first sight of Notre Dame.
He slowed, awed, wanting to weep from the sheer
beauty of it. But there was no time. Behind him he
could hear the roar of the crowds, the droning of the
tanks' engines. He wanted a place where he could
see, so he went inside. Already there were people
there. He went toward the front, took his place
beside a sullen-looking man in workman's clothing.
He didn't have long to wait. He could hear the roar
of the crowds, the approach of the tanks, and then
the tanks were quiet and a roar went up.

"De Gaulle, de Gaulle, de Gaulle!"

And three quick shots.

Ed felt his heart slow. The man beside him jerked,
but did not attempt to leave. Ed was moving. Jesus

Christ, it had happened outside and he'd missed it. And why hadn't he gone to someone in authority with the story, instead of talking it over with Hemingway over brandy? He had no great love for de Gaulle, but he could see him marching down that magnificent, tree-lined boulevard, head back, taller than real life, Charles of Gaul, king, hero. Dead.

Firing broke out in small volleys and then became a scattered roar, like a fire fight of company size. He was halfway down the aisle. And he could see, through the open doors, the head of de Gaulle, standing above the crowd, moving, with a calm face, toward the cathedral.

"Get down, get down," he whispered, but de Gaulle came on, oblivious of the firing.

He was going to make it. He *would* make it, being de Gaulle. He made it. He came in through the Portal of the Last Judgment and came toward Ed, who had returned to his place beside the workman. He had almost two hundred feet to go to get to the place of honor when shots rang out and the crowded cathedral echoed with them and the man beside Ed was bringing his hand up with a German hand weapon in it and Ed was moving, not thinking, slapping down hard with a closed fist, the gun going off in his ear. He lashed out with his other fist and got in a solid blow. The man in workman's clothing staggered, dropped his weapon, and Ed was looking to see de Gaulle, walking confidently while people tried to crawl under the seats.

"*Vive de Gaulle!*" someone yelled.

That fantastic man walked to the head of the aisle, head high, not looking to right or left. Firing made the cathedral sound like the blacksmith shop of hell.

De Gaulle took his place in front of the priest. He

shouted back the correct phrases of the *Magnificat*. And the firing stopped and de Gaulle had France.

The man who had tried to kill de Gaulle had slipped away when Ed looked back.

"My God," he said, looking at de Gaulle's straight, tall back. "What are you going to do for an encore, walk on water?"

31

"MADY?" TEDDY WHISPERED. She had rolled over, opened her eyes. "Hey, Mady?"

She looked at him and screamed, low, eerily. He felt the pain himself. "It's me. It's me," he whispered, and she stopped making the sound.

"Teddy?"

"Yes."

"Don't touch me, please," she said, as his hand went out. He withdrew it.

"She has undergone a great shock," the doctor had told Teddy. "At first I feared that she would not be able to recover from it, but she is strong. She will be a bit difficult, for some time, I fear. What she needs is gentleness, reassurance. I have seen this type of case. A skilled sadist can effectively destroy a human psyche. At first she said that she wanted to die."

"But she's not badly hurt, is she?" Teddy had asked.

"Not physically," the doctor told him. "The hurt,

the terrible wound, is on the inside. You see, in doing the things he did to her, the German showed her that she was nothing, nothing, that she was merely a creature of pain and shame to be treated as he wished. It is a dehumanizing experience. I take it, from your concern, that you and she were more than, ah, acquaintances?''

"Yes," Teddy said.

"Then be very careful, my boy. It was a man who took away her humanity, made her nothing more than a sniveling animal. She may not be able to stand the touch of a man, ever again.''

Oh Christ. "Don't touch me, please," she said.

"Help me, Doctor," Teddy had begged. "Tell me what to do. I'll do whatever it takes.''

"Time," the doctor said.

He would take time. To hell with the war. To hell with the RAF. To hell with all of them. They'd sent him on a fool's errand. As it had turned out, the uprising that everyone had tried to stop had most probably been the major factor in liberating Paris without severe damage. To hell with them. He'd stay.

"All right, Mady," he said. "But I'm here. I'll be here. Sleep now.''

She slept as he heard the far-off and familiar sound and went tense. It was a large group, coming from the northeast. He judged them to be over a hundred as he went to a window, opened it, saw the dark city spread out and away from him. Mady had been moved, by the director, to a more luxurious room high up in the hotel, and he had a good view.

He'd heard the sound before as the German aerial armadas approached London, and he was helpless.

He did not even have a Spitfire handy to use to climb into the night sky to try to spot the exhaust flare of the Heinkels. He could only watch. They came over the Bois de Vincennes and then he could hear and feel the distant bursts, could see the glow of incendiary-induced fires. And the scream of the air-raid sirens. Ah, God. And for a long while he was back in London with Weeping Willie wailing and *she* was there.

"Jeanna, Jeanna," he whispered aloud. She would understand. He knew she would understand if, some-how, she could. look down and see him standing guard over a wounded girl, a hurt girl, a woman who was to take her place, a woman *they* were trying to take away from him as her own people had taken Jeanna from him.

The planes of Luftflotte 3 wafted safely through the night sky. There were no antiaircraft guns, no fighters. Only the drifting, unloading bombers and the sky was beginning to glow with the fires and people were dying and he could remember how Jacques Delmas had wept when he agreed to light flares in one of the least densely populated areas of the city to lead the Germans to the least damaging target. It went on forever, but forever was a half hour and then there were only the fires.

Ed Raine had somehow slept through the air raid. By the following morning he knew he'd had enough. De Gaulle had escaped death at the cathedral, and now there was only the matter of trying to place the blame, but Ed knew. He knew that a bloodied and hurt woman had whispered that the Communists were going to kill de Gaulle. However, it was a story he could not write.

Ed was on the way home. He'd covered the liberation of Paris; let others tail the Third Army into Germany. It was going to be a long fight, for, partly as the result of the diversion of supplies to Paris, Patton's tanks were grinding to a standstill, out of gas. But others could write of it, analyze it, measure an intact Paris against the deaths that would come to young Britons, Americans, French, as the Germans were given time to regroup and make their stand behind the West Wall. He was going home.

He had a stop to make on the way. He liberated a jeep and headed out of Paris the way he'd come in, down the road that was still lined with the dead and charred vehicles of the Second Armored.

It was a lovely August day and a lovely girl was, he imagined, waiting in Lougjumeau. He could not get her out of his mind. Monique. How disappointed he would have been if he'd come to France without meeting at least one girl named Monique. He would, he decided, give her all the cigarettes he had left, all the cash except what he needed to get to an air-corps base to hitch a ride, by whatever route, back to Washington and the OWI.

He came into the virtually undamaged town in midmorning, a ten o'clock scholar eager to find teacher, in the form of Monique, tell her what a ray of sunshine she'd been in his life, tell her good-bye. He thought he could remember the route she'd taken to get to her small house, but he was lost within a few minutes. There were people up ahead—a crowd, growling, jeering, making ugly noises. He edged the jeep forward, then stopped at an intersection.

Down the street at right angles to where he had stopped, two women were walking. Their heads had been cropped close to their skulls. Their dresses had been torn. One clasped her ripped garment with one hand, walking with her head down, her dingy slip showing under the torn dress. The other walked with her head high, eyes glaring at the jeering, hooting crowds that lined the sidewalks. Her dress, too, had been torn down off her shoulders, but she made no attempt to hold it up, letting it fall to her waist where she held it with arms clasped in front of her stomach, and the slip she wore was lacy and one bra strap had been broken and there were bruises on her face. He didn't recognize her at first. She had a well-shaped head, but, without hair, her nose seemed too large. Then he knew her. It was Monique.

"What is it?" he asked an old man who came up to stare at his correspondent's insignia in puzzlement.

"Those?" The old man spat. "Whores. They slept with the boches."

Ah, Monique. Oh, Goddamn it all to hell—this war, and all those who had anything to do with it.

She was gone, walking with her head high, glaring back at the jeering crowd, her back straight. Then she was blocked from his view by the surging crowds. He jerked the jeep into motion, set it off after her, to get her away from the people. Then he stopped, because he had not lived in the town through four years of occupation and he knew her only from that one, lovely night. Fervently he wished that he had not come, that he had never known.

Monique. Young, sweet, accomplished in the art of love. What had she gone through to be in such a position? He would never know. He did not want to know. He wanted only to get the hell out of Europe, where all the fucking world wars started, and leave the contentious bastards to fight their own battles in the future, never to have another young American die on British or French or German soil.

32

NOW IT WAS cold in Paris. And it was cold in the Ardennes, that beautiful and unlikely place for war, and once again German tanks were on the move in heavy fog, slashing through the elements of four American divisions to encircle another in Bastogne. Teddy didn't care much. He had never reported in. He had stayed on at the Ritz, and that famous old hotel was coming back to life. He did his job as steward, because that was the only way he could be near her. He didn't care if the Germans counterattacked, for he knew, in the end, that it would be victory for the Allies. And he'd done his part. He had more important considerations now. He had a wounded girl to cure.

Mady was back at her work. She was thin, and she drank a lot of coffee, which was available again. She seemed to be grateful to him for sticking by her, but she had told him, quietly, sadly, that she could never love him. She could never marry him. He didn't have to ask why. Even an accidental touch would cause her to shiver. Externally, there was no sign left of her afternoon with the sadistic Wolf, but inside . . .

Soon it would be Christmas. De Gaulle was in firm control of France. The Third Army was moving to relieve the defenders of Bastogne.

"Teddy," Mady said, one day in late December, with the holidays only days away, "I have to make a trip."

"Need company?"

"Would you mind?"

"Not at all."

They boarded a train, rode toward the south. He didn't ask the destination. They rode through a winter landscape and then he knew.

It was Saumur. There hadn't been time nor money to rebuild the school entirely, but it was back in operation in makeshift Quonset huts, General Issue. The Cavalry School was a part of French tradition, a part of the French Army, and it had been set working again, with a new batch of young cadets.

The instructor who greeted them had lost an arm. He was quick to inform them that he'd been with the Second Armored during the liberation of Paris. He knew of Blaise Deschaises, of course. Survivors of the stand made by the Saumur cadets had told of young Blaise's heroism there, and tales of his deeds in Paris were legion. The veteran invited Mady and Teddy to accompany him to the chapel. There, in a place of honor, were the pictures of the cadets who had died, and Blaise was prominent among them.

"The school will always honor him," the veteran told them. "He is the spirit of France."

"He asked me to bring this back to you," Mady

said, extending the heavy package, which she'd insisted on holding all the way down on the train.

"Ah," the instructor said.

"Open it, please," Mady said.

His face showed his astonishment, then he wept. He held the Egyptian horse up and the tears streamed down his face.

"My son told me," Mady said proudly, "that the horse was the only reason why he left, that if he had not had the horse to save from the Germans, he would have stayed to fight on."

"Yes, yes," the one-armed man said, weeping quietly. "He was the spirit of France."

They walked the grounds together. Here and there was a depression, an old crater that had been filled in and then sunken slightly. Overhead a hundred contrails told of still another B-19 raid heading deep into Germany.

"Mady, you can be proud of him," Teddy said.

"Yes."

She didn't seem to want to talk. They walked in silence down the long slope up which the German Panzer division had attacked.

"I think it's time for you to go back to the war," she said, breaking the silence.

"I don't think it's missed me," he said. "I can't do the job I trained for."

"It doesn't seem right, somehow," she said.

"It's the war that isn't right," he said. "I won't go back to a desk. If I could fly, it would be another matter."

"I think I understand," she said.

"One war took your husband," he said. "Another your son."

"But you have lost someone, too."

"Yes." He'd told her about Jeanna. He'd thought, at the time, that it might cause her to forget her own ordeal, to think of him.

"And now you've lost again," she said.

"I don't know about that."

"I am no longer a woman," she said, her face averted.

"You're very much a woman, a beautiful one,"

She walked away. Their train would leave in another hour. He followed her slowly, and as they were approaching the station she stopped and turned to face him. "We will not go back tonight," she said, her face showing strain.

"Yes," he said, "we can take rooms at a hotel."

They found a small place. Before he could speak to the concierge she said, "My husband and I want a room, with bath, please."

He looked at her in wonder and hope. "There is no luggage," she said, "for we had intended going back to Paris."

The room was not luxurious, but it was clean and comfortable. They ordered food and wine. She sat across a small table from him, not looking up.

"Mady, are you sure?" he asked, when they had finished eating, and the wine had been drunk, and it was dark and growing late.

"Come," she said, rising, pulling off her clothing as she walked toward the bed.

He pulled the sheet up over her body when she lay down. He undressed, slid in carefully beside her, not touching. When he did put out a finger and touched her arm she jumped, as if not expecting his touch. Somehow he knew, however, that it was now or never.

"Mady, I love you," he said. He rolled onto his

side, put one arm gently around her, lowered his face. She was trembling. He pulled away and looked down at her. Her eyes were closed.

"No," she said, reaching for him. "Don't leave me."

"Never," he said.

He paid tribute to her beauty with gentle fingertips, with his lips, with his words, with his heart, and gradually her trembling stopped and her breathing deepened and she clung to him tight, with her fingernails digging into his back.

But when he entered her she cried out and, for a moment, tried to escape, her body trembling again.

"No, Mady" he whispered. "I love you."

And then she was clinging again, and forcing herself to move, and later, she laughed and said. "I've been as the English say, a bloody fool. How much patience you've had!"

She was his, all soft woman and sweetness, and she was laughing, and teasing him and demanding, and he grinned wryly.

"I told you the first time," she said, as she did things to call his attention to certain portions of their anatomy, "that you had made a mistake, that you would only make me want more and more of you. Soon you'll be begging to be allowed to go back to your war."

He didn't beg to go back, but in January he made it known that Group Commander Teddy Werner had, after all, survived the mission in Paris. He saw the man who had sent him on the fool's errand and promised to tell the newspapermen certain aspects of the training he'd been given before going into the city, and somehow things were ironed out.

He came home to the Ritz in uniform. He'd been given a job in Paris. That had been one of his stipulations, because he didn't intend to let his new wife get out of his sight.